J. J. Connington and The Murder Room

〉〉〉 This title is part of The Murder Room, our series dedicated to making available out-of-print or hard-to-find titles by classic crime writers.

Crime fiction has always held up a mirror to society. The Victorians were fascinated by sensational murder and the emerging science of detection; now we are obsessed with the forensic detail of violent death. And no other genre has so captivated and enthralled readers.

Vast troves of classic crime writing have for a long time been unavailable to all but the most dedicated frequenters of second-hand bookshops. The advent of digital publishing means that we are now able to bring you the backlists of a huge range of titles by classic and contemporary crime writers, some of which have been out of print for decades.

From the genteel amateur private eyes of the Golden Age and the femmes fatales of pulp fiction, to the morally ambiguous hard-boiled detectives of mid twentieth-century America and their descendants who walk our twenty-first century streets, The Murder Room has it all. 〉〉〉

The Murder Room
Where Criminal Minds Meet

themurderroom.com

J. J. Connington (1880–1947)

Alfred Walter Stewart, who wrote under the pen name J. J. Connington, was born in Glasgow, the youngest of three sons of Reverend Dr Stewart. He graduated from Glasgow University and pursued an academic career as a chemistry professor, working for the Admiralty during the First World War. Known for his ingenious and carefully worked-out puzzles and in-depth character development, he was admired by a host of his better-known contemporaries, including Dorothy L. Sayers and John Dickson Carr, who both paid tribute to his influence on their work. He married Jessie Lily Courts in 1916 and they had one daughter.

Tragedy at Ravensthorpe

J. J. Connington

An Orion book

Copyright © The Professor A. W. Stewart Deceased Trust 1927, 2012

The right of J. J. Connington to be identified as the author of this work
has been asserted in accordance with the Copyright, Designs and Patents
Act 1988.

This edition published by
The Orion Publishing Group Ltd
Orion House
5 Upper St Martin's Lane
London WC2H 9EA

An Hachette UK company
A CIP catalogue record for this book is available from the British Library

ISBN 978 1 4719 0595 7

www.orionbooks.co.uk

CONTENTS

Introduction
by
Curtis Evans

During the Golden Age of the detective novel, in the 1920s and 1930s, J. J. Connington stood with fellow crime writers R. Austin Freeman, Cecil John Charles Street and Freeman Wills Crofts as the foremost practitioner in British mystery fiction of the science of pure detection. I use the word 'science' advisedly, for the man behind J. J. Connington, Alfred Walter Stewart, was an esteemed Scottish-born scientist. A 'small, unassuming, moustached polymath', Stewart was 'a strikingly effective lecturer with an excellent sense of humour, fertile imagination and fantastically retentive memory', qualities that also served him well in his fiction. He held the Chair of Chemistry at Queens University, Belfast for twenty-five years, from 1919 until his retirement in 1944.

During roughly this period, the busy Professor Stewart found time to author a remarkable apocalyptic science fiction tale, *Nordenholt's Million* (1923), a mainstream novel, *Almighty Gold* (1924), a collection of essays, *Alias J. J. Connington* (1947), and, between 1926 and 1947, twenty-four mysteries (all but one tales of detection), many of them sterling examples of the Golden Age puzzle-oriented detective novel at its considerable best. 'For those who ask first of all in a detective story for exact and mathematical accuracy in the construction of the plot', avowed a contemporary *London Daily Mail* reviewer, 'there is no author to equal the distinguished scientist who writes under the name of J. J. Connington.'[1]

Alfred Stewart's background as a man of science is reflected in his fiction, not only in the impressive puzzle plot mechanics he devised for his mysteries but in his choices of themes and depictions of characters. Along with Stanley Nordenholt of *Nordenholt's Million*, a novel about a plutocrat's pitiless efforts to preserve a ruthlessly remolded remnant of human life after a global environmental calamity, Stewart's most notable character is Chief Constable Sir Clinton Driffield, the detective in seventeen of the twenty-four Connington crime novels. Driffield is one of crime fiction's most highhanded investigators, occasionally taking on the functions of judge and jury as well as chief of police.

Absent from Stewart's fiction is the hail-fellow-well-met quality found in John Street's works or the religious ethos suffusing those of Freeman Wills Crofts, not to mention the effervescent novel-of-manners style of the British Golden Age Crime Queens Dorothy L. Sayers, Margery Allingham and Ngaio Marsh. Instead we see an often disdainful cynicism about the human animal and a marked admiration for detached supermen with superior intellects. For this reason, reading a Connington novel can be a challenging experience for modern readers inculcated in gentler social beliefs. Yet Alfred Stewart produced a classic apocalyptic science fiction tale in *Nordenholt's Million* (justly dubbed 'exciting and terrifying reading' by the *Spectator*) as well as superb detective novels boasting well-wrought puzzles, bracing characterization and an occasional leavening of dry humour. Not long after Stewart's death in 1947, the Connington novels fell entirely out of print. The recent embrace of Stewart's fiction by Orion's Murder Room imprint is a welcome event indeed, correcting as it does over sixty years of underserved neglect of an accomplished genre writer.

Born in Glasgow on 5 September 1880, Alfred Stewart had significant exposure to religion in his earlier life. His father was William Stewart, longtime Professor of Divinity and Biblical Criticism at Glasgow University, and he married Lily Coats, a daughter of the Reverend Jervis Coats and member of one of Scotland's preeminent Baptist families. Religious sensibility is entirely absent from the Connington corpus, however. A confirmed secularist, Stewart once referred to one of his wife's brothers, the Reverend William Holms Coats (1881–1954), principal of the Scottish Baptist College, as his 'mental and spiritual antithesis', bemusedly adding: 'It's quite an education to see what one would look like if one were turned into one's mirror-image.'

Stewart's J. J. Connington pseudonym was derived from a nineteenth-century Oxford Professor of Latin and translator of Horace, indicating that Stewart's literary interests lay not in pietistic writing but rather in the pre-Christian classics ('I prefer the *Odyssey* to *Paradise Lost*,' the author once avowed). Possessing an inquisitive and expansive mind, Stewart was in fact an uncommonly well-read individual, freely ranging over a variety of literary genres. His deep immersion in French literature and super-natural horror fiction, for example, is documented in his lively correspondence with the noted horologist Rupert Thomas Gould.[2]

It thus is not surprising that in the 1920s the intellectually restless Stewart, having achieved a distinguished middle age as a highly regarded man of science, decided to apply his creative energy to a new endeavour, the writing of fiction. After several years he settled, like other gifted men and women of his generation, on the wildly popular mystery genre. Stewart was modest about his accomplishments in this particular field of light fiction, telling Rupert Gould later in life that 'I write these things [what Stewart called tec yarns] because they amuse me in parts when I am putting them together and because they are the only writings of mine that the public will look at. Also, in a minor degree, because I like to think some people get pleasure out of them.' No doubt Stewart's single most impressive literary accomplishment is *Nordenholt's Million*, yet in their time the two dozen J. J. Connington mysteries did indeed give readers in Great Britain, the United States and other countries much diversionary reading pleasure. Today these works constitute an estimable addition to British crime fiction.

After his 'prentice pastiche mystery, *Death at Swaythling Court* (1926), a rural English country-house tale set in the highly traditional village of Fernhurst Parva, Stewart published another, superior country-house affair, *The Dangerfield Talisman* (1926), a novel about the baffling theft of a precious family heirloom, an ancient, jewel-encrusted armlet. This clever, murderless tale, which likely is the one that the author told Rupert Gould he wrote in under six weeks, was praised in *The Bookman* as 'continuously exciting and interesting' and in the *New York*

Times Book Review as 'ingeniously fitted together and, what is more, written with a deal of real literary charm'. Despite its virtues, however, *The Dangerfield Talisman* is not fully characteristic of mature Connington detective fiction. The author needed a memorable series sleuth, more representative of his own forceful personality.

It was the next year, 1927, that saw J. J. Connington make his break to the front of the murdermongerer's pack with a third country-house mystery, *Murder in the Maze*, wherein debuted as the author's great series detective the assertive and acerbic Sir Clinton Driffield, along with Sir Clinton's neighbour and 'Watson', the more genial (if much less astute) Squire Wendover. In this much-praised novel, Stewart's detective duo confronts some truly diabolical doings, including slayings by means of curare-tipped darts in the double-centered hedge maze at a country estate, Whistlefield. No less a fan of the genre than T. S. Eliot praised *Murder in the Maze* for its construction ('we are provided early in the story with all the clues which guide the detective') and its liveliness ('The very idea of murder in a box-hedge labyrinth does the author great credit, and he makes full use of its possibilities'). The delighted Eliot concluded that *Murder in the Maze* was 'a really first-rate detective story'. For his part, the critic H. C. Harwood declared in *The Outlook* that with the publication of *Murder in the Maze* Connington demanded and deserved 'comparison with the masters'. 'Buy, borrow, or – anyhow – get hold of it', he amusingly advised. Two decades later, in his 1946 critical essay 'The Grandest Game in the World', the great locked-room detective novelist John Dickson Carr echoed Eliot's assessment of the novel's virtuoso setting, writing: 'These 1920s [. . .] thronged with sheer brains. What would be one of the best possible settings for violent death? J. J. Connington found the answer, with *Murder in the Maze*.' Certainly in retrospect *Murder in the Maze* stands as one of the finest English country-house mysteries of the 1920s, cleverly yet fairly clued, imaginatively detailed and often grimly suspenseful. As the great American true-crime writer Edmund Lester Pearson noted in his review of *Murder in the Maze* in *The Outlook*, this Connington novel had everything that one could desire in a detective story: 'A shrubbery maze, a hot day, and somebody potting at you with an air gun loaded with darts covered with a deadly South-American arrow-poison – *there* is a situation to wheedle two dollars out of anybody's pocket.'[3]

Staying with what had worked so well for him to date, Stewart the same year produced yet another country-house mystery, *Tragedy at Ravensthorpe*, an ingenious tale of murders and thefts at the ancestral home of the Chacewaters, old family friends of Sir Clinton Driffield. There is much clever matter in *Ravensthorpe*. Especially fascinating is the author's inspired integration of faerie folklore into his plot. Stewart, who had a lifelong – though skeptical – interest in paranormal phenomena, probably was inspired in this instance by the recent hubbub over the Cottingly Faeries photographs that in the early 1920s had famously duped, among other individuals, Arthur Conan Doyle.[4] As with *Murder in the Maze*, critics raved about this new Connington mystery. In the *Spectator*, for example, a reviewer hailed *Tragedy at Ravensthorpe* in the strongest terms, declaring of the novel: 'This is more than a good detective tale. Alike in plot, characterization, and literary style, it is a work of art.'

In 1928 there appeared two additional Sir Clinton Driffield detective novels, *Mystery at Lynden Sands* and *The Case with Nine Solutions*. Once again there was great praise for the latest Conningtons. H. C. Harwood, the critic who had so much admired *Murder in the Maze*, opined of *Mystery at Lynden Sands* that it 'may just fail of being the detective story of the century', while in the United States author and book reviewer Frederic F. Van de Water expressed nearly as high an opinion of *The Case with Nine Solutions*. 'This book is a thoroughbred of a distinguished lineage that runs back to "The Gold Bug" of [Edgar Allan] Poe,' he avowed. 'It represents the highest type of detective fiction.' In both of these Connington novels, Stewart moved away from his customary country-house milieu, setting *Lynden Sands* at a fashionable beach resort and *Nine Solutions* at a scientific research institute. *Nine Solutions* is of particular interest today, I think, for its relatively frank sexual subject matter and its modern urban setting among science professionals, which rather resembles the locales found in P. D. James' classic detective novels *A Mind to Murder* (1963) and *Shroud for a Nightingale* (1971).

By the end of the 1920s, J. J. Connington's critical reputation had achieved enviable heights indeed. At this time Stewart became one of the charter members of the Detection

Club, an assemblage of the finest writers of British detective fiction that included, among other distinguished individuals, Agatha Christie, Dorothy L. Sayers and G. K. Chesterton. Certainly Victor Gollancz, the British publisher of the J. J. Connington mysteries, did not stint praise for the author, informing readers that 'J. J. Connington is now established as, in the opinion of many, the greatest living master of the story of pure detection. He is one of those who, discarding all the superfluities, has made of deductive fiction a genuine minor art, with its own laws and its own conventions.'

Such warm praise for J. J. Connington makes it all the more surprising that at this juncture the esteemed author tinkered with his successful formula by dispensing with his original series detective. In the fifth Clinton Driffield detective novel, *Nemesis at Raynham Parva* (1929), Alfred Walter Stewart, rather like Arthur Conan Doyle before him, seemed with a dramatic dénouement to have devised his popular series detective's permanent exit from the fictional stage (read it and see for yourself). The next two Connington detective novels, *The Eye in the Museum* (1929) and *The Two Tickets Puzzle* (1930), have a different series detective, Superintendent Ross, a rather dull dog of a policeman. While both these mysteries are competently done – the railway material in *The Two Tickets Puzzle* is particularly effective and should have appeal today – the presence of Sir Clinton Driffield (no superfluity he!) is missed.

Probably Stewart detected that the public minded the absence of the brilliant and biting Sir Clinton, for the Chief Constable – accompanied, naturally, by his friend Squire

Wendover – triumphantly returned in 1931 in *The Boathouse Riddle*, another well-constructed criminous country-house affair. Later in the year came *The Sweepstake Murders*, which boasts the perennially popular tontine multiple-murder plot, in this case a rapid succession of puzzling suspicious deaths afflicting the members of a sweepstake syndicate that has just won nearly £250,000.[5] Adding piquancy to this plot is the fact that Wendover is one of the imperiled syndicate members. Altogether the novel is, as the late Jacques Barzun and his colleague Wendell Hertig Taylor put it in *A Catalogue of Crime* (1971, 1989), their magisterial survey of detective fiction, 'one of Connington's best conceptions'.

Stewart's productivity as a fiction writer slowed in the 1930s, so that, barring the year 1938, at most only one new Connington appeared annually. However, in 1932 Stewart produced one of the best Connington mysteries, *The Castleford Conundrum*. A classic country-house detective novel, Castleford introduces to readers Stewart's most delightfully unpleasant set of greedy relations and one of his most deserving murderees, Winifred Castleford. Stewart also fashions a wonderfully rich puzzle plot, full of meaty material clues for the reader's delectation. *Castleford* presented critics with no conundrum over its quality. 'In *The Castleford Conundrum* Mr Connington goes to work like an accomplished chess player. The moves in the games his detectives are called on to play are a delight to watch,' raved the reviewer for the *Sunday Times*, adding that 'the clues would have rejoiced Mr. Holmes' heart.' For its part, the *Spectator* concurred in the *Sunday Times*' assessment of the novel's masterfully constructed plot: 'Few detective stories show such sound reasoning as that by which the Chief Constable brings the crime home to the culprit.' Additionally, E. C. Bentley, much admired himself as the author of the landmark detective novel *Trent's Last Case*, took time to praise Connington's purely literary virtues, noting: 'Mr Connington has never written better, or drawn characters more full of life.'

With *Tom Tiddler's Island* in 1933 Stewart produced a different sort of Connington, a criminal-gang mystery in the rather more breathless style of such hugely popular English thriller writers as Sapper, Sax Rohmer, John Buchan and Edgar Wallace (in violation of the strict detective fiction rules of Ronald Knox, there is even a secret passage in the novel). Detailing the startling discoveries made by a newlywed couple honeymooning on a remote Scottish island, *Tom Tiddler's Island* is an atmospheric and entertaining tale, though it is not as mentally stimulating for armchair sleuths as Stewart's true detective novels. The title, incidentally, refers to an ancient British children's game, 'Tom Tiddler's Ground', in which one child tries to hold a height against other children.

After his fictional Scottish excursion into thrillerdom, Stewart returned the next year to his English country-house roots with *The Ha-Ha Case* (1934), his last masterwork in this classic mystery setting (for elucidation of non-British readers, a ha-ha is a sunken wall, placed so as to delineate property boundaries while not obstructing views). Although

The Ha-Ha Case is not set in Scotland, Stewart drew inspiration for the novel from a notorious Scottish true crime, the 1893 Ardlamont murder case. From the facts of the Ardlamont affair Stewart drew several of the key characters in *The Ha-Ha Case*, as well as the circumstances of the novel's murder (a shooting 'accident' while hunting), though he added complications that take the tale in a new direction.[6]

In newspaper reviews both Dorothy L. Sayers and 'Francis Iles' (crime novelist Anthony Berkeley Cox) highly praised this latest mystery by 'The Clever Mr Connington', as he was now dubbed on book jackets by his new English publisher, Hodder & Stoughton. Sayers particularly noted the effective characterisation in *The Ha-Ha Case*: 'There is no need to say that Mr Connington has given us a sound and interesting plot, very carefully and ingeniously worked out. In addition, there are the three portraits of the three brothers, cleverly and rather subtly characterised, of the [governess], and of Inspector Hinton, whose admirable qualities are counteracted by that besetting sin of the man who has made his own way: a jealousy of delegating responsibility.' The reviewer for the *Times Literary Supplement* detected signs that the sardonic Sir Clinton Driffield had begun mellowing with age: 'Those who have never really liked Sir Clinton's perhaps excessively soldierly manner will be surprised to find that he makes his discovery not only by the pure light of intelligence, but partly as a reward for amiability and tact, qualities in which the Inspector [Hinton] was strikingly deficient.' This is true enough, although the classic Sir Clinton emerges a number of times in the novel, as in his subtly sarcastic recurrent backhanded praise of Inspector Hinton: 'He writes a first class report.'

Clinton Driffield returned the next year in the detective novel *In Whose Dim Shadow* (1935), a tale set in a recently erected English suburb, the denizens of which seem to have committed an impressive number of indiscretions, including sexual ones. The intriguing title of the British edition of the novel is drawn from a poem by the British historian Thomas Babington Macaulay: 'Those trees in whose dim shadow/The ghastly priest doth reign/The priest who slew the slayer/And shall himself be slain.' Stewart's puzzle plot in *In Whose Dim Shadow* is well clued and compelling, the kicker of a closing paragraph is a classic of its kind and, additionally, the author paints some excellent character portraits. I fully concur with the *Sunday Times*' assessment of the tale: 'Quiet domestic murder, full of the neatest detective points [. . .] These are not the detective's stock figures, but fully realised human beings.'[7]

Uncharacteristically for Stewart, nearly twenty months elapsed between the publication of *In Whose Dim Shadow* and his next book, *A Minor Operation* (1937). The reason for the author's delay in production was the onset in 1935–36 of the afflictions of cataracts and heart disease (Stewart ultimately succumbed to heart disease in 1947). Despite these grave health complications, Stewart in late 1936 was able to complete *A Minor Operation*, a first-rate Clinton Driffield story of murder and a most baffling disappearance.

A *Times Literary Supplement* reviewer found that *A Minor Operation* treated the reader 'to exactly the right mixture of mystification and clue' and that, in addition to its impressive construction, the novel boasted 'character-drawing above the average' for a detective novel.

Alfred Stewart's final eight mysteries, which appeared between 1938 and 1947, the year of the author's death, are, on the whole, a somewhat weaker group of tales than the sixteen that appeared between 1926 and 1937, yet they are not without interest. In 1938 Stewart for the last time managed to publish two detective novels, *Truth Comes Limping* and *For Murder Will Speak* (also published as *Murder Will Speak*). The latter tale is much the superior of the two, having an interesting suburban setting and a bevy of female characters found to have motives when a contemptible philandering businessman meets with foul play. Sexual neurosis plays a major role in *For Murder Will Speak*, the ever-thorough Stewart obviously having made a study of the subject when writing the novel. The somewhat squeamish reviewer for *Scribner's Magazine* considered the subject matter of *For Murder Will Speak* 'rather unsavory, at times', yet this individual conceded that the novel nevertheless made 'first-class reading for those who enjoy a good puzzle intricately worked out'. 'Judge Lynch' in the *Saturday Review* apparently had no such moral reservations about the latest Clinton Driffield murder case, avowing simply of the novel: 'They don't come any better'.

Over the next couple of years Stewart again sent Sir

Clinton Driffield temporarily packing, replacing him with a new series detective, a brash radio personality named Mark Brand, in *The Counsellor* (1939) and *The Four Defences* (1940). The better of these two novels is *The Four Defences*, which Stewart based on another notorious British true-crime case, the Alfred Rouse blazing-car murder. (Rouse is believed to have fabricated his death by murdering an unknown man, placing the dead man's body in his car and setting the car on fire, in the hope that the murdered man's body would be taken for his.) Though admittedly a thinly characterised academic exercise in ratiocination, Stewart's *Four Defences* surely is also one of the most complexly plotted Golden Age detective novels and should delight devotees of classical detection. Taking the Rouse blazing-car affair as his theme, Stewart composes from it a stunning set of diabolically ingenious criminal variations. 'This is in the cold-blooded category which [. . .] excites a crossword puzzle kind of interest,' the reviewer for the *Times Literary Supplement* acutely noted of the novel. 'Nothing in the Rouse case would prepare you for these complications upon complications [. . .] What they prove is that Mr Connington has the power of penetrating into the puzzle-corner of the brain. He leaves it dazedly wondering whether in the records of actual crime there can be any dark deed to equal this in its planned convolutions.'

Sir Clinton Driffield returned to action in the remaining four detective novels in the Connington oeuvre, *The Twenty-One Clues* (1941), *No Past is Dead* (1942), *Jack-in-the-Box* (1944) and *Commonsense is All You Need* (1947), all of which were written as Stewart's heart disease steadily worsened and reflect to some extent his diminishing physical and mental energy. Although *The Twenty-One Clues* was inspired by the notorious Hall-Mills double murder case – probably the most publicised murder case in the United States in the 1920s – and the American critic and novelist Anthony Boucher commended *Jack-in-the-Box*, I believe the best of these later mysteries is *No Past Is Dead*, which Stewart partly based on a bizarre French true-crime affair, the 1891 Achet-Lepine murder case.[8] Besides providing an interesting background for the tale, the ailing author managed some virtuoso plot twists, of the sort most associated today with that ingenious Golden Age Queen of Crime, Agatha Christie.

What Stewart with characteristic bluntness referred to as 'my complete crack-up' forced his retirement from Queen's University in 1944. 'I am afraid,' Stewart wrote a friend, the chemist and forensic scientist F. Gerald Tryhorn, in August 1946, eleven months before his death, 'that I shall never be much use again. Very stupidly, I tried for a session to combine a full course of lecturing with angina pectoris; and ended up by establishing that the two are immiscible.' He added that since retiring in 1944, he had been physically 'limited to my house, since even a fifty-yard crawl brings on the usual cramps'. Stewart completed his essay collection and a final novel before he died at his study desk in his Belfast home on 1 July 1947, at the age of sixty-six. When death came to the author he was busy at work, writing.

More than six decades after Alfred Walter Stewart's death, his J. J. Connington fiction is again available to a wider audience of classic-mystery fans, rather than strictly limited to a select company of rare-book collectors with deep pockets. This is fitting for an individual who was one of the finest writers of British genre fiction between the two world wars. 'Heaven forfend that you should imagine I take myself for anything out of the common in the tec yarn stuff,' Stewart once self-deprecatingly declared in a letter to Rupert Gould. Yet, as contemporary critics recognised, as a writer of detective and science fiction Stewart indeed was something out of the common. Now more modern readers can find this out for themselves. They have much good sleuthing in store.

1. For more on Street, Crofts and particularly Stewart, see Curtis Evans, *Masters of the 'Humdrum' Mystery: Cecil John Charles Street, Freeman Wills Crofts, Alfred Walter Stewart and the British Detective Novel, 1920–1961* (Jefferson, NC: McFarland, 2012). On the academic career of Alfred Walter Stewart, see his entry in *Oxford Dictionary of National Biography* (London and New York: Oxford University Press, 2004), vol. 52, 627–628.

2. The Gould–Stewart correspondence is discussed in considerable detail in *Masters of the 'Humdrum' Mystery*. For more on the life of the fascinating Rupert Thomas Gould, see Jonathan Betts, *Time Restored: The Harrison Timekeepers and R. T. Gould, the Man Who Knew (Almost) Everything* (London and New York: Oxford University Press, 2006) and *Longitude,* the 2000 British film adaptation of Dava Sobel's book *Longitude: The True Story of a Lone Genius Who Solved the Greatest Scientific Problem of His Time* (London: Harper Collins, 1995), which details Gould's restoration of the marine chronometers built by in the eighteenth century by the clockmaker John Harrison.

3. Potential purchasers of *Murder in the Maze* should keep in mind that $2 in 1927 is worth over $26 today.

4. In a 1920 article in *The Strand Magazine,* Arthur Conan Doyle endorsed as real prank photographs of purported fairies taken by two English girls in the garden of a house in the village of Cottingley. In the aftermath of the Great War Doyle had become a fervent believer in Spiritualism and other paranormal phenomena. Especially embarrassing to Doyle's admirers today, he also published *The Coming of the Faeries* (1922), wherein he argued that these mystical creatures genuinely existed. 'When the spirits came in, the common sense oozed out,' Stewart once wrote bluntly to his friend Rupert Gould of the creator of Sherlock Holmes. Like Gould, however, Stewart had an intense interest in the subject of the Loch Ness Monster, believing that he, his wife and daughter had sighted a large marine creature of some sort in Loch Ness in 1935. A year earlier Gould had authored *The Loch Ness Monster and Others*, and it was this book that led Stewart, after he made his 'Nessie' sighting, to initiate correspondence with Gould.

5. A tontine is a financial arrangement wherein shareowners in a common fund receive annuities that increase in value with the death of each participant, with the entire amount of the fund going to the last survivor. The impetus that the tontine provided to the deadly creative imaginations of Golden Age mystery writers should be sufficiently obvious.

6. At Ardlamont, a large country estate in Argyll, Cecil Hambrough died from a gunshot wound while hunting. Cecil's tutor, Alfred John Monson, and another man, both of whom were out hunting with Cecil, claimed that Cecil had accidentally shot himself, but Monson was arrested and tried for Cecil's murder. The verdict delivered was 'not proven', but Monson was then – and is today – considered almost certain to have been guilty of the murder. On the Ardlamont case, see William Roughead, *Classic Crimes* (1951; repr., New York: New York Review Books Classics, 2000), 378–464.

7. For the genesis of the title, see Macaulay's 'The Battle of the Lake Regillus', from his narrative poem collection *Lays of Ancient Rome*. In this poem Macaulay alludes to the ancient cult of Diana Nemorensis, which elevated its priests through trial by

combat. Study of the practices of the Diana Nemorensis cult influenced Sir James George Frazer's cultural interpretation of religion in his most renowned work, *The Golden Bough: A Study in Magic and Religion*. As with *Tom Tiddler's Island* and *The Ha-Ha Case* the title *In Whose Dim Shadow* proved too esoteric for Connington's American publishers, Little, Brown and Co., who altered it to the more prosaic *The Tau Cross Mystery*.

8. Stewart analysed the Achet-Lepine case in detail in 'The Mystery of Chantelle', one of the best essays in his 1947 collection *Alias J. J. Connington*.

Tragedy at Ravensthorpe

CHAPTER I

THE FAIRY HOUSES

"Got fixed up in your new house yet, Sir Clinton?" asked Cecil Chacewater, as they sauntered together up one of the paths in the Ravensthorpe grounds. "It must be a bit of a change from South Africa—settling down in this backwater."

Sir Clinton Driffield, the new Chief Constable of the county, nodded affirmatively in reply to the question.

"One manages to be fairly comfortable; and it's certainly been less trouble to fit up than it would have been if I'd taken a bigger place. Not that I don't envy you people at Ravensthorpe," he added, glancing round at the long front of the house behind him. "You've plenty of elbow-room in that castle of yours."

Cecil made no reply; and they paced on for a minute or more before Sir Clinton again spoke.

"It's a curious thing, Cecil, that although I knew your father so well, I never happened to come down here to Ravensthorpe. He often asked me to stay; and I wanted to see his collection; but somehow we never seemed able to fix on a time that suited us both.

1

It was at the house in Onslow Square that I always saw you, so this is all fresh ground to me. It's rather like the irony of fate that my first post since I came home should be in the very district I couldn't find time to visit when your father was alive."

Cecil Chacewater agreed with a gesture.

" I was very glad when I saw you'd been appointed. I wondered if you'd know me again after all that time ; but I thought we'd better bring ourselves to your notice in case we could be of any help here—introduce you to people, and all that sort of thing, you know."

" I hardly recognized you when you turned up the other day," Sir Clinton admitted frankly. " You were a kiddie when I went off to take that police post in South Africa ; and somehow or other I never seem to have run across you on any of my trips home on leave. It must have been ten years since I'd seen you."

" I don't wonder you didn't place me at once. Ten years makes a lot of difference at my advanced age. But you don't look a bit changed. I recognized you straight off, as soon as I saw you."

" What age are you now ? " asked Sir Clinton.

" About twenty-three," Cecil replied. " Maurice is twenty-five, and Joan's just on the edge of twenty-one."

" I suppose she must be," Sir Clinton confirmed.

A thought seemed to cross his mind.

" By the way, this masked ball, I take it, is for Joan's coming-of-age ? "

" You got an invitation ? Right ! I've nothing

to do with that part of the business." Then, answering Sir Clinton's inquiry : " Yes, that's so. She wanted a spree of some sort ; and she generally gets what she wants, you know. You'll hardly know *her* when you see her. She's shot up out of all recognition from the kid you knew before you went away."

" She used to be pretty as a school-girl."

" Oh, she hasn't fallen off in that direction. You must come to this show of hers. She'll be awfully pleased if you do. She looks on you as a kind of unofficial uncle, you know."

Sir Clinton's expression showed that he appreciated the indirect compliment.

" I'm highly flattered. She's the only one of you who took the trouble to write to me from time to time when I was out yonder. All my Ravensthorpe news came through her."

Cecil was rather discomfited by this reminder. He changed the subject abruptly.

" I suppose you'll come as Sherlock Holmes ? Joan's laid down that everyone must act up to their costume, whatever it is ; and Sherlock wouldn't give you much trouble after all your detective experience. You'd only have to snoop round and pick up clues and make people uncomfortable with deductions."

Sir Clinton seemed amused by the idea.

" A pretty programme ! Something like this, I suppose ? " he demanded, and gave a faintly caricatured imitation of the Holmes mannerisms.

" By Jove, you know, that's awfully good ! " Cecil commented, rather taken aback by the complete change

3

in Sir Clinton's voice and gait. " You ought to do it. You'd get first prize easily."

Sir Clinton shook his head as he resumed his natural guise.

" The mask wouldn't cover my moustache ; and I draw the line at shaving that off, even in a good cause. Besides, a Chief Constable can't go running about disguised as Sherlock Holmes. Rather bad taste, dragging one's trade into one's amusements. No, I'll come as something quite unostentatious : a pillar-box or an Invisible Man, or a spook, probably."

" I forgot," Cecil hastened to say, apologetically, " I shouldn't have asked you about your costume. Joan's very strong on some fancy regulation she's made that no one is to know beforehand what anyone else is wearing. She wants the prize awarding to be absolutely unbiased. So you'd better not tell me what you're going to do."

Sir Clinton glanced at him with a faint twinkle in his eye.

" That's precisely what I've been doing for the last minute or two," he said, dryly.

" What do you mean ? " Cecil asked, looking puzzled. " You haven't told me anything."

" Exactly."

Cecil was forced to smile.

" No harm done," he admitted. " You gave nothing away."

" It's a very useful habit in my line of business."

But Sir Clinton's interest in the approaching masked ball was apparently not yet exhausted.

4

" Large crowd coming ? " he asked.

" Fairish, I believe. Most of the neighbours, I suppose. We're putting up a few people for the night, of course ; and there are three or four visitors on the premises already. It should be quite a decent show. I can't give you even rough numbers, for Joan's taken the invitation side of the thing entirely into her own hands—most mysterious about it, too. Hush ! Hush ! Very Secret ! and all that kind of thing. She won't even let us see her lists for fear of making it too easy to recognize people ; so she's had to arrange the catering side of the thing on her own as well."

" She always was an independent kind of person," Sir Clinton volunteered.

Cecil took no notice of the interjection.

" If you ask me," he went on, " I think she's a bit besotted with this incognito notion. She doesn't realize that half the gang can be spotted at once by their walk, and the other half will give themselves away as soon as they get animated and begin to jabber freely. But it's her show, you know, so it's no use anyone else butting in with criticisms and spoiling her fun before it begins."

Sir Clinton nodded his assent ; but for a moment or two he seemed to be preoccupied with some line of thought which Cecil's words had started in his mind. Suddenly, however, something caught his eye and diverted his attention to external things.

" What's that weird thing over there ? " he asked.

As he spoke, he pointed to an object a little way off

5

the path on which they were standing. It was a tiny building about a yard in height and a couple of yards or more in length. At the first glance it seemed like a bungalow reduced to the scale of a large doll's house ; but closer inspection showed that it was windowless, though ventilation of a sort appeared to have been provided. A miniature door closed the entrance, through which a full-grown man could gain admittance only by lying flat on the ground and wriggling with some difficulty through the narrow opening provided.

" That ? " Cecil answered carelessly. " Oh, that's one of the Fairy Houses, you know. They're a sort of local curiosity. No matter where you are, you'll find one of them within a couple of hundred yards of you, anywhere in the grounds."

" Only in the grounds ? Aren't there any outside the estate ? " inquired Sir Clinton. " At the first glance I took it for some sort of archæological affair."

" They're old enough, I dare say," Cecil admitted, indifferently. " A century, or a century and a half, or perhaps even more. They're purely a Ravensthorpe product. I've never seen one of them outside the boundary."

Sir Clinton left the path and made a closer examination of the tiny hut ; but it presented very few points of interest in itself. Out of curiosity, he turned the handle of the door and found it moved easily.

" You seem to keep the locks and hinges oiled," he said, with some surprise.

Pushing the door open, he stooped down and glanced inside.

"Very spick and span. You keep them in good repair, evidently."

"Oh, one of the gardeners has the job of looking after them," Cecil explained, without showing much interest.

"I've never seen anything of the sort before. They might be Picts' dwellings, or something of that kind ; but why keep them in repair ? And, of course, they're not prehistoric at all. They're comparatively modern, from the way they're put together. What are they ?"

"Ask me another," said Cecil, who seemed bored by the subject. "They're an ancestral legacy, or an heirloom, or a tenant's improvement, or whatever you like to call it. Clause in the will each time, to provide for them being kept in good repair, and so forth."

Sir Clinton seemed to prick up his ears when he heard of this provision, though his tone showed only languid interest when he put his next inquiry.

"Anything at the back of it all ? It seems a rum sort of business."

"The country-people round about here will supply you with all the information you can believe about it— and a lot you're not likely to swallow, too. By their way of it, Lavington Knoll up there "—he pointed vaguely to indicate its position—" was the last of the fairy strongholds hereabouts ; and when most of the fairies went away, a few stayed behind. But these ones didn't care much for the old Knoll after that. Reminded them of past glories and cheery company too much, I suppose ; and so they made a sort of treaty with an ancestor of ours. He was to provide houses for them, and they were to look after the general prosperity side of Ravensthorpe."

Sir Clinton seemed amused by Cecil's somewhat scornful summary.

" A case of ' Farewell rewards and fairies,' it seems, Cecil."

Then, half to himself, he hummed a few lines of Corbet's song :

> Witness those rings and roundelayes
> Of theirs, which yet remaine ;
> Were footed in queene Maries dayes
> On many a grassy playne.
> But since of late Elizabeth . . .

" Do you go as far back as Elizabeth, here at Ravens-thorpe, by any chance, Cecil ? "

" So far as the grounds go, yes. The house was partly destroyed in Cromwell's time ; and some new bits were built on in place of the old stuff. But there's a lot of the old part left yet, in quite good repair."

Sir Clinton still seemed interested in the compact with the Fairies.

" Was there any penalty clause in the contract about these Houses ? There's usually some drawback to these affairs—like the Luck of Edenhall, for instance."

" There used to be some legend or other that unless the Fairies found their houses always in good order, the Family Curse would come home to roost, one-time.

No one believes in that sort of stuff nowadays ; but it's kept alive by this clause that's put into every will —a kind of family custom, you know, that no one cares to be the first to break. If you call it a damned old wives' tale, I shan't blame you."

Sir Clinton could not be sure whether Cecil's indifference in the matter was natural or assumed ; but in any case he thought it tactful to pursue the subject no further. Closing the door of the Fairy House again, he made his way back to the path where his companion was waiting for him.

As the Chief Constable rejoined him, Cecil looked round the horizon with feeble interest.

" Not much else to show you, I'm afraid," he said. Then, with an after-thought : " Care to see rather a good view ? The best one hereabouts is just up above us—through the wood here—if you think it worth the trouble of the climb. It's not very far. We've plenty of time before lunch."

Sir Clinton acquiesced, and they began to mount a further slope in the path which now led them up through a sparse pine-wood.

" There seems to be a good sound foundation to this path," the Chief Constable commented, as they walked on.

" There used to be a carriage-drive, at one time, leading up to the top. I suppose the old birds used to drive up here and sit out having tea and admiring the view on fine days. But it's been neglected for long enough. Hardly anyone goes up to the top now, except once in a blue moon or else by accident."

9

Sir Clinton gave a nod of acquiescence.

" Anyone can see the path's hardly ever used."

" Just beyond this brow," Cecil explained as they moved on, " there's an old quarry cut in the further side of the hill. It's a very old place, rather picturesque nowadays. Most of the stone for Ravensthorpe came from it in the old days, and during the rebuilding. After that, the quarry dropped out of use gradually ; and finally someone had the notion of letting water in at the foot of it and having a sort of model lake there, with the cliff of the quarry at one end of it. We're making for the top of the cliff by going this way ; and when you get out of the wood into the open, you'll find rather a good outlook over the country."

A short walk took them through the rest of the pine-wood. On the further side they came into a belt of open ground beyond which, on a slight eminence, a little spinney blocked part of the view.

" That's where we're making for," Cecil explained. ' The best view-point is on the other side of these trees. The old birds, a century back, chose it carefully and did some laying out at the top ; so I suppose they must have been keen on the place."

As they approached the spinney, Sir Clinton noticed a fence running down from each side of it. Cecil followed the direction of the Chief Constable's glance.

" That's barbed wire," he pointed out. " The spinney's at the top of the quarry ; but there's a bad drop down towards the hollow on either side—a dangerous bit, practically precipitous—and so the wire was put up to prevent anyone wandering near the edge and tripping over."

Cutting through the fringe of trees, they emerged at the top of the cliff. Here the ground had been levelled and paved. Along the precipice, a marble balustrade had been erected as a safeguard. Further back, a curved tier of marble seats faced the view ; and here and there in the line rose pedestals carrying life-sized marble statues which faced out towards the gulf.

" This is really very elaborate," Sir Clinton commented. " Evidently your ancestors liked the view, if they took so much trouble to put up this affair."

He moved across the paved space, leaned on the balustrade, and looked down into the depths.

" I don't wonder you fenced that in with barbed wire on each side," he said. " It's a nasty drop down there—well over a fifty-foot fall at least."

" It's nearer a hundred, really," Cecil corrected him. " The height's a bit deceptive from here. And a fall into that pool would be no joy, I can tell you ! It's full of sharp spikes of rock jutting up from the bottom. You'd get fairly well mauled if you happened to drop on any of them. You can't see them for that green stuff in the water ; but they're all present and correct under the surface."

Sir Clinton looked down at the weed-grown little lakelet. The dense green fronds gave the water an unpleasant appearance ; and in some tiny backwaters the surface was covered with a layer of scum.

" Why don't you get all that stuff cleared out ? " he demanded. " It looks rather beastly. Once you

11

got rid of it you could stock the pool with trout or perch, easily enough. I see there's some flow of water through it from a spring at the east end."

Cecil seemed to have no interest in the suggestion.

" If you want some fishing," he said, " we've got quite a decent stream that runs through another part of the grounds. This place used to be kept in good order ; but since the war and all that, you know, the fine edge has been rather off things hereabouts. It's in a bad state, right enough. Just a frog-pond."

" Is the water deep ? " Sir Clinton inquired.

" Oh, ten to fifteen feet in parts. Quite deep just in front of the cave at the bottom of the cliff below here. We used to have great times playing robbers and so forth when we were kids. There's our old raft at the far end. It was well tarred and I see it's still afloat. It was the only way of getting at the cave-mouth, you see."

He dismissed the subject.

" Suppose we sit down for a while."

Sir Clinton followed him to one of the marble benches. Before them, the view of the Ravensthorpe grounds stretched out, closed on the horizon by a line of woodland. In the foreground, beyond a fence at the end of the lake, sheep were grazing on some meadow-land.

" One of your ancestors ? " inquired Sir Clinton, nodding towards the nearest statue. " Or merely Phœbus Apollo ? "

Cecil turned to glance at the statue.

" I think I'd back your second choice," he said.

" If it was an ancestor, it must have been one of the ancient Britons. It's a bit short of clothes for anything later than that ; and even for an ancient Briton it seems a trifle undressed. No woad, you know."

He took out his cigarette-case, offered it to Sir Clinton, and then began to smoke. Sir Clinton seemed to be admiring the view in front of him for a few minutes ; but when he spoke again it was evident that something more than scenery had been in his mind.

" I'm not altogether easy in my mind over this masked ball of Joan's. Speaking as a Chief Constable responsible for the good behaviour of the district, Cecil, it seems to me that you're running some risks over it. A dance is all very well. You know all your guests by headmark and no one can get in on false pretences. But once you start masks, it's a different state of affairs altogether."

Cecil made no comment ; and Sir Clinton smoked in silence for a time before continuing :

" It's this craze of Joan's for anonymity that seems to me to open the door to all sorts of things. I take it that there'll be no announcing of individual guests, because of this incognito stunt of hers. But unfortunately that means you'll have to admit anyone who chooses to present himself as Winnie-the-Pooh or Felix the Cat or Father Christmas. You don't know who he is. You can't inquire at the start. Anybody might get in. Considering the amount of good portable stuff there is in the collection at Ravensthorpe, do

13

you think it's quite desirable to have no check whatever on your guests ? "

Cecil seemed struck by this view of the case.

" I never thought of that," he said. " I suppose we ought to have issued uniform entrance-tickets, or something of that sort ; but the thing never crossed any of our minds. Somehow, it seems a bit steep to take precautions against people when one's inviting them to one's house."

" It's not *invited* guests I'm thinking about," Sir Clinton hastened to explain more definitely. " This affair must have been talked about all over the country-side. What's to hinder some enterprising thief dressing up as a tramp and presenting himself along with the rest ? He'd get in all right. And once he was inside, he might be tempted to forget the laws of hospitality and help himself. Then, if he made himself scarce before the unmasking at midnight, he'd get clean away and leave no trace. See it ? "

Cecil nodded affirmatively ; but to Sir Clinton's slight surprise he did not appear to be much perturbed on the subject. The Chief Constable seemed to see an explanation of this attitude.

" Perhaps, of course, you're shutting up the collections for the evening."

Cecil shook his head.

" No. Joan insists on having them on view—all of them. It's a state occasion for her, you know ; and she's determined to have all the best of Ravensthorpe for her guests. What she says goes, you know. If she can't get her own way by one road she takes

another. It's always easier to give in to her at once
and be done with it. She has such a way of making
one feel a beast if one refuses her anything ; and yet
she never seems to get spoiled with it all."

Sir Clinton seemed rather taken aback by the news
about the collections.

" Well, it's your funeral, not mine, if anything does
happen," he admitted.

" Maurice's—not mine," Cecil corrected him with
a touch of bitterness which Sir Clinton failed to understand at the moment.

" I've nothing to do with Ravensthorpe nowadays,"
Cecil went on, after a pause. " I live there, that's all.
The whole affair went to Maurice—lock, stock, and
barrel—when my father died. I've really no more
right in these grounds than you have. I might be
kicked out any day."

Sir Clinton was puzzled by Cecil's tone. It was
only natural that Ravensthorpe should go down into
the hands of Maurice, since he was the elder brother.
There could be no particular grievance in that. And
yet Cecil's voice had betrayed something deeper than
a mere mild resentment. The asperity in his last
remark had been unmistakable.

For a few minutes Cecil remained silent, staring
moodily out at the landscape. Sir Clinton refrained
from interrupting his thoughts. The matter certainly had excited his curiosity ; but until Cecil chose
to say more, there seemed to be no reason for intruding
into the private affairs of the Ravensthorpe household.
Even the privileges of an old friend did not seem to

Sir Clinton a sufficient excuse for probing into family matters.

But the Chief Constable, without any voluntary effort, had the gift of eliciting confidences without soliciting them. Cecil's brooding came to an end and he turned round to face his companion.

" I suppose I've said either too much or too little already," he began. " I don't see why I shouldn't tell you about the affair. It's nearly common talk as it is, and you're sure to hear something about it sooner or later. You may as well get it first-hand and be done with it."

Sir Clinton, having solicited no confidence, contented himself with merely listening, without offering any vocal encouragement.

" You knew my father well," Cecil went on, after a short pause in which he seemed to be arranging his ideas in some definite order. " He was one of the best, if you like. No one would say a word against him—it's the last thing I'd think of doing myself, at any rate."

Sir Clinton nodded approvingly.

" The bother was," Cecil continued, " that he judged everyone by himself. He couldn't understand that anyone might not be as straight as he always was. He never made an allowance for some kinds of human nature, if you see what I mean. And, another thing, he had a great notion of the duties of the head of the family. He took them pretty seriously and he looked after a lot of people who had no claim on him, really, except that they belonged to the clan."

" He was always generous, I know," Sir Clinton confirmed. " And he always trusted people. Sometimes, perhaps, he overdid it."

Cecil made a gesture of agreement and continued :

" He overdid it when he drew up his will. Maurice, of course, was bound to be the next head of the family, once my father had gone ; so my father took it for granted that things would go on just the same. The head of the family would run the show with an eye to the interests of the rest of us, and all would be right on the night. That was the theory of the business, as my father saw it ; and he drafted his will on that basis."

Cecil sat up suddenly and flung away his cigarette with a vehemence which betrayed the heat of his feelings.

" That was the theory of the business, as I said. But the practice wasn't quite so satisfactory. My father left every penny he had to Maurice ; he left him absolutely every asset ; and, of course, Ravensthorpe's entailed, so Maurice got that in the normal course. Joan, my mother, and myself, were left without a farthing to bless ourselves with. But there was a suggestion in the will—not a legally binding thing, but merely a sort of informal direction—that Maurice was to look after us all and give us some sort of income each. I suppose my father hardly thought it worth while to do more than that. Being the sort of man he was, he would rely implicitly on Maurice playing the game, just as he'd have played the game himself—had played it all his life, you know."

17

Sir Clinton showed no desire to offer any comment ; and in a moment or two Cecil went on once more :

" Last year, there was nothing to complain about. Maurice footed our bills quite decently. He never grumbled over our expenses. Everything seemed quite sound. It never crossed my mind to get things put on a business footing. In fact, you know, I'd hardly have had the nerve to suggest anything of the sort. It would have looked a bit grasping, wouldn't it ? "

Cecil glanced inquiringly at Sir Clinton, but the Chief Constable seemed averse from making any comment at this stage. Cecil took his case from his pocket and lit a fresh cigarette before continuing his story.

" You don't remember Una Rainhill, I suppose ? "

Sir Clinton shook his head.

" She's a sort of second cousin of ours," Cecil explained. " Probably you never came across her. Besides, she'd hardly be out of the nursery when you went off to South Africa. Well, she's grown up now —just about a year or two younger than Joan. You'll see her for yourself. She's staying with us just now for this coming-of-age of Joan's."

Sir Clinton had no great difficulty in guessing, behind Cecil's restraint, his actual feelings about the girl. His voice gave him away if the words did not.

" No use making a long story of it, is there ? " Cecil continued. " Both Maurice and I wanted Una. So did a good many others. But she didn't want Maurice. She was quite nice about it. He'd nothing to complain of in that way. He got no encouragement from her at all. But he wouldn't take 'no' for an answer. He was really extra keen, and I think he overdid it instead of making the best of a bad business. And finally he realized that it was me that he was up against. Una and I aren't officially engaged, or anything like that—you'll see why in a moment—but it's a case of two's company and three's none ; and Maurice knows he's Number Three."

There was more than a tinge of rancour in Cecil's voice when he came to this last sentence. Sir Clinton raised his eyebrows slightly. He did not quite admire this malevolence on the part of the successful lover against his defeated rival. Cecil apparently noticed the slight change in the Chief Constable's expression.

" Wait a minute," he said. " You haven't heard it all yet. Before I go on, just bear in mind that there was plenty of money for all of us in the family. My father always took it for granted that I'd have enough to keep me. He'd never thought of my going into business. I've got some sort of turn for writing ; and I think he hoped that I'd make some kind of name as an author. And, of course, with what I supposed was an assured income behind me, I haven't hurried much in the way of publishing my stuff. I could afford to let it lie—or so I thought."

A slight gesture of Sir Clinton showed his approval of this outlook on authorship. It seemed to him that Cecil at his age could hardly have much to tell the world that it didn't know already ; but he had no intention of expressing any such discouraging views.

" You see how it is," Cecil continued. " As things stand, I haven't the ghost of a chance of earning a decent income for years and years. And that was the weak joint that Maurice saw and went for—damn him ! He took it upon himself to tell me that I was here more or less on sufferance. He'd been generous in the past—he actually reminded me of that !—but he didn't see how he was to continue to subsidize me indefinitely. You see his game ? If he couldn't have Una himself, he'd take care that I shouldn't have her either. Damned dog-in-the-manger ! That's a nice sort of brother for you ! I wonder what his father would think about him if he knew of this trick."

He pitched away the stub of his unfinished cigarette as though with it he could rid himself of some of his feelings.

" Of course there was friction—I'm putting it mildly—but there was no open row. My mother's not in good health and I couldn't afford to have her worried over my affairs. So we settled down to some sort of armed neutrality, although the thing's more or less evident to most people. That's what I meant when I said I might be kicked out any day. It's only a question of time, it seems to me. He still thinks that if I were out of the way he'd have a chance with Una ; and sooner or later I expect him to give me an express-ticket into the wide world. I'm trying to get some sort of job ; but so far I haven't succeeded in lighting on anything that seems to offer the slightest prospects. It's no pleasure to stay here on sufferance, I can tell you."

Now that Sir Clinton had received Cecil's unsoli-
cited confidences, he hardly knew what to do with
them. After all, he reflected, he had heard only one
side of the story ; and it was scarcely fair to judge the
case on the strength of an *ex-parte* statement. It was
not quite the Ravensthorpe which he had expected, he
admitted ruefully to himself as he bent his efforts to
bringing Cecil back to normal again. Money and a
girl : the two things that seemed to lie behind most
troubles—and even crimes, as he knew from experience. It seemed an unkind Fate that had forced these
two factors to the front in an environment where
trouble of the kind was the last that might have been
expected. One never knew what this sort of thing
might lead to in the end.

" I'd like to have a look at your father's collections
some time or other," he said at last, to change the
subject, when he had succeeded in getting Cecil into a
somewhat cooler frame of mind. " I saw a good many
of the things in London from time to time, as he
bought them ; but there must be a lot here at Ravensthorpe that will be new to me. Anything your father
bought will be worth looking at. He had wonderful
taste."

Rather to his vexation, Sir Clinton found that he
had only shifted the conversation from one sore point
to another.

" If you want to see anything," Cecil snapped
" you'd better pay your visit as soon as you can arrange
it. Maurice is going to sell the lot."

Sir Clinton was completely taken aback by this news.

" Sell the stuff ? What on earth would he want to do that for ? He's got all the money he needs, surely."

Cecil dissociated himself from any connection with the matter.

" No business of mine, now. Maurice can do as he likes. Of course, I hate the idea of all these things of my father's being sold off when there seems no need for it ; but it's not my affair. The Maurice boy isn't all we thought him ; and since he's come into Ravensthorpe, he seems to think of very little else but money and how to get more of it. Anything for the dibs, it appears."

" But surely he isn't selling everything. He might get rid of some minor things ; but he'll hardly break up the whole collection."

" Every damned thing, Sir Clinton. Why at this very moment he's got a Yankee agent—a man Foss—staying at Ravensthorpe and chaffering for the star pieces of the collection : the Medusa Medallions."

Sir Clinton shook his head.

" They must be fresh acquisitions since my day. I've never even heard of them."

" Ever see the picture of Medusa in the Uffizi Gallery ? It's attributed to Leonardo da Vinci ; but some people say it's only a student's copy of the original Leonardo which has disappeared. It seems my father came across three medallions with almost exactly the same Medusa on one side and a figure of Perseus on the reverse. And what's more, he was able to get documentary proof that these things were

22

really Leonardo's own work—strange as it seems. The thing's quite admitted by experts. So you can imagine that these Medusas are quite the star pieces in the museum. And Maurice calmly proposes to sell them to Kessock, the Yank millionaire ; and Kessock has sent this man Foss over here to negotiate for them."

" It seems rather a pity to part with them," Sir Clinton said, regretfully.

" Maurice doesn't feel it so," Cecil retorted, rather bitterly. " He got a friend of mine, Foxy Polegate, to make him electrotypes of them in gold—Foxy's rather good at that sort of thing for an amateur—and Maurice thinks that the electrotypes will look just as well as the originals."

" H'm ! Cenotaphs, I suppose," Sir Clinton commented.

" Quite so. In Memoriam. The real things being buried in the U.S.A."

Cecil paused for a moment and then concluded :

" You can imagine that none of us like this damned chandlering with these things that my father spent so much thought over. It's enough to make him turn in his grave to have all his favourites scattered—and just for the sake of Maurice's infernal miserliness and greed for cash."

Sir Clinton rose from his seat and took a last glance at the view before him.

" What about moving on now ? "

Cecil agreed ; and they retraced their steps towards the pine-wood. As they entered the spinney, Sir

Clinton noticed another of the Fairy Houses set back among the trees at a little distance from the path.

" Another of those things ? "

Rather to his surprise, Cecil moved over to examine the little edifice, and, bending down, opened the door and glanced inside.

" The Fairy's not at home at present," he said, standing aside to let Sir Clinton look in.

Something in Cecil's voice forced itself on the attention of the Chief Constable. The words seemed to be pointless ; but in the tone there was an ill-suppressed tinge of what might almost have been malicious glee at some unexplained jest. Sir Clinton was too wary to follow up this track, wherever it might lead to. He did not quite like the expression on Cecil's face when the remark was made ; and he sought for some transition which would bring them on to a fresh subject.

" You must have some curiosities in Ravensthorpe itself, if parts of it are as old as they seem to be. Any priest's holes, or secret passages, or things of that sort ? "

" There are one or two," Cecil admitted. " But we don't make a show of them. In fact, even Joan doesn't know how to get into them. There's some sort of *Mistletoe Bough* story in the family : a girl went into one of the passages, forgot how to work the spring to get out again, lost her nerve apparently, and stayed there till she died. It so happened that she was the only one of the family in the house at the time, so there was no one to help her out. Since then, we've kept the secret of the springs from our girls. No use running risks."

" And even Joan hasn't wheedled it out of you ? "

" No, not even Joan. Maurice and I are the only ones who can get into these places."

Sir Clinton evidently approved of this.

" Short of opening the passages up altogether, that seems the best thing to do. One never knows one's luck. By the way, in an old place like this you ought to have a stock of family legends. You've got these Fairy Houses. Is there anything else of general interest ? "

Cecil seemed to have recovered something of his normal good humour ; and his face betrayed almost a grin of amusement as he replied :

" Oh, yes ! We've got a family ghost—or so the country-folk say. I've never come across it myself ; but it's common talk that the family spectre is a White Man who walks in the woods just before the head of the family dies. All rot, you know. Nobody believes in it, really. But it's quite an old-established tradition round about here."

Sir Clinton laughed.

" You certainly don't seem to take him very seriously. What about Family Curses ? Are you well supplied ? "

" You'd better apply to Maurice if you're keen on Family Curses. He seems to have specialized in that branch, if you ask me."

CHAPTER II

"How time flies !" said Joan Chacewater, in mock despondency. "To-night I'm in my prime. To-morrow I shall be twenty-one, with all my bright youth behind me. Five years after that, I shall quite possibly be married to Michael here, if I'm still alive and he hasn't died in the meantime. Then I shall sit o' nights darning his socks in horn-rimmed spectacles, and sadly recalling those glad days when I was young and still happy. It's dreadful ! I feel I want to cry over it. Give me something to cry into, Michael ; I seem to have mislaid my bag."

Michael Clifton obligingly held out a handkerchief. Joan looked at it disparagingly.

"Haven't you anything smaller than that ? It discourages me. I'm not going to cry on a manu-facturing scale. It wouldn't be becoming."

Una Rainhill laid her cigarette down on the ash-tray beside her.

"If you're going to be as particular as all that, Joan, I think I'd be content with a gulp or two of emotion or perhaps a lump in the throat. Cheer up ! You've one more night before the shadows fall."

"Ah, there it is !" said Joan, tragically. "You're young, Una, and you never had any foresight, anyway. But I can see it all coming. I can see the fat ankles" —she glanced down at her own slim ones—" and the

26

artificial silk stockings at three-and-eleven the pair ;
because Michael's business will always be mismanaged,
with him at the head of it.   And I'll have that red nose
that comes from indigestion ; because after Michael
ends up in bankruptcy, we won't be able to keep a
maid, and I never could cook anything whatever.
And then Michael will grow fat, and short of breath,
and bald . . ."

"That'll be quite enough for the present," interrupted the outraged Michael.   "I'm not so sure
about letting you marry me at all, after that pleasant
little sketch."

"If you can't drop those domineering ways of
yours, Michael, I shall withdraw," Joan warned him,
coldly.   "You can boss other people as much as you
choose ; I rather like to see you doing it.   But it
doesn't go with me, remember.   If you show these
distressing signs of wanting your own way, I shall
simply have to score you off my list of possibles.   And
that would no doubt be painful to both of us—to you,
at any rate."

"Oh, to both of us, to both of us, I'm sure.   I
wouldn't dream of contradicting you, Joan.   Where
would you be, if the only serious candidate dropped
out ?   Anything rather than that."

"Well, it's a blessing that one man seems to have
some sense," Joan admitted, turning to the others.
"One can't help liking Michael, if it's only for the
frank way he acknowledges when he's in the wrong.
Skilful handling does a lot with the most unpromising
material, of course."

Cecil leaned over in his chair and peered athwart the greenery which surrounded the nook in the winter-garden in which they were sitting.

" There's Foxy wandering round."

He raised his voice :

" Are you looking for us, Foxy ? We're over here."

Foxton Polegate's freckled face, surmounted by a shock of reddish hair, appeared at the entrance to their recess.

" Been hunting about for you," he explained as he sat down. " Couldn't make out where you'd got to."

He turned to Joan.

" Dropped across this evening on important business. Fact is, I've lost my invitation-card and the book of words. Didn't read it carefully when it came. So thought I'd drop over and hear what's what. Programme, I mean, and all that sort of thing, so there'll be no hitch."

Una leaned over and selected a fresh cigarette from the box.

" You're hopeless, Foxy," she pronounced. " One of these memory courses is what you need badly. Why not treat the thing as a practical joke instead of in earnest ? *Then* you'd have no difficulty. Jokes are the only things you ever seem to take seriously."

" Epigrams went completely out before you were born, Una," Foxy retorted. " Don't drag 'em from their graves at this hour of the century. And don't interrupt Joan in her instructions to the guest of the evening. Don't you see she's saying 'em over nervously to herself for fear she forgets 'em ? "

" There's a bit too much of the harassed nursemaid about you, Foxy, with all your ' don'ts,' " Joan broke in. " Now take your stylus and tablets and jot this down carefully, for I won't repeat it under a shilling a page. Here's the programme. Ten p.m. : Arrival of distinguished guests. (They're all distinguished, except you, Foxy.) Brilliant and animated conversation by those who can manage it ; the rest can listen intelligently. (You may try listening, Foxy, if it isn't too much of a strain.) The cloak-room, picture-gallery, museum, and poultry-yard will be thrown open for inspection by the public absolutely free of charge. It won't cost you a cent. Bridge-tables will be provided for the curiosities who don't dance. Dancing will begin straightway and will be continued up to 11.45, when the judges will take their seats. As soon as they are comfortable, the march-past will start. All guests must present themselves at this without fail, Foxy. At five minutes to twelve the identity of the prize-winners will be disclosed. When midnight strikes, all guests will remove their masks, even at the cost of shocking the company in some cases. Dancing will then be resumed and will continue into the dewy dawn. And that's how it will take place according to plan."

" There's just one point," said Foxy, hesitatingly. " Are the prizes portable things, or shall I have to hire a van to take mine away with me ? "

" I shouldn't worry a bit about that, Foxy," said Una, comfortingly. " We've decided to keep the prizes in the family, you see. Joan gets one, because it will be her birthday. I get the other for the best female costume. Cecil, Maurice, and Michael are going to toss odd-man-out for the two men's prizes. So you can come as a Teddy Bear without pockets if you like. It won't be of any consequence. You'll have nothing to carry away."

" Can't say fairer than that," Foxy admitted. " Always liked that plain, straightforward way of doing things myself."

A recollection of his talk with Sir Clinton passed across Cecil Chacewater's mind, and without reflection he communicated it to the others :

" By the way, Sir Clinton seemed a trifle worried over this affair. He pointed out to me that some scallywag might creep in amongst the guests and play Old Harry in the museum if he got the chance."

Just at this moment, Maurice Chacewater passed along the alley in the winter-garden from which the nook opened.

" Maurice ! " Joan called to her brother. " Come here for a moment, please."

Maurice turned back and entered the recess. He seemed tired ; and there was a certain hesitancy in his manner as though he were not quite sure of himself. His sister made a gesture inviting him to sit down, but he appeared disinclined to stay.

" What's the trouble ? " he asked, with a weary air.

" Cecil's been suggesting that it's hardly safe to leave the collections open to-morrow night, in case a stranger got in with a mask on. Hadn't we better have someone to stay in the museum and look after them ? "

" Cecil needn't worry his head," Maurice returned, ignoring his brother. " I'm putting one of the keepers on to watch the museum."

He turned on his heel and went off along the corridor. Foxy gazed after him with a peculiar expression on his face.

" Maurice looks a bit done-up, doesn't he ? " he finally said, turning back towards the group about him. " He hasn't been quite all right for a while. Seems almost as if he expected a thunderbolt to strike him any minute, doesn't he ? A bit white about the gills and holding himself in all the time."

Before anyone could reply to this, Joan rose and beckoned to Michael.

" Come along, Michael. I'll play you a hundred up, if you like. There'll be no one in the billiard-room."

Michael Clifton rose eagerly from his chair and followed her out. Foxy looked after them.

" As an old friend of the family, merely wanting to know, *are* those two engaged or not ? They go on as if they were and as if they weren't. It's most confusing to plain fellows like me."

" I doubt if they know themselves," said Una, " so I'd advise you not to waste too much brain-matter over it, Foxy. What do boys of your age know about such things ? "

" Not much, not much, I admit. Cupid seems to pass me by on his rounds. Perhaps it's the red hair. Or maybe the freckles. Or because I'm not the strong, talkative sort like Michael. Or just Fate, or something."

31

" I expect it's just Something, as you say," Una confirmed in a sympathetic tone. " That seems, somehow, to explain everything, doesn't it ? "

" As it were, yes," retorted Foxy. " But don't let the fact that you've ensnared Cecil—poor chap—lead you into putting on expert airs with me. Betrays inexperience at once, that. Only the very young do it."

His face lighted up.

" I've just thought of something. What a joke ! Suppose we took the Chief Constable's tip and engineered a sham robbery to-morrow night ? Priceless, what ? Carry it through in real good style. Make Maurice sit up for a day or two, eh ? Do his liver good if he'd something to worry about."

Cecil's face showed indecision.

" I shouldn't mind giving Maurice a twinge or two just to teach him manners," he confessed. " But I don't see much in the notion as it stands, Foxy. Maurice is posting a keeper in the museum, you know ; and that complicates things a bit. The keeper would spot any of us tampering with things. He knows us all as well as his own brother."

" Not in fancy dress, with a mask on, dear boy. Don't forget that part of it.

> Fancy me in fancy dress,
> Fancy me as Good Queen Bess ! "

he hummed softly. " Only I don't think I'll come as Good Queen Bess, after all."

Cecil knitted his brows slightly and seemed to be considering Foxy's idea.

" I wouldn't mind giving Maurice a start," he admitted half-reluctantly. " And your notion might be good enough if one could work it out properly. Question is, can you ? Suppose you suddenly make a grab for some of the stuff. The keeper'll be down on you like a shot. He'll yell for help ; and you'll be pinched for a cert. before you could get away. There doesn't seem to be anything in it, Foxy."

" Hold on for a minute. I'll see my way through it."

Foxy took a cigarette, lighted it, and seemed to cogitate deeply over the first few puffs.

" I've got it ! " he announced. " It's dead easy. Suppose one of us grabs the keeper while the other helps himself to the till ? We could easily knock out the keeper between us and get off all right without an alarm being raised."

Cecil shook his head.

" No, I draw the line at using a sand-bag or a knuckle-duster on our own keeper. That's barred, Foxy. Think again."

" There's aye a way," Foxy assured him sententiously. " Give me another jiffy or two. This is how it goes. We mustn't knock out the keeper. We mustn't be recognized. We've got to get away scot-free, or the joke would be on us. These the conditions ? "

Cecil nodded.

" This is where pure genius comes in," Foxy announced with pride. " How does one recognize anyone ? By looking at 'em. So if the keeper can't look at us, he won't recognize us. That's as sound as Euclid, if not sounder."

" Well ? " asked Una, joining in the conversation.

" Well, he won't recognize us if the place is dark, then," explained Foxy, triumphantly. " All we have to do is to get the light in the room switched off, and the thing's as good as done."

" That seems to hit the mark," Cecil agreed. " But that makes it a three-handed job, you know : one to grab the keeper ; one to snaffle the stuff ; and one to pull out the fuse of the museum light from the fuse-box. Where's our third man ? "

Una leaned forward eagerly.

" I'll do that part for you ! I'd like to make Maurice sit up. He hasn't been very nice to me lately ; and I want to pay him out just a little."

" Nonsense, Una," Cecil interrupted. " You can't be mixed up in a joke of this sort. There's almost bound to be a row after it. It doesn't matter in my case ; Maurice has his knife into me anyway, you know. But there's no need for you to be getting your fingers nipped."

Una brushed the suggestion aside.

" What can Maurice do to me even if he does find out ? I've nothing to do with him. And, besides, how is he going to find out anything about it ? I suppose you'll just keep the things for a day or two and then return them by some way that he can't trace. He'll never know who did it, unless we let it out ourselves. And we mustn't let it out, of course."

Foxy nodded his agreement. Cecil was longer in

his consideration ; but at last he seemed to fall in with the arrangement.

" Well, so long as Una's name isn't mixed up in it, Foxy, I'm your man. It's a silly caper ; but I'm not above going into it for the sport of vexing my good brother."

" Right ! " said Foxy, with relief. " Now the next article : What's the best thing to go for ? It must be portable, of course."

Cecil pondered for a moment ; then, as a thought struck him, he laughed.

" Here's the game. It may be news to you, Foxy, but my good brother is taking steps to sell off our collection."

Foxy was quite plainly staggered by this news.

" All the stuff your father got together ? Surely not ! Well, that's the limit ! "

" Quite," confirmed Cecil. " I'd prevent it if I could ; but he's got the whip-hand, and that's all there is to it."

Foxy seemed still slightly incredulous.

" Why, your Governor loved that stuff as if it were a child ! And Maurice doesn't need the money he'll get for it. It's . . . it's shameful ! My word ! If I were in your shoes, Cecil, I believe I'd really steal the stuff instead of only pretending to grab it."

" I'm sorely tempted," said Cecil, half-grimly. " Now here's the point. It seems Maurice has got into touch with Kessock, the Yank millionaire. Kessock wants to buy the Medusa Medallions—the very thing my father set most store by in the whole lot. Kessock's sent over an agent of his—this fellow Foss who's staying here just now—to settle up the business, see to the genuineness of the things, and so forth. I've nothing against Foss. He's only doing his job and he seems all right. I don't like some of his American manners ; but that's neither here nor there. The point is, the deal's just going to be closed. Now if we lift these medallions, won't Maurice look an extra-sized ass ? "

" Absoluto ! " said Foxy. " I see what you're after. We lift 'em. Foss wants 'em at once. He can't get 'em. P'raps the deal's off—for the time at least. And Maurice looks a prize ape."

" Yes," Cecil snapped, angrily. " That'll perhaps teach him a lesson."

Una Rainhill had been thinking while this last part of the conversation had been going on.

" There's one thing you haven't provided against, Foxy," she pointed out. " Suppose you manage everything as you've arranged. Even if you get clear away from the museum, there's almost certain to be someone in the passage outside who'll see you rush out. And then the game would be up. It's not enough to dowse the light in the museum. You'll need to put all the house lights out as well."

" That's sound," Foxy agreed at once. " That means that you'll need to pull out the main switch instead of just the fuse of the museum. It's an even easier job, with no chance of a mistake in it. And what a spree it'll be. The whole shop will be buzzing like an overturned hive ! It'll be great sport. And, of course, there'll be such a wild confusion before they get the lights on again, that we'll come out of it absolutely O.K. All we have to do is to saunter quietly out of the museum and help to restore order among the rabble in the dark. By the time the lights go on again, we'll be anywhere it suits us to be. That's a master-stroke of yours, Una. Couldn't be bettered."

Cecil glanced at his wrist-watch.

" Time's getting on, Foxy. We've sketched the general idea, but we must get this thing down to dots now. Everything will depend on synchronizing things exactly. We can't afford to leave affairs to the last moment ; for we mustn't be seen together, you know, to-morrow night."

Foxy nodded assent and pulled out a notebook.

" Here it is, then," he declared. " I'll make three copies—one for each of us—and we can burn 'em once we've memorized 'em later on. Now, first of all, we can't start our game too early. That'd be a mistake. Let 'em all get well mixed up in dancing and so forth, before we begin operations."

Cecil and Una assented to this at once.

" Midnight's the limit at the other end," Foxy pointed out. " Can't afford to wait for the unmasking, for then the keeper would know us and remember we'd been in the museum when the thing happened."

His fellow-conspirators made no objection.

" In between those limits, I think this would be about right," Foxy proposed. " First of all, we set our three watches to the same time. Better do it now, for fear of forgetting."

When this had been done, he continued :

" At 11.40 Una goes to the main switch. You'll have to show her where it is, Cecil, either to-night or to-morrow morning. At 11.40, also, Cecil and I wander independently into the museum. I remember quite well where the medallions are kept."

" Wait a moment," interrupted Cecil. " Just remember that the three real medallions and your three electrotypes are lying side by side in the glass case. The real medallions are in the top row ; your electros are the bottom row."

Foxy made a note of this and then went on :

" Your business, Cecil, will be to mark down the keeper. Get so near him that you can jump on him for certain the very instant the lights go out. Make sure you can get his hands or his wrists at the first grab. You mustn't fumble it or you'll shipwreck the whole caboodle."

" I'll manage it all right," Cecil assured him.

" In the meantime I'll be stooping over the medallion case, looking at the stuff, with something in my hand to break the glass. I'll have a thick glove, so as not to get cut with the edges when I put my hand in."

" That's sound," said Cecil, " I hadn't thought of the splinters."

" Blood would give us away at once," Foxy pointed out. " Now comes the real business. At a quarter to twelve precisely Una pulls out the switch. As soon as the light goes, Cecil jumps on the keeper while I smash the glass of the case and grab the top row of the medallions. After that, we both cut for the door and mingle with the mob. And remember, not a word said during the whole affair. Our voices would give us away to the keeper."

He scribbled two extra copies of his time-table and handed one of these to each of the other conspirators.

" Now, for my sake, don't botch this business," he added. " I've played a joke or two in my time, but this is the best I've ever done, and I don't want it spoiled by inattention to details. It'll be worth all the trouble to see Maurice's face when he finds what's happened."

CHAPTER III

THE THEFT AT THE MASKED BALL

"I'M thankful I took my wings off," said Ariel, leaning back in her chair with a soft sigh of satisfaction. "You've no notion how much you long to sit down when you know you daren't do it for fear of crushing the frames of these things. It's not tiredness ; it's simply tantalization."

She turned her eyes inquisitively on the bearded figure of her partner.

"I wonder who you're supposed to be ? " she mused. "You ought to have a ticket, with a costume like that. I can't guess who you imagine you are—or who you really are, for that matter."

Her companion showed no desire to enlighten her on the last point.

" ' My quaint Ariel, hark in thine ear,' " he quoted, but she failed to recognize the tones of his voice.

"Oh, now I see ! We did *The Tempest* one year at school. So you're Prospero, are you ? Well, don't let's begin by any misunderstandings. If you think you're entitled to act your part by ordering me about, you're far mistaken. My trade union positively refuses to permit any overtime."

"I've left my book and staff in the cloak-room," Prospero confessed, laughingly, " otherwise, malignant spirit . . . "

" ' That's my noble master ! ' " quoted Ariel,

ironically. "Prospero was a cross old thing. I
suppose you couldn't even throw in a bit of conjuring to keep up appearances? It's almost expected
of you."

Prospero looked cautiously round the winter-garden
in which they were sitting.

"Not much field here for my illimitable powers,"
he grumbled disparagingly, "unless you'd like me to
turn Falstaff over there into a white rabbit. And that
would startle his partner somewhat, I'm afraid, so
we'd better not risk it."

He pondered for a moment.

"I hate to disappoint you, Ariel. What about a
turn at divination? Would it amuse you if I told
your fortune, revealed the secrets of your soul, and
what not? This is how I do it; it's called Botano-
mancy, if you desire to pursue your studies on a more
convenient occasion."

He stretched up his hand and plucked a leaf from
the tropical plant above his head. Ariel watched him
mischievously from behind her mask.

"Well, Prospero, get along with it, will you? The
next dance will be starting sooner than immediately."

Prospero pretended to study the leaf minutely before
continuing.

"I see a girl who likes to play at having her own
way . . . and isn't too scrupulous in her methods
of getting it. She is very happy . . . happier, perhaps, than she has ever been before. . . . I see two
Thresholds, one of which she has just crossed, the
other which she will cross after this next dance, I

think. Yes, that is correct. There's some influence in the background. . . ."

He broke off and regarded Ariel blandly.

" So much for the signs. Now for the interpretation. You are obviously in the very early twenties ; so I infer that the Threshold you are about to cross lies between your twentieth and twenty-first birthday. Putting that along with the character which the leaf revealed . . . Why, Ariel, you must be Miss Joan Chacewater, and you've just got engaged ! "

" You seem to know me all right, Prospero," Joan admitted. " But how about the engagement ? It's too dim in here for you to have seen my ring ; and besides, I've had my hand in the folds of my dress ever since I sat down."

" Except for one moment when you settled the band round your hair," Prospero pointed out. " The ring you're wearing is more than a shade too large for your finger—obviously it's so new that you haven't had time to get it altered to fit, yet."

" You seem to notice things," Joan admitted. " I wonder who you are."

Prospero brushed her inquiry aside.

" A little parlour conjuring to finish up the part in due form ? " he suggested. " It's almost time for our dance. Look ! "

He held out an empty hand for Joan's inspection, then made a slight snatch in the air as if seizing something in flight. When he extended his hand again, a small diamond star glittered in the palm.

" Take it, Joan," said Sir Clinton in his natural

voice. " I meant to send it to you to-morrow ; but at the last moment I thought I might as well bring it with me and have the pleasure of giving it to you myself. It's your birthday present. I'm an old enough friend to give you diamonds on a special occasion like this."

" You took me in completely," Joan admitted, after she had thanked him. " I couldn't make out who you were ; and I thought you were the limit in insolence when you began talking about my private affairs."

" It's Michael Clifton, of course ? " Sir Clinton asked.

" Why ' of course ' ? One would think he'd been my last chance, by the way you put it. This living on a magic island has ruined your manners, my good Prospero."

" Well, he won't let you down, Joan. You—shall I say, even you, to be tactful—couldn't have done better in the raffle."

Before Joan could reply, a girl in Egyptian costume came past their chairs. Joan stopped her with a gesture.

" Pin this pretty thing in the front of my band, please, Cleopatra. Be sure you get it in the right place."

She held out the diamond star. Cleopatra took it without comment and fastened it in position hastily.

" Sit down," Joan invited, " your next partner will find you here when he comes. Tell us about Cæsar and Antony and all the rest of your disreputable past. Make it exciting."

Cleopatra shook her head.

" Sorry I can't stop just now. Neither Julius nor Antony put in an appearance to-night, so I'm spending my arts on a mere centurion. He's a stickler for punctuality—being a Roman soldier."

She glanced at her wrist-watch.

" I must fly at once. O reservoir ! as we say in Egypt, you know."

With a nod of farewell, she hastened along the alley and out of the winter-garden.

" She seems a trifle nervous about something," Sir Clinton commented, indifferently.

Joan smoothed down her filmy tunic.

" Isn't it time we moved ? " she asked. " I see Falstaff's gone away, so you can't turn him into a white rabbit now ; and there doesn't seem to be anything else you could enchant just at present. The orchestra will be starting in a moment, anyhow."

She rose as she spoke. Sir Clinton followed her example, and they made their way out of the winter-garden.

" What costume is Michael Clifton wearing to-night ? " asked Sir Clinton as the orchestra played the opening bars of the dance. " I ought to congratulate him ; and it's easier to pick him up at a distance if I know how he's dressed."

" Look for something in eighteenth-century clothes and a large wig, then," Joan directed. " He says he's Macheath out of the *Beggar's Opera*. I suppose he's quite as like that as anything else. You'll perhaps recognize him best by a large artificial mole at the left corner of his mouth. I observed it particularly myself."

She noticed that her partner seemed more on the alert than the occasion required.

" What are you worried about ? " she demanded. " You seem to be listening for something ; and you can't hear anything, you know, even if you tried, because of the orchestra."

Sir Clinton shook off his air of preoccupation.

" The fact is, Joan, I've been worried all evening. I'm really afraid of something happening to-night. I don't much like this mask business with all that stuff in the collections. I've a feeling in my bones that there might be trouble."

Joan laughed at his gloomy premonitions.

" You won't be kept on the rack much longer, that's one good thing. There's just this dance, then the march-past for judging the costumes, and then it will be midnight when everybody must unmask. So you'll have to make the best of your fears in the next half-hour. After that there'll be no excuse for them."

" Meanwhile, on with the dance, eh ? " said Sir Clinton. " I see it's no use trying to give you a nightmare. You're too poor a subject to repay the labour and trouble. Besides, this music's terribly straining on the vocal cords if one tries to compete with it."

As he spoke, however, the orchestra reached a diminuendo in the score and sank to comparative quietness. Joan looked here and there about the room as they danced and at last detected the figure for which she was searching.

" That's Michael over there," she pointed out, " the one dancing with the girl dressed as . . ."

Across the sound of the music there cut the sharp report of a small-calibre pistol fired in some adjacent room. On the heels of it came the crash and tinkle of falling glass, and, almost simultaneously, a cry for help in a man's voice.

Sir Clinton let Joan's hand go and turned to the door ; but before he could take a step, the lights above them vanished and the room was plunged in darkness. Joan felt a hand come out and grip her arm.

" That you, Joan ? "

" Yes."

" They've taken out the main switch," Sir Clinton said hurriedly. " Get hold of some man at once and show him where it is. We want the lights as quick as possible. I can trust you not to lose your head. Take a man with you for fear of trouble. We don't know what's happening."

" Very well," Joan assured him.

" Hurry ! " Sir Clinton urged.

His hand dropped from her arm as he moved invisibly away towards the door. In the darkness around her she could hear movements and startled exclamations. The orchestra, after mechanically playing a couple of bars, had fallen to silence. Someone blundered into her and passed on before she could put out her hand.

" Well, at least I know where the door is," she assured herself ; and she began to move towards it.

Meanwhile the cries for help continued to come

from the museum. Then, abruptly, they were hushed; and she shuddered as she thought of what that cessation might mean. She moved forward and came to what seemed an unobstructed space on the floor, over which she was able to advance freely.

Her whole senses were concentrated on reaching the exit ; but her mind appeared to work independently of her own volition and to conjure up possibilities behind this series of events. Sir Clinton had evidently expected some criminal attempt that night ; and he had assumed that the museum would be the objective. But suppose he were wrong. Perhaps the affair in the museum was only a blind to draw towards it all the men outside the ball-room. Then, when they were disposed of, there might come an incursion here. Most of the women had taken advantage of their fancy dress to deck themselves out with jewellery, and a few armed men could easily reap a small fortune in a minute or two. Despite the soundness of her nerves, she began to feel anxious, and to conjure up still more appalling pictures.

Suddenly her eyes were dazzled by a flash of light as a man beside her struck a match. Almost at the same moment she felt a hand on her shoulder and she was pulled backwards so brusquely that she almost lost her balance and slipped.

" Put out that match, you fool ! " said Michael's voice. " Do you want to have these girls' dresses in a blaze ? "

The flare of the match had revealed a circle of startled faces. The room was filled with excited voices and a sound of confused movements. Over at the orchestra a music-stand fell with a clash of metal. Then, close beside her in the darkness, Joan heard a girl's voice repeating monotonously in tones of acute fear : " What does it mean ? Oh, what does it mean ? "

" Much good *that* does anyone," Joan muttered, contemptuously. Then, aloud, she called : " Michael ! "

Before he could reply, there came a sharp exclamation in a man's voice :

" Stand back, there ! My partner's fainted."

The possibilities involved in a panic suddenly became all too clear in Joan's mind. If half a dozen people lost their heads, the girl might be badly hurt.

Michael's voice was lifted again, in a tone that would have carried through a storm at sea :

" Everybody stand fast ! You'll be trampling the girl underfoot if you don't take care. Stand still, confound you ! Pull the blinds up and throw back the curtains. It's a moonlight night."

There was a rustling as those nearest the windows set about the execution of his orders. Light suddenly appeared, revealing the strained faces and uneasy attitudes of the company. Joan turned to Michael.

" Come with me and put in the switch, Michael. Sir Clinton's gone to the museum. We must get the lights on quick."

Michael, with a word to his partner, followed his fiancée towards the door. A thought seemed to strike him just as he was leaving the room :

" Wait here, everybody, till we get the lights on again. You'll just run risks by moving about in the

dark outside. It's nothing. Probably only a fuse
blown."

" Now then, Joan, where's that switch ? " he added
as they passed out of the door.

It was pitch-dark in the rest of the house ; but
Joan knew her way and was able to grope along the
corridors without much difficulty. As they came near
the switch-box, the lights flashed up again. One of
the servants appeared round a corner.

" Someone had pulled out the switch, sir," he
explained. " It took me some time to make my way
to it and put it in again."

" Stout fellow ! " said Michael, approvingly.

At that moment, a voice shouted above the confused noises of the house :

" Come on, you fellows ! He's got away. Lend
hand to chase him."

And a sound of running steps filled the hall, as the
male guests poured out in answer to the summons.

" You don't need me any longer, Joan ? " Michael
questioned. " Right ! Then I'm off to lend a hand."

He ran to join the rest.

Left alone, Joan retraced her steps to the ball-
room ; but instead of re-entering it, she passed on in
the direction of the museum, whither a number of
the guests were making their way also.

" I hope nobody's got badly hurt," she thought to
herself as she hurried along. " I do wish I'd taken
the hint and not asked to have that collection thrown
open to-night."

Much to her relief, she found Sir Clinton sitting on

a chair beside the museum door. In the doorway stood the keeper, looking none the worse and busying himself with fending off the more inquisitive among the guests who wished to enter the room. Joan noticed that the museum itself was in darkness though the lights were burning in the rest of the house.

"You're not hurt, are you, Sir Clinton?" she asked as she came up to him.

"Nothing to speak of. The fellow kicked me on the ankle as he came out. I'm temporarily lamed, that's all. Nothing to worry about, I think."

He rubbed his ankle as he spoke.

"Are you all right, Mold?" Joan inquired.

The keeper reassured her.

"No harm done, Miss Joan. They didn't hurt me. But I'm sorry, miss, I didn't manage to get hold of them. They were on me before I could do anything, me being so taken aback by the lights going out."

"What's happened?" Joan questioned Sir Clinton. "Has anything been stolen?"

"We don't know yet what's gone," he replied, answering her last question first. "The bulb of the lamp's smashed in there"—he nodded towards the museum—"and until they bring a fresh one, we can't find out what damage has been done. As to what happened, it seems rather confused at present ; but I expect we shall get it cleared up eventually. There seems to have been a gang at work ; and I'm afraid some things may be missing when we begin to look over the collection."

"I wish I'd taken your hint," Joan admitted,

frankly. " It's partly my blame, I feel, for neglecting your advice. I was silly to laugh at you when you spoke about it."

" I shouldn't worry about it, if I were you, Joan," Sir Clinton reassured her. " It was really only one chance in a million that anything of the sort would happen to-night. Besides, if we manage to nail this fellow that they're all after, we may be able to get some clue to his confederates. Quite evidently there was a gang at work, and he may be induced to split on his friends if we can lay hands on him ; and then we'll get the stuff back again without much trouble, I hope."

He glanced at her, as though to see the effect of his words ; then, as his eyes caught her mask, he seemed struck by another idea.

" That reminds me," he said, " we must get these masks off. Send someone round at once, please, Joan, to order everyone to unmask now. And have all the outer doors shut, too. It's a futile precaution, I'm afraid ; because anyone could slip out during the confusion when there was no light : but we may as well do what we can even at this stage."

He removed his own mask as he spoke, and pulled away the false beard which he had worn as Prospero. Joan loosened her mask and went off to give the necessary orders. In a few moments she returned.

" Now tell me what did happen," she demanded.

" There's no one killed, or even hurt," Sir Clinton assured her. " This ankle of mine's the only casualty, so far as I know ; and I expect I'll be able to limp about quite comfortably by to-morrow."

51

" I'm thankful it's no worse," said Joan, with relief.

" All I know about the business comes from Mold, here," Sir Clinton went on. " It seems he was patrolling the museum at the time the thing happened, under your brother's orders. Perhaps half a dozen people—under a dozen, he says, at any rate—were in the place then. Some of them were examining the cases in the bays ; some of them were looking at the things in the big centre case. Mold doesn't remember what costumes they were wearing. I don't blame him. People had been passing in and out all through the evening ; and there was no reason why he should take particular note of the guests at that special moment."

Sir Clinton glanced up at the keeper, who was looking rather ashamed at his inability to furnish better information.

" Don't you worry, Mold. I doubt if I'd have had any more to tell, myself, if I'd been there. One can't be expected to remember everything."

He turned back to Joan.

" The next thing that happened was a pistol-shot, and the light went out. Some light filtered in from the door of the room, for the lamps in the hall here were still blazing ; but before Mold could do any-thing, someone gripped him from behind and got his wrists twisted behind his back. In the struggle Mold was swung round, so that he couldn't see the central case even in what light there was. Then the lights outside were switched off and he heard a smashing of glass. There was a bit of a struggle, apparently ; and then all at once he felt himself let loose. As soon as he got free, he lit a match and posted himself at the door to prevent anyone getting away ; and he stayed there until the lights went on again. Then he made all his prisoners unmask and those whom he didn't recognize himself he kept there until someone he knew came to identify them. They're all people you know quite well, Joan. More than half of them were girls, who seem rather unlikely people to go in for robbery with violence, to put it mildly. Mold made a list of them, if we happen to need it. But I don't think we're likely to find the criminal amongst them. This affair was too well planned for that. The real gang have got clean away, I'm pretty sure."

" And what about your ankle ? " demanded Joan.

" Oh, that ? I happened to arrive at the door fairly quickly after the lights went out. Just as I got to it, a fellow came dashing out ; and I made a grab at him as well as I could in the dark. But one can't see what one's doing ; and I didn't get a decent grip on him as he charged out on top of me. He landed me a fairly effective kick—right on the ankle-bone, by bad luck—and then, before I could get my hands on him properly he tore himself clear and was off down the hall towards the front door. I hobbled after him as best I could ; and there he was—a fellow dressed in Pierrot costume—running quite leisurely over the gravel sweep and making for the woods. I couldn't go after him ; but he was quite clear in the moonlight and he'd a long way to go before getting into cover ; so I raised a hue and cry at once, and quite a crowd of stout fellows are after him. He'll have to run a bit faster than he was doing, if he expects to get off. These pine-woods have no undergrowth to speak of ; and he'll find it difficult to conceal himself in a hurry."

As Sir Clinton ended his narrative a servant came hurrying up the hall, bringing a tall pair of steps with him.

" Is that the new lamp ? " Sir Clinton demanded. " All right. Light a match or two, Mold, to let him see where to put the steps. And don't tramp about too much while you're fixing them up, please. I want to see things undisturbed as far as possible."

CHAPTER IV

THE CHASE IN THE WOODS

IN earlier days, Michael Clifton had been reckoned among the more creditable runners in the School Mile ; and he had never allowed himself to fall out of training. Thus as he joined the throng of would-be pursuers emerging from the house, he felt a certain confidence that the fugitive would at any rate have to put his best foot foremost if he was to avoid being run down. Before he had covered twenty yards, however, Michael found himself handicapped by his costume. The full-bottomed wig dropped off almost immediately, and the shoes were not so troublesome as he had feared ; but the sleeves of his coat interfered with his movements, and the long skirts hampered his legs.

" I wonder if these coves in the eighteenth century ever ran a step," he grumbled. " If they did it in this kit, they must have been wonders. I must get rid of the truck."

He pulled up and stripped off the full-skirted coat ; then, as an after-thought, he removed the long waist-coat as well. While doing this, he glanced ahead to see how the chase was progressing. The light of the full moon, now at its highest in the cloudless heavens, lit up the whole landscape before him almost as clearly as daylight. Far ahead, he could see the white figure of the escaping thief as it ascended the long, gentle slope towards the pine-woods.

" I wonder what tempted the beggar to choose *that* particular costume on a night like this," Michael speculated. " It's the most conspicuous affair he could have put on. Well, all the better for us."

The quarry had evidently secured a fair start, for the nearest group of pursuers was still a considerable distance behind him. The hunters were strung out in an irregular file, knotted here and there with groups of three or four runners ; and the line extended back almost to Michael's position. Behind him, he could hear fresh reinforcements emerging from the house, shouting as they came.

" They'd better save their breath," Michael commented critically to himself. " That long rise'll take it out of a good many of them."

He settled down to his favourite stride ; and very soon began to overtake the laggards at the tail of the chase. In front of him he saw a Cardinal Richelieu with kilted cassock ; but the Cardinal found his costume too much for him and pulled out of the race as Michael passed him. Shortly after, Michael drew level with an early nineteenth-century dandy and for a few seconds they raced neck and neck. The dandy, however, was unable to stay the pace.

" It's these damned Johnny Walker boots," he gasped, as he fell behind.

Michael, running comfortably, began to take a faint amusement in the misfortunes of his colleagues. He could not help smiling as he passed a Minotaur, sitting beside the track and making furious efforts to , disentangle himself from his pasteboard bull's head which seemed to have become clamped in position. But as he found two more of the hunters by the wayside, a fresh point of view occurred to him.

" If they're going to drop out at this rate, there won't be many of us left at the finish to tackle the beggar ; and he's armed.   We'll need all the men we can scrape up, if we're to make sure of him."

Glancing ahead again, he was relieved to see that he had gained a fair amount of ground on the fugitive ; and now he began to pass runner after runner, as the rising slope told on the weaker pursuers.   He reached the group at the head of the chase just as the escaping burglar dashed into the shadow of the woods a hundred yards in advance.

" He'll dodge us now, if he can," Michael warned his companions, who evidently were unacquainted with the ground.   " Keep your eyes on him at any cost."

But as they entered the pine arcades, Michael found that he was mistaken.   The quarry maintained his lead; but he made no effort to leave the beaten track.   Ahead of them they could see his white-clad figure dappled with light and darkness as he sped up the broad pathway.

Suddenly, Michael remembered what lay beyond the pine-wood.   Without raising his voice, for fear the runner in front should hear him, he explained the situation.

" He doesn't know what he's running into.   There's a big quarry up there, with barbed wire fences on each side.   If we can keep him straight for it, we'll have him pinned."

On went the fugitive, still maintaining his lead and glancing over his shoulder from time to time, as though he were gauging the distance which separated him from his closest pursuers.

" The beggar can run, certainly," Michael admitted to himself. " But running isn't going to help him much in a minute or two. We have him on toast."

In a few moments the moon shone bright through the trees ahead. As they reached the edge of the wood, the white figure in front of them showed up clearly as it sprinted across the strip of open ground, straight for the spinney which bounded the quarry cliff. With a gesture, Michael called his motley group to a halt.

" Wait a minute," he ordered. " You, Mephistopheles, get off to the left there, outside the spinney. Go on until you strike barbed wire. Take this Prehistoric Man—oh, it's you, is it, Frankie? Well, both of you get down there and act as stoppers, so that he can't sneak off along the fence. Oliver Cromwell and you in the funny coat! You're to do the same over yonder on the right. Put some hurry into it, now! And don't move in towards him till you get the word. The rest of you, extend a bit along the near edge of the spinney. Not too close ; give yourselves a chance of spotting him if he breaks cover. And don't yell unless you actually see him. We've got him shut in now, and we can afford to wait for reinforcements. Here they come ! "

Two panting runners breasted the hill as he spoke. At this moment there came from beyond the spinney the sound of a splash. Michael was taken aback.

" The beggar can't have dived over, surely. It's

full of rocks down below. We'll have to hurry up.
He might get away, after all, if he's extra lucky."

A fresh group of pursuers gave him the reinforcements he needed ; and he fed them into his cordon at
its weak points.

" Pass the word for the whole line to close in ! "

The cordon began to contract around the spinney,
the wide gaps in it closing up as it advanced.

" The beggar's probably got a pistol ; look out for
yourselves among the trees," Michael cautioned them
as they reached the boundary of the plantation.
" Don't hurry. And keep touch, whatever you do."

He himself was at the centre of the line and was the
first to enter the tiny wood. The advance was slow ;
for here there was some undergrowth which might
offer a hiding-place to the fugitive ; and this was carefully scrutinized, clump by clump, before the line
moved forward as a whole. Michael meant to make
certain of capturing the burglar ; and he could afford
now to go about the matter deliberately. Fresh reinforcements in twos and threes were still streaming in
from the pine-wood.

It took only a few minutes, however, to draw his
screen through the spinney ; for the belt of trees was
a narrow one. Every instant he expected to hear a
shout indicating that the quarry had been run to earth ;
but none came. His line emerged intact from the
trees, forming an arc of which the cliff-face was the
chord ; and as his men came out into the moonlight,
Michael had to admit to himself that no one could well
have crept through any gap in the cordon.

" He must be out here, hiding among these seats,"
he shouted. " Don't break your line any more than
you can help. Advance to that balustrade in front.
Rush him, if he shows up."

Now that he was sure of his quarry, Michael at last
had leisure to note the tincture of the bizarre in the
scene before him. The high-riding moon whitened
the terrace and touched with glamour the motley
costumes of the hunters preparing for their final
swoop. Here Robin Hood and a hatless Flying
Dutchman were stooping to peer below one of the
marble seats. Farther along the line Lohengrin and
a Milkman discussed something eagerly in whispers.
On the left the Prehistoric Man loomed up like a
Troglodyte emerging from his cave ; while beyond
him Mephistopheles leaned upon the railing, scanning
the water below. From the inky shadow of the
spinney Felix the Cat stole softly out to join the
cordon.

" A weird-looking gang we are," Michael commented to himself as he gazed about him.

Only a few steps separated the hunters from the
clear floor of the terrace. In a second or two at most,
the man they were chasing must break cover and make
a dash for liberty or else tamely surrender. Slowly
the line crept forward.

" We've got him now ! " a voice cried, exultantly.

But the living net swept on past the marble tier
without catching anything in its meshes. Between it
and the balustrade was nothing but the untenanted
paving of the terrace.

" He's got away ! " ejaculated someone in tones of complete amazement. " Well, I'm damned if I see how he managed it."

The chain broke up into individuals, who hurried hither and thither on the esplanade searching even in the most unlikely spots for the missing fugitive. All at once Michael's eye caught something which had been concealed in the shadows thrown by the moon.

" Here's a rope, you fellows ! He's gone down the face of the cliff. Swum the lake, probably."

Mephistopheles dissented in a languid drawl.

" Not he, Clifton. I've had my eye on the water ever since I got up to the barbed wire. You could spot the faintest ripple in this moonshine. He didn't get off that way."

" Sure of that ? " demanded Michael.

" Dead sure. I watched specially."

Michael hesitated for a moment or two, considering the situation. Then his face cleared.

" I see it ! I remember there's a cave right below here, in the cliff-face. He's gone to ground there. Half of you get through the barbed wire on the right ; the rest take the left side. Line up on the banks when you get down to the water. He may swim for it yet if we don't hurry."

They raced off to carry out his instructions, while Michael pulled up the rope and flung it on the terrace.

" That cuts off his escape in this direction," he said to himself. " Now we can dig him out at leisure."

Without hurrying, he made his way down to the water.

" There used to be a raft of sorts here," he explained.
" If we can rout it out, we'll be able to ferry across to
the cave-mouth without much bother. I doubt if
he'll show fight once we lay our hands on him ; for he
hasn't an earthly chance of getting away."

He poked about among the sedge on the rim of the
lakelet and at last discovered the decrepit raft.

" This thing'll just bear two of us. Do we dig the
beggar out or starve him out ? Dig him out, eh ?
Well, I want someone to go with me. Here, you,
Frankie "—he turned to the Prehistoric Man—
" you'd better come along. If it comes to a ducking,
you've got fewer clothes to spoil than the rest of us."

Nothing loath, the Prehistoric Man scrambled
aboard the raft, which sank ominously under the extra
weight.

" I can't find anything to pole with," grumbled
Michael. " Paddle with your flippers, Frankie. It's
the only thing to do. Get busy with it."

Under this primitive method of propulsion, the
progress of the raft was slow ; but at last they succeeded in bringing it under the cliff-face, after which
they were able to work it along by hand. Gradually
they manœuvred it into position in front of the cave-
mouth, which stood only a yard or so above water-
level. Michael leaned forward to the entrance.

" You may as well come out quietly," he warned the
inmate. " It's no good trying to put up a fight. You
haven't a dog's chance."

There was no reply of any sort.

" Hold the damned raft steady, Frankie ! You

nearly had me overboard," expostulated Michael. " I'm going to light a match. The cave's as black as the pit, and I can see nothing."

He pulled a silver match-box from his trousers pocket.

" Lucky I hadn't this in my coat ; for you don't look as if you had a pocket of any sort on you, Frankie."

The first match, damped by the moisture on his hands, sputtered and died out.

" *Hurry* up, Guvnor," shouted Mephistopheles, cheerfully, from the bank. " Don't keep us up all night with your firework display. It's getting a bit chilly, paddling about amongst this sedge. Not at all the temperature I'm accustomed to at home."

Michael felt for another match and lighted it successfully. Standing up on the raft, he held the light above his head and peered into the cavity in the rock. The Prehistoric Man heard him exclaim in amazement.

" Damnation, Frankie ! He's not here ! It's hardly a cave at all."

He put his hands on the cave floor.

" Hold tight with the raft. I'm going in to make sure."

He scrambled up into the hollow ; but almost immediately his face appeared again in the moonlight.

" Nothing here. The hole's barely big enough to take me in."

" Then where's he gone ? " demanded the Prehistoric Man, who was a creature of few words.

" I dunno ! Must have given us the slip somehow.

If he isn't here, he must be somewhere else. No getting round that."

He shouted the news to the watchers on the banks ; and a confused sound of argument rose from amongst the sedge.

" Not much use hanging round the old home, Frankie. Pull for the shore, sailor. We'd best man-handle her along the face of the cliff. I've had enough of that paddling."

When they touched firm ground again they were surrounded by their friends, most of whom seemed to doubt whether the search of the cave had been pro-perly carried out.

" I tell you," declaimed the exasperated Michael, " I got right into the damned hole ! It's so small that I nearly broke my nose against the back wall as I heaved myself inside. It would have been a tight fit for me and a squirrel together. He's not there, whether you like it or not. . . . I can't help your troubles, Tommy ; you can go and look for yourself, if you like the job of lying on your tummy on a raft that's awash. I shan't interfere with your simple pleasures."

" But . . ."

" We've lost him. Is that plain enough ? There's nothing to be done but go home again with our tails between our legs. I'm going now."

He accompanied his friends to the top of the cliff again ; but when he reached the terrace a fresh thought struck him, and he loitered behind while the others, soaked and disconsolate, made their way down into the

pine-wood. When the last of them had disappeared,
Michael retraced his steps to the edge of the cliff.

" He reached here all right," he assured himself.
" And he didn't break back through the cordon."

He stooped down, picked up the rope, and refastened
it round one of the pillars of the balustrade.

" Everyone knows there are secret passages about
Ravensthorpe," he mused. " Perhaps this beggar has
got on to one of them. And quite possibly the end of
the passage is in that cave down there. That would
explain the rope. I'll slide down and have another
look round."

He got into the cave-mouth without difficulty and
used up the remainder of his matches in a close examination of the interior of the cavity ; but even the
closest scrutiny failed to reveal anything to his eyes.

" Nothing there but plain rock, so far as I can
see," he had to admit to himself as the last match
burned out. " That's a blank end in more senses
than one."

Without much difficulty he swarmed up the rope
again, untied it from the balustrade, and coiled it over
his arm.

" A nice little clue for Sir Clinton Driffield to puzzle
over," he assured himself. " Sherlock Holmes would
have been on to it at once ; found where it was sold
in no time ; discovered who bought it before five
minutes had passed ; and paralysed Watson with the
whole story that same evening over a pipeful of shag.
We shall see."

He threw a last glance round the empty terrace and

then moved off into the spinney. As he passed into the shadow of the trees he saw, a few yards to one side, the outline of the Fairy House dappled in the moonshine which filtered through the leaves overhead. Half-unconsciously, Michael halted and looked at the little building.

" They could never have overlooked that in the hunt, surely. Well, no harm in having a peep to make certain."

He dropped his coil of rope, stepped across to the house, and, stooping down, flung open the door. Inside, he caught a flash of some white fabric.

" It's the beggar after all ! Here ! Come out of that ! "

He gripped the inmate roughly and hauled him by main force out of his retreat.

" Pierrot costume, right enough ! " he said to himself as he extracted the man little by little from his refuge. Then, having got his victim into the open :

" Now we'll turn you over and have a look at your face . . . Good God ! Maurice ! "

For as he turned the man on his back, it was the face of Maurice Chacewater that met his eyes. But it was not a normal Maurice whom he saw. The features were contorted by some excessive emotion the like of which Michael had never seen.

" Let me alone, damn you," Maurice gasped, and turned over once more on his face, resting his brow on his arm as though to shut out the spectacle of Michael's astonishment.

" Are you ill ? " Michael inquired, solicitously.

66

" For God's sake leave me alone. Don't stand there gaping. Clear out, I tell you."

Michael looked at him in amazement.

" I'm going to have a cheerful kind of brother-in-law before all's done, it seems," he thought to himself.

" Can I do anything for you, Maurice ?

" Oh, go to hell ! "

Michael turned away.

" It's fairly clear he doesn't like my company," he reflected, as he stepped across and picked up his coil of rope from the ground. " But I've known politer ways of showing it, I must say."

With a final glance at the prostrate figure of Maurice, he walked on and took the road back to Ravensthorpe. But as he went a vision of Maurice's face kept passing before his mind's eye.

" There's something damned far wrong with that beggar, whether it's an evil conscience or cramp in the tummy. It might be either of them, by the look of him. He didn't seem to want any assistance from me. That looks more like the evil conscience theory."

He dismissed this with a laugh ; but gradually he grew troubled.

" There he was, in white—same as the burglar. He's in a bit of a bate at being discovered, that's clear enough. He didn't half like it, to judge by his chat."

A discomforting hypothesis began to frame itself in his mind despite his efforts to stifle it.

" He's the fellow, if there is one, who would know all these secret passages about here. Suppose there really is one leading out of that cave. He could have swarmed down the rope, got into the cave, sneaked up the subterranean passage, and got behind us that way."

A fresh fact fitted suddenly in.

" And of course the other end of the passage may be in that Fairy House ! That would explain his being there. He'd be waiting to see us off the premises before he could venture out in his white costume."

He pondered over the problem as he hurried with long strides towards the house.

" Well," he concluded, " I'm taking no further steps in the business. It's no concern of mine to go probing into the private affairs of the family I'm going to marry into. And that's that."

Then, as a fresh aspect of the matter came to his mind, he gave a sigh of relief.

" I must be a stricken idiot ! No man would ever dream of burgling his own house. What would he gain by it, if he did ? The thing's ridiculous."

And the comfort which this view brought him was sufficient to lighten his steps for the rest of his way.

CHAPTER V

"THERE's the light on again in the museum," Sir Clinton observed. "I think we'll go in and have a look round, now, to see if the place suggests anything."

Mold stood aside to let them pass, and then resumed his watch at the door to prevent anyone else from entering the room. The servant had just finished fitting the new globe in its place and was preparing to remove the steps which he had used, when Sir Clinton ordered him to leave them in position and to await further instructions.

The museum was a room about forty feet square, with a lofty ceiling. To judge by the panelling of the walls, it belonged to the older part of Ravensthorpe ; but the parquet of the floor seemed to be much more modern. Round the sides were placed exhibition cases about six feet high ; and others of the same kind jutted out at intervals to form a series of shallow bays. In the centre of the room, directly under the lamp, stood a long, flat-topped case ; and the floor beside it was littered with broken glass.

"I think we'll begin at the beginning," said Sir Clinton.

He turned to the servant who stood waiting beside the steps.

"Have you got the remains of the broken lamp there ? "

"You can go now," he added. "We shan't need you further."

When he had received the smashed lamp, he examined it.

"Not much to be made out of that," he admitted. "It's been one of these thousand candle-power gas-filled things ; and there's practically nothing left of it but the metal base and a few splinters of glass sticking to it."

He looked up at the fresh lamp hanging above them.

"It's thirty feet or so above the floor. Nothing short of a fishing-rod would reach it. Evidently they didn't smash it by hand."

He stooped down and sorted out one or two small fragments of glass from the debris at his feet.

"These are more bits of the lamp, Joan," he said, holding them out for her to look at. "You see the curve of the glass ; and you'll notice that the whole affair seems to have been smashed almost to smithereens. There doesn't seem to be a decent-sized fragment in the whole lot."

He turned to the keeper.

"I think we'll shut the door, Mold. We'd better conduct the rest of this business in private."

The keeper closed the door of the museum, much to the disappointment of the group of people who had clustered about the entrance and were watching the proceedings with interest.

"Now, Joan, would you mind going round the wall-cases and seeing if anything has been taken from them ? "

Joan obediently paced round the room and soon came back to report that nothing seemed to have been removed.

" All the cases were locked, you know," she explained. " And there's no glass broken in any of them. So far as I can see, nothing's missing from the shelves."

" What about that safe let into the wall over yonder ? " Sir Clinton inquired.

" It's used to house one or two extra valuable things from time to time," Joan explained. " But to-night everything was put on show, and the safe's empty."

She went over and swung the door open, showing the vacant shelves within.

" We do take precautions usually," she pointed out. " The museum door itself is iron-plated and has a special lock. It was only to-night that we had everything out in the show-cases."

Sir Clinton refrained from comment, as he knew the girl was still blaming herself for her share in the catastrophe. He turned to examine the rifled section of the central case.

" What's missing here, Joan, can you make out ? "

Obediently, Joan came to his side and ran her eye over the remaining articles in the compartment.

" They've taken the Medusa Medallions ! " she exclaimed, turning pale as she realized the magnitude of the calamity. " They've got the very pick of the collection, Sir Clinton. My father would have parted with all the rest rather than with these, I know."

71

" Nothing else gone ? "

Joan looked again at the case.

" No, nothing else, so far as I can see. Wait a bit, though ! They've taken the electrotype copies as well. There were three of each : three medallions and an electrotype from each that Foxton Clifford made for us. The whole six are gone."

She cast a final glance at the compartment.

" No, there's nothing else missing, so far as I can see. Some of the things are displaced a bit ; but everything except the medallions and the electros seems to be here."

" You're quite sure ? "

" Certain."

Sir Clinton seemed satisfied.

" Of course we'll have to check the stuff by the catalogue to make sure," he said, " but I expect you're right. The medallions alone would be quite a good enough haul for a minute or two's work ; and probably they had their eyes on the things as the best paying proposition of the lot."

" But why did they take the electros as well ? " Joan demanded.

Then a possible explanation occurred to her.

" Oh, of course, they wouldn't know which was which, so they took the lot in order to make sure."

" Possibly," Sir Clinton admitted. " But don't let's be going too fast, Joan. We'd better not get ideas into our minds till we've got all the evidence, you know."

" Oh, I see," said Joan, with a faint return of her

normal spirits, " I'm to be Watson, am I ? And you'll prove in a minute or two what an ass I've made of myself. Is that the idea ? "

" Not altogether," Sir Clinton returned, with a smile. " But let's have the facts before the theories."

He turned to the keeper.

" Now we'll take your story, Mold ; but give us the things in the exact order in which they happened, if you can. And don't be worried if I break in with questions."

Mold thought for a moment or two before beginning his tale.

" I'm trying to remember how many people there were in the room just before the lights went out," he explained at last, " but somehow I don't quite seem able to put a figure on it, Sir Clinton. I've a sort of feeling that some of 'em must ha' got away before I stopped the door—sneaked off in the dark. At least I know I felt surprised when I saw how few I'd got left when they began to come up to me to be let out. But that's all I can really say, sir."

Sir Clinton evidently approved of the keeper's caution.

" Now tell us exactly what happened when the light went out. This is the bit where I want you to be careful. Tell us everything you can remember." •

Mold fixed his eye on the corner of the room near the safe.

" I was patrollin' round the room, sir, most of the night. I didn't stand in one place all the time. Now just when the light was about to go out, I was walkin'

73

away from this case here "—he nodded towards the rifled central case—" and as near as may be, I'd got to the entrance to that second-last bay, just before you come to the safe. I just turned round to come back, when I heard a pistol goin' off."

" That was the first thing that attracted your attention ? " questioned Sir Clinton. " It's an important point, Mold."

" That was the first thing out o' the common that happened," Mold asserted. " The pistol went bang, and out went the light, and I heard glass tinkling all over the place."

" Shot the light out, did they ? " Sir Clinton mused.

He glanced up at the carved wooden ceiling, but evidently failed to find what he was looking for.

" Have you a pair of race-glasses, Joan ? Prismatics, or even opera-glasses ? Tell Mold where he can get them, please."

Joan gave the keeper instructions and he left the room.

" Knock when you come back again," Sir Clinton ordered. " I'm going to lock the door to keep out the inquisitive."

As soon as the keeper was out of earshot, Sir Clinton turned to Joan.

" This fellow Mold, is he a reliable man ? Do you know anything about him, Joan ? "

" He's our head keeper. We've always trusted him completely."

She glanced at Sir Clinton, trying to read the expression on his face.

" You don't think *he's* at the bottom of the business, do you ? I never thought of that ! "

" I'm only collecting facts at present. All I want to know is whether you know Mold to be reliable."

" We've always found him so."

" Good. We'll make a note of that ; and if we get the thing cleared up, then we'll perhaps be able to confirm that opinion of yours."

In a few minutes a knock came at the door and Sir Clinton admitted the keeper.

" Prismatics ? " he said, taking the glasses from Mold. " They'll do quite well."

Adjusting the focus, he subjected the ceiling of the room to a minute scrutiny. At last he handed the glasses to Joan.

" Look up there," he said, indicating the position.

Joan swept the place with the glasses for a moment.

" I see," she said. " That's a bullet-hole in the wood, isn't it ? "

Sir Clinton confirmed her guess.

" That's evidently where the bullet went after knocking the lamp to pieces. Pull the steps over there, Mold. I want to have a closer look at the thing."

With some difficulty, owing to his injured ankle, he ascended the steps and inspected the tiny cavity.

" It looks like a ·22 calibre. One could carry a Colt pistol of that size in one's pocket and no one would notice it."

His eye traced out the line joining the bullet-mark and the lamp.

" The shot was evidently fired by someone in that bay over there," he inferred. " Just go to where you were standing when the light went out, Mold. Can you see into this bay here ? "

Mold looked round and discovered that a show-case interposed between him and the point from which the pistol had been fired.

" They evidently thought of everything," Sir Clinton said, when he heard Mold's report. " If a man had brandished his pistol in front of Mold, there was always a chance that Mold might have remembered his costume. Firing from that hiding-place, he was quite safe, and could take time over his aim if he wanted to."

He climbed down the steps and verified the matter by going to the position from which the shot had been fired. It was evident that the shooter was out of sight of the keeper at the actual moment of the discharge.

" Now what happened after that, Mold ? " Sir Clinton demanded, coming back to the central case again.

Mold scratched his ear as though reflecting, then hurriedly took his hand down again.

" This pistol went off, sir ; and the lamp-glass tinkled all over the place. I got a start—who wouldn't ?—with the light going out, and all. Before I could move an inch, someone got a grip of my wrists and swung me round. He twisted my arms behind my back and I couldn't do anything but kick —and not much kickin' even, or I'd have gone down on my face."

" Did you manage to get home on him at all ? "

" I think I kicked him once, sir ; but it was only a graze."

" Pity," Sir Clinton said. " It would have always been something gained if you'd marked him with a good bruise."

" Oh, there'll be a mark, if that's all you want, sir. But it wouldn't prevent him runnin' at all."

" And then ? " Sir Clinton brought Mold back to his story.

" Then, almost at once when the lights went out, I heard glass breakin'—just as if you'd heaved a stone through a window. It seemed to me—but I couldn't take my oath on it—as if there was two smashes, one after t'other. I couldn't be sure. Then there was a lot of scufflin' in the dark ; but who did it, I couldn't rightly say. I was busy tryin' to get free from the man who was holdin' me then."

Sir Clinton moved over to the rifled compartment and inspected the broken glass thoughtfully for a moment or two.

" Are you looking for finger-marks ? " asked Joan, as she came to his side.

Sir Clinton shook his head.

" Not much use hunting for finger-marks round here. Remember how many people must have leaned on this case at one time or other during the evening, when they were looking at the collection before the robbery. Finger-prints would prove nothing against anyone in particular, I'm afraid, Joan. What I'm really trying to find is some evidence confirming Mold's notion that he heard two smashes after the light went out. It certainly looks as if he were right. If you look at the way that bit of glass there is cracked, you'll see two series of lines in it. It might have been cracked here "—he pointed with his finger—" first of all : long cracks radiating from a smash over in this direction. Then there was a second blow—about here—which snapped off the apices of the spears of glass left after the first smash. But that really proves nothing. The same man might easily have hit the pane twice."

He turned back to the keeper.

" Can you give me an estimate, Mold, of how long it was between the two crashes you heard ? "

Mold considered carefully before replying.

" So far's I can remember, Sir Clinton, it was about five seconds. But I'll not take my oath on it."

" I wish you could be surer," said the Chief Constable. " If it really was five seconds, it certainly looks like two separate affairs. A man smashing glass with repeated blows wouldn't wait five seconds between them.

He scanned the broken glass again.

" There's a lot of jagged stuff round the edge of the hole but no blood, so far as I can see. The fellow must have worn a thick glove if he got his hand in there in the dark without cutting himself in the hurry."

He turned back to the keeper.

" You can go outside, Mold, and keep people off the doorstep for a minute or two. Perhaps we shall have news of the man-hunt soon. If anyone wants to see me on business, let him in ; but keep off casual inquirers for the present."

Obediently Mold unlocked the door and took his stand on the threshold outside, shutting the door behind him as he went. When he had gone, Sir Clinton turned to Joan.

" Were these medallions insured, do you know ? "

Fortunately, Joan was able to supply some information.

" Maurice insured them, I know, But I've heard him say that he wasn't content with the valuation put on them by the company. It seems they wouldn't take his word for the value of the things—they thought it was a speculative one or something—and in case of a loss they weren't prepared to go beyond a figure which Maurice thought too small."

" The electros weren't insured for any great amount, I suppose ? "

Joan shook her head.

" I don't think they were specially insured. They were just put under the ordinary house policy, I think. But you'd better ask Maurice. He knows all about it."

Sir Clinton glanced round the room once more.

" I doubt if there's much more to find out here," he concluded. " It doesn't give us much to go on, does it ? Perhaps we'll have better luck when these fellows come in from their hunt. They may have some news for us. But as things stand, we can't even be sure whether it was two men or two gangs that were at work. One can't blame Mold for not giving us better information ; but what he gave us doesn't seem to amount to very much at present."

He turned, as though to leave the room ; but at that moment the door opened and Mold appeared.

" There's a Mr Foss wants to see you, sir. He says he's got something to tell you that won't wait. He's been looking for you all over the house."

" That's the American, isn't it ? " Sir Clinton asked Joan in a low voice.

" Yes. He's been here for a day or two, consulting with Maurice about these medallions."

" Well, if he can throw any light on this business, I suppose we'd better let him in and see what he has to say. You needn't go, Joan. You may as well hear his story, whatever it may be."

He turned to the keeper.

" Let Mr Foss in, Mold ; and wait outside the door yourself."

CHAPTER VI

MR FOSS had nothing distinctively American in his appearance, Sir Clinton noted ; and when he spoke, his accent was so faint as to be hardly detectable. He was a stout man of about fifty, with a cleanshaven face and more than a trace of a double chin : the kind of man who might readily be chosen as an unofficial uncle by children. Sir Clinton's first glance showed him that the American was troubled about something.

Foss seemed surprised to find the Chief Constable in the guise of Prospero. He himself, in preparation for an official interview, had exchanged his masquerade costume for ordinary evening clothes.

" We haven't met before, Sir Clinton," he explained, rather unnecessarily, " but I've something to tell you " —his face clouded slightly—" which I felt you ought to know before you go any further in this business. I've been hunting all over the house for you ; and it was only a minute or two ago that I got directed in here."

" Yes ? " said Sir Clinton, interrogatively.

Foss glanced at Joan and seemed to find some difficulty in opening the subject.

" It's a strictly private matter," he explained.

Joan refused to take the implied hint.

" If it has any connection with this burglary, Mr

Foss, I see no reason why I should not hear what you have to say. It's a matter that concerns me as one of the family, you know."

Foss seemed taken aback and quite evidently he would have preferred to make his confidence to Sir Clinton alone.

" It's rather a difficult matter," he said, with a feeble endeavour to deflect Joan from her purpose.

Joan, however, took no notice of his diffidence.

" Come, Mr Foss," she said. " If it's really important, the sooner Sir Clinton hears of it the better. Begin."

Foss glanced appealingly at Sir Clinton ; but apparently the Chief Constable took Joan's view of the matter.

" I'm rather busy at present, Mr Foss," he said, dryly. " Perhaps you'll give us your information as concisely as possible."

Having failed in his attempt, Foss made the best of it ; though it was with obvious reluctance that he launched into his subject.

" Last night after dinner," he began, " I went into the winter-garden to smoke a cigar. I had some business affairs which I wanted to put straight in my mind ; and I thought I could stow myself away in a corner there and be free from interruption. So I sat down at one side of the winter-garden behind a large clump of palms where no one was likely to see me ; and I began to think over the points I had in mind."

" Yes ? " prompted Sir Clinton, who seemed anxious to cut Foss's narrative down to essentials.

"While I was sitting there," the American continued, "some of the young people came into the winter-garden and sat down in a recess on the side opposite to where I was. At first they didn't disturb me. I thought they'd be almost out of earshot, on the other side of the dome. I think you were one of them, Miss Chacewater : you, and your brother, and Miss Rainhill, and someone else whom I didn't recognize."

"I was there," Joan confirmed, looking rather puzzled as to what might come next.

"You may not know, Miss Chacewater," Foss continued, "that your winter-garden is a sort of whispering-gallery. Although I was quite a long way off from your party, your voices came quite clearly across to where I was sitting. They didn't disturb me at all—I've got the knack of concentration when I'm thinking about business affairs. But although I wasn't listening intentionally, the whole conversation was getting in at my ear while I was thinking about other things. I suppose I ought to have gone away or let you know I was there ; but the fact is, I'd just got to a point where I was seeing my way through a rather knotty tangle, and I didn't want to break my chain of thought. I wasn't eavesdropping, you understand ? "

"Yes ? " repeated Sir Clinton, with a slight acidity in his tone. " And then ? "

But the American failed to take the hint. Evidently he laid great stress on explaining exactly how things had fallen out.

" After a while," he went on, with an evident effort to be accurate, " Miss Chacewater and someone else left the party."

" Quite true," Joan confirmed. " We went to play billiards."

The American nodded.

" When you had gone," he continued, " someone else joined the party—a red-haired young man whom they called Foxy."

Sir Clinton glanced at Joan.

" That's Foxton Polegate," Joan explained. " He's a neighbour of ours. He made these electrotypes of the medallions for us."

Foss waited patiently till she had finished her interjection. Then he resumed his narrative.

" Shortly after that, my ear caught the sound of my own name. Naturally my attention was attracted, quite without any intention on my part. It's only natural to prick up your ears when you hear your own name mentioned."

He looked apologetically at them both as if asking them to condone his conduct.

" The next thing I heard—without listening intentionally, you understand ?—was ' Medusa Medallions.' Now, as you know, I've been sent over here by Mr Kessock to see if I can arrange to buy these medallions from Mr Chacewater. It's my duty to my employer to get to know all I can about them. I wouldn't be earning my money if I spared any trouble in the work which has been put into my hands. So when I heard the name of the medallions mentioned, I . . . frankly,

I listened with both ears. It seemed to me my duty
to Mr Kessock to do so."

He looked appealingly at their faces as though to
plead for a favourable verdict on his conduct.

" Go on, please," Sir Clinton requested.

" I hardly expected you'd look on it as I do," Foss
confessed rather shamefacedly. " Of course, it was
just plain eavesdropping on my part by that time. But
I felt Mr Kessock would have expected me to find out
all I could about these medallions. To be candid, I'd
do the same again ; though I didn't like doing it."

Sir Clinton seemed to feel that he had been rather
discouraging.

" I shouldn't make too much of it, Mr Foss. What
happened next ? "

Foss's face showed that he was at last coming to a
matter of real difficulty.

" It's rather unfortunate that I came to be mixed up
in the thing at all," he said, with obvious chagrin. " I
can assure you, Miss Chacewater, that I don't like
doing it. I only made up my mind to tell you about
it because it seems to me to give a chance of hushing
this supposed burglary up quietly before there's any
talk goes round."

" *Supposed* burglary," exclaimed Joan. " What's
your idea of a real burglary, if this sort of thing is only
a supposed one ? "

She indicated the shattered show-case and the litter
of glass on the floor.

Foss evidently decided to take the rest of his narrative in a rush.

"I'll tell you," he said. "The next thing I over-heard was a complete plan for a fake burglary—a practical joke—to be carried out to-night. The light in here was to be put out ; the house-lights were to be extinguished : and in the darkness, your brother and this Mr Foxy How-d'you-call-him were to get away with the medallions."

"Ah, Mr Foss, now you become interesting," Sir Clinton acknowledged.

"I heard all the details," Foss went on. "How Miss Rainhill was to see to extinguishing the lights ; how Mr Chacewater was to secure the keeper ; and how meanwhile his friend was to put on a thick glove and take the medallions out of the case there. And it seems to me that it was a matter that interested me directly," he added, dropping his air of apology, "for I gathered that the whole affair was planned with some idea of making this sale to Mr Kessock fall through at the last moment."

"Indeed ? "

Sir Clinton's face showed that at last he saw some-thing more clearly than before.

"That was the motive," Foss continued. "Now the whole thing put me in a most awkward position."

"I think I see your difficulty," Sir Clinton assured him, with more geniality than he had hitherto shown.

"It was very hard to make up my mind what to do," Foss went on. "I'm a guest here. This was a family joke, apparently—one brother taking a rise out of another. It was hardly for me to step in and perhaps cause bad feelings between them. I thought

the whole thing was perhaps just talk—not meant
seriously in the end. A kind of ' how-would-we-do-
it-if-we-set-about-it ' discussion, you understand."

Sir Clinton nodded understandingly.

" Difficult to know what to do, in your shoes,
undoubtedly."

Foss was obviously relieved by the Chief Constable's
comprehension.

" I thought it over," he continued, with a less
defensive tone in his voice, " and it seemed to me that
the soundest course was to let sleeping dogs lie—to
let them lie, at any rate, until they woke up and bit
somebody. I made up my mind I'd say nothing about
the matter at all, unless something really did happen."

" Very judicious," Sir Clinton acquiesced.

" Then came to-night," Foss resumed. " Their
plan went through. I don't know what success they
had—the house is full of all sorts of rumours. But I
heard that the Chief Constable was on the spot and
was taking up the case himself ; and as soon as I
heard that, I felt I ought to tell what I knew. So I
hunted you out, so as to avoid your taking any steps
before you knew just how the land lay. It's only a
practical joke and not a crime at all. I don't know
anything about your English laws, and I was afraid
you might be taking some steps, doing something or
other that would make it impossible to stop short of
the whole affair coming out in public. I'm sure the
family wouldn't like that."

He glanced at Joan's face, but evidently found
nothing very encouraging in her expression.

" It's been a most unfortunate position for me," he complained.

Sir Clinton took pity on him.

" It was very good of you to give me these facts," he said with more cordiality than he had hitherto shown. " You've cleared up the thing and saved us from putting our foot in it badly, perhaps. Thanks very much for your trouble, Mr Foss. You've been of great assistance."

His tone showed that the interview was at an end ; but, tactfully, as though to spare the obviously ruffled feelings of the American, he accompanied him to the door. When Foss had left the room, Sir Clinton turned back to Joan.

" Well, Joan, what about it ? "

" Oh, it sounds accurate enough," Joan admitted, though there was an undercurrent of resentment in her tone. " Foss couldn't have known what sort of person Foxy is ; and it's as clear as daylight that Foxy was at the bottom of this. He's a silly ass who's always playing practical jokes."

She paused for a moment. Then relief showed itself in her voice as she added :

" It's rather a blessing to know the whole affair has been just spoof, isn't it ? You can hush it up easily enough, can't you ? Nobody need know exactly what happened ; and then we'll be all right. If this story comes out, all our little family bickerings will be common talk ; and one doesn't want that. I'm not exactly proud of the way Maurice has been treating Cecil."

Sir Clinton's face showed that he understood her position ; but, rather to her surprise, he gave no verbal assurance.

" It *is* all right ! " she demanded.

" I think we'll interview your friend Foxy first of all," Sir Clinton proposed, taking no notice of her inquiry.

Going to the door, he gave some orders to the keeper.

" You were rather stiff with our good Mr Foss," he said, turning to Joan as he closed the door again. " What would you have done yourself, if you'd been in his position ? "

Joan had her answer ready.

" I suppose he couldn't help overhearing things ; but when this affair came to light, I think if I'd been in his shoes I'd have gone to Cecil instead of coming to us with the tale. Once Cecil found the game was up, he'd have been able to return the medallions in some way or other, without raising any dust."

" That was one way, certainly."

" What I object to is Foss coming to you," Joan explained. " He didn't know you're an old friend of ours. All he knew was that you were the Chief Constable. So off he hies to you, post-haste, to give the whole show away ; when he might quite well have come to me or gone to Cecil. I don't like this way of doing things—no tact at all."

" I can't conceive how Cecil came to take up a silly prank like this," said Sir Clinton. " It's a schoolboy's trick."

" You don't know everything," said Joan, in defence of her brother.

" I know a good deal, Joan," Sir Clinton retorted in a decisive tone. " Perhaps I know more than you think about this business."

In a few minutes the keeper knocked at the door.

" Well ? " demanded Sir Clinton, opening it.

" I can't find Mr Polegate anywhere, sir," Mold reported. " No one's seen him ; and he's not in the house."

" He was here to-night," Joan declared. " I recognized him when I was dancing with him. You can't mistake that shock of hair ; and of course his voice gave him away when he spoke."

Sir Clinton did not seem perturbed.

" Bring Mr Cecil, Mold," he ordered, and locked the door again as the keeper went off on his fresh errand.

This task Mold completed in a very short time. Sir Clinton opened at his knock and Cecil Chacewater came into the museum. He was dressed as a Swiss admiral and behind him came Una Rainhill in the costume of Cleopatra.

Sir Clinton wasted no time in preliminaries.

" I've sent for you, Cecil, because I want to know exactly what part you played in this business to-night."

Cecil Chacewater opened his eyes in astonishment.

" You seem to be a bit of a super-sleuth ! How did you spot us so quickly ? "

Quite obviously Cecil was not greatly perturbed at being found out, as Sir Clinton noted with a certain relief. So far as he was concerned, the thing had been only a prank.

" Tell me exactly what happened after you came in here before the lights went out," the Chief Constable demanded in a curt tone.

Cecil glanced at Una. Sir Clinton caught the look.

" We know all about Miss Rainhill's part in the affair," he explained bluntly.

" Oh, in that case," said Cecil, " there's no particular reason why I should keep back anything. Una, Foxy, and I planned it between us. I take full responsibility for that. I wanted to upset this sale, if I could. I'm not ashamed of that."

" I know all about that," Sir Clinton pointed out, coldly. " What I wish to know is exactly what happened after you came in here to steal these medallions."

Cecil seemed impressed by the Chief Constable's tone.

" I'll tell you, then. We've nothing to conceal. I came in here at about twenty to twelve and sauntered about the room, pretending to look at the cases as if I'd never seen them before. My part was to mark down Mold and prevent him interfering."

Sir Clinton nodded to show that he knew all this.

" Rather before I expected it, the light went out. Oh, there was a shot fired just then. I didn't understand that part of it, but I supposed that Foxy had brought a pistol with him and fired a blank cartridge just to add a touch of interest to the affair. It wasn't on the bill of fare, so I imagine it must have been one of these last-minute improvements. Anyhow, I did my part of the business : jumped on Mold and held him while Foxy got away with the stuff. Then, when he'd had time to get away, I let Mold go and made a bee-line for the door myself. I could swear no one spotted me in the dark, and I was well mixed up in the mob before the lights went on again."

" Did you pay particular attention to what Polegate was doing while you were busy with the keeper ? "

" No. Mold gave me all I wanted in the way of trouble."

" You're sure it was Mold you got hold of ? You didn't make any mistake ? "

Cecil reflected for a moment.

" I don't see how I could have gripped the wrong man. I'd marked him down while the light was on."

" Can you remember anything about sounds of breaking glass ? "

Cecil pondered before replying.

" It seemed to me that there was a lot of glass-breaking—more than I'd expected. The light was hardly out before there was a smash and tinkle all over the place. Foxy must have got to work quicker than I'd allowed for. And I remember hearing quite a lot of hammering and smashing going on after that, as if he'd found it difficult to make a big enough hole in the glass of the case. I thought he'd bungled the business, and it was all I could do to keep my grip on Mold long enough to get the thing safely through."

Sir Clinton dismissed that part of the subject. He turned to Una.

" Now, Miss Rainhill, I believe your part in the affair was to pull out the main switch of the house ? "

" Yes," Una admitted, looking rather surprised at the extent of his knowledge.

" Did you carry out your part of the arrangement punctually, or were you late in getting the current off ? "

" I pulled out the switch to the very second. I had my hand on it and my eye on my wrist-watch ; and when it came to 11.45 I jerked it out and the lights went off. I was absolutely right to a second, I'm sure."

" And you thought Miss Rainhill had been a shade before her time, Cecil ? "

" So it seemed to me. I hadn't a chance of looking at my watch ; and of course after the lights went off I couldn't spare time to look."

At this moment another knock came to the door and Foxy Clifford burst into the museum. Sir Clinton noticed that he was masquerading as a Harlequin.

" Heard you'd been asking for me, Sir Clinton," he broke out as he came into the room. " Seems the keeper had been inquiring for me. So I came along as soon as I heard about it."

He glanced inquisitively at Cecil and Una, as though wondering what they were doing there.

Sir Clinton wasted no words.

" The medallions, Mr Polegate, please."

Foxy made a very good pretence of astonishment at the demand ; but Cecil cut him short.

" You may as well hand them over, Foxy. They seem to know all about the joke."

" Oh, they do, do they ? " Foxy exclaimed. " They

seem to have been mighty swift about it. That little joke's gone astray, evidently."

He seemed completely taken aback by the exposure. " The medallions ? " he repeated. " I'll get 'em for you in a jiffy."

He walked across to the show-case, fumbled for a moment at the flat base near one of the legs, and from below this he drew out three medallions.

" Stuck 'em there with plasticine as soon as I'd got 'em. After that anyone would have turned out my pockets if they'd wanted, see ? "

Sir Clinton held out his hand and took the medallions from Foxy. For a moment or two he examined them, then he passed them to Cecil.

" Have you any way of telling easily whether these are the real things or the replicas ? "

Cecil inspected them one by one with minute care.

" These are the real things," he announced. " What else could they be ? "

" You've no doubt about it ? " questioned Sir Clinton.

" Not a bit," Cecil assured him. " When Foxy made the replicas, my father had a tiny hole—just a dot—drilled in the edge of each electrotype so as to distinguish the real things from the sham. There are no holes here ; so these are the real Leonardos."

Sir Clinton swung round suddenly on Foxy.

" Now, Mr Polegate," he said, sternly, " you've given a lot of trouble with this silly joke of yours. I'm not concerned with your taste in humour, or I might say a few things you wouldn't care to hear. But you can repair the damage to some extent if you give me a frank account of your doings in here to-night. I want the whole story, please."

Foxy was evidently completely taken aback by Sir Clinton's tone.

" Come, we're waiting. There's no time to lose," Sir Clinton said, curtly, as Foxy seemed to hesitate. Joan and the others showed by their faces that they could not quite understand the reason for the Chief Constable's asperity.

" We planned that . . ."

" I know all about that," said Sir Clinton, brusquely. " Begin at the point where you came in here at twenty to twelve or so."

Foxy pulled himself together. The Chief Constable's manner was not encouraging.

" I came in here as arranged, and worked my way over to the central case there—slowly, so as not to attract the keeper's attention. One or two other people were hanging round it then, too. I remember noticing a chap in a white Pierrot costume alongside me. Suddenly there was a pistol-shot and the light went out according to plan."

" How do you account for the pistol-shot ?" demanded Sir Clinton.

" Try next door," said Foxy. " I thought it was a fancy tip that Cecil had thrown in at the last moment. It wasn't in the book of words."

" You were ready to get to work when the light went out ? " inquired Sir Clinton.

Foxy considered for a moment.

" It took me rather by surprise," he admitted. " I'd counted on having at least another minute, according to the time-table."

" What happened next ?   Be careful now."

" As soon as the light went out, I pulled on a thick pair of gloves and got a bit of lead pipe out of my slap-stick.   But there was a bit of a scuffle in the dark round the show-case, and someone must have put their elbow through the glass.   I heard it go crash in the dark.   I shoved along till I was opposite the medallion section of the case—luckily someone made way for me just then—and I got to work with my lead pipe.   The glass smashed easily—it must have been cracked before. So I put my hand in and groped about.   I could find only three medallions instead of six ; but I hooked them out, slabbed on some plasticine, stuck them under the case for future reference, and cut my stick for the door.   Someone was ahead of me there, and I heard some sort of mix-up in the dark.   Then I wandered out into the garden by the east door, as soon as I could find it in the dark.   And I've been out there having a smoke till now.   When I came in again, I heard you'd been asking for me, so I came along."

Sir Clinton considered for a moment.

" I want to be quite clear on one point," he said with no relaxation of his manner.   " You say that you heard the glass crack before you began your work.   Are you certain of that ? "

" Quite," said Foxy.

" And when you got your hand into the case you could find only three medallions ? "

" That was all. I was groping for the top row of the six ; and naturally it surprised me when I felt only three altogether. I'm quite certain about it."

" So you were evidently the second thief at the case to-night ? " Sir Clinton concluded.

Foxy flushed at the word " thief " but a glance at the face of the Chief Constable evidently persuaded him that it would be best not to argue on philology at that moment. He contented himself with nodding sullenly in response to Sir Clinton's remark.

Joan relieved the tension.

" Anyhow, we've got the medallions safe, and that's all that really matters," she pointed out. " Let's have a look at them, Cecil."

She took them from his hand and scrutinized them carefully.

" Yes, these are the real Leonardos," she affirmed, without hesitation. " That's all right."

" Quite all right," admitted Sir Clinton, with a wry smile, " except for one point : Why were the replicas stolen and the real things left untouched ? "

" That certainly seems to need explaining," Una admitted. " Can you throw any light on it, Foxy ? You're the only one of us who was near the case."

There was no hint of accusation in her tone ; but Foxy seemed to read an insinuation into her remark.

" I haven't got the replicas, if that's what you mean, Una," he protested angrily. " I just took what was left—and it turns out to be the real things. Whoever was ahead of me took the duds."

97

Cecil considered the point, and then appealed to Sir Clinton.

" Doesn't that seem to show that an outsider's been at work—someone who knew a certain amount about the collection, but not quite enough ? An outsider wouldn't know we had the replicas in the case alongside the real things. He'd just grab three medallions and think he'd got away with it."

Sir Clinton shook his head.

" Your hypothetical outsider, Cecil, must have had a preliminary look at the case before the lights went out—just to make sure of getting to the right spot in the dark. Therefore he must have seen the six medallions there ; and he'd have taken the lot instead of only three, when he had his chance."

" That upsets your applecart, Cecil," said Joan. " It's obvious Sir Clinton's right. Unless "—a fresh idea seemed to strike her—" unless the thief knew of the replicas and had wrong information, so that he imagined he was taking the Leonardos when he really was grabbing the replicas. I mean he may have thought that the replicas were in the top row instead of the lower one."

She glanced at Sir Clinton's face to see what he thought of her suggestion ; but he betrayed nothing.

" Wouldn't you have taken the whole six, Joan, if you had been in his shoes ? "

Joan had to admit that she would have made certain by snatching the complete set.

" There's more in it than that," was all that Sir Clinton could be induced to say.

Before any more could be said, the door opened again. This time it was Michael Clifton who entered the museum.

" You've got him, Michael ? " cried Joan. " Who was he ? "

Michael shook his head.

" He got away from us. It's a damned mysterious business how he managed it ; but he slipped through our fingers, Joan."

" Well, tell us what happened—quick ! " Joan ordered. " I didn't think you'd botch it, Michael."

Michael obeyed her at once and launched into an account of the moonlight chase of the fugitive. Sir Clinton listened attentively, but interposed no questions until Michael had finished his story.

" Let's have this quite clear," the Chief Constable said, when the tale had been completed. " You had him hemmed in at the cliff top ; you heard a splash, but there was no sign of anyone swimming in the lake ; you discovered a rope tied to the balustrade and lying down the cliff-face to the cave-mouth ; he wasn't in the cave when you looked for him there. Is that correct ? "

" That's how it happened."

" You're sure he didn't break back through your cordon ? "

" Certain."

" And you found Maurice in one of the Fairy Houses in the spinney ? "

" Yes. He seemed in a queer state."

Sir Clinton, glancing at Cecil's face, was surprised

to see on it the same expression of almost malicious glee which he had surprised on the day when they examined that very Fairy House during their walk. Quite obviously Cecil knew something more than the Chief Constable did.

" Does that suggest anything to you, Cecil ? " he demanded point-blank.

At the query, Cecil's face came back to normal suddenly.

" To me ?   No, why should it ? "

" I merely wondered," said Sir Clinton, without seeming to notice anything.

It was clear that whatever Cecil knew, it was something which he was not prepared to tell.

Foxy had listened intently to Michael's narrative, and as the Chief Constable seemed to have come to the end of his interrogations, Foxy put a question of his own.

" You say Maurice was wearing a white Pierrot costume ? So was the fellow you were chasing. So was the man next me at the case when the lights went out."

" I suppose you're suggesting that Maurice is at the bottom of the business, Foxy," Michael replied at once.   " I'll swallow that if you'll answer one question. Why should a man burgle his own house ? "

" Lord alone knows," Foxy admitted humbly. " I've no brain-wave on the subject."

" It seems rather improbable," observed Sir Clinton.   " I think you'll have to produce a motive before that idea could be accepted."

He glanced round at the door as he spoke and added :

" Here's Maurice himself."

Maurice Chacewater had entered the room while the Chief Constable was speaking. He had discarded his fancy costume and wore ordinary evening-dress, against the black of which his face looked white and drawn. He came up to the group and leaned on the show-case as if for support.

" So you've muddled it, Michael," he commented, after a pause. " You didn't get your hands on the fellow, after all ? "

Dismissing Michael with almost open contempt, he turned to Sir Clinton.

" What's the damage ? Did the fellow get away with anything of value ? "

" Nothing much : only your three replicas of the Leonardo medallions, so far as we can see."

As he spoke, his glance telegraphed a warning to the rest of the group. It seemed unnecessary that Maurice should know all the inns and outs of the night's doings.

But Foxy evidently failed to grasp the meaning of the Chief Constable's look.

" We saved the real medallions for you, Maurice. Vote of thanks to us, eh ? "

" How did you manage that ? " Maurice demanded, with no sign of gratitude in his voice.

Quite oblivious of the warning looks thrown at him by the rest of the group, Foxy launched at once into a detailed account of the whole practical joke and its sequel. Maurice listened frowningly to the story. When it was completed, he made no direct comment.

"Who's got the medallions? You, Joan? I'll take them."

When she had handed them over, he scrutinized them carefully.

"These seem to be the Leonardo ones," he confirmed.

Sir Clinton interposed a question.

"Were the medallions and the replicas in their usual places to-night, Maurice? I mean, were the real things in the top row and the electros down below?"

Maurice gave a curt nod of assent. He weighed the three medallions unconsciously in his hand for a moment, then moved over to the safe in the wall of the museum.

"These things will be safer under lock and key, now," he said.

He opened the safe, inserted the medallions, closed the safe-door with a clang, and busied himself with the combination of the lock.

Before saying anything further, Sir Clinton waited until Maurice had returned to the group.

"There's one thing," he said. "I shall have to look into this affair officially now. It's essential that things shall be left as they are. Especially the place where that fellow gave you the slip, Clifton. Nobody must be wandering about there, up at the spinney, until I've done with the ground. There may be clues left, for all one can tell; and we can't run the risk of them being destroyed."

Maurice looked up gloomily.

"Very well. I'll give orders to the keepers to patrol the wood and turn everyone back. That do?"

"So long as no one sets foot on anything beyond the wood, I'll be quite satisfied. But it's important, Maurice. Impress that on your keepers, please."

Maurice indicated his comprehension with a nod.

"I'll begin dragging the lakelet up there to-morrow morning," Sir Clinton added. "Something must have gone into the water to make the splash that was heard; and perhaps we shall find it. I don't mind anyone going down by the lake side. It's the top of the cliff that I want kept intact."

He looked at his watch.

"You're on the 'phone here? I must ring up the police in Hincheldene now and make arrangements for to-morrow. Show me your 'phone, please, Joan. And as I must get some sleep to-night, I'll say good-bye to the rest of you now. Come along, Ariel. Lead the way."

CHAPTER VII

WHAT WAS IN THE LAKE

"I WAS afraid of it," Sir Clinton observed, as he lifted the dripping pole with which he had been sounding the water of the lakelet. " The net will be no good, Inspector. With these spikes of rock jutting up from the bottom all over the place, you couldn't get a clean sweep ; and if there's anything here at all, it's pretty sure to have lodged in one of the cavities between the spikes."

It was the morning after the masked ball at Ravensthorpe. The Chief Constable had made all his arrangements over-night, so that when he reached the shore of the artificial lake, everything was in readiness. The decrepit raft had been strengthened ; a large net had been brought for the purpose of dragging the pool ; and several grapnels had been procured, in case the net turned out to be useless. Sir Clinton had gone out on the raft to sound the water and discover whether the net could be utilized ; but the results had not been encouraging.

Inspector Armadale listened to the verdict with a rather gloomy face.

" It's a pity," he commented regretfully. " Dragging with the grapnel is a kind of hit-or-miss job, Sir Clinton ; and it'll take far longer than working with the net."

Sir Clinton acquiesced with a gesture.

" We'd better start close in under the cliff-face," he said. " If anything came down from the top, it can't have gone far before it sank. One of the people last night was watching the pool and he saw nothing on the surface after the splash, so it ought to be somewhere near the cave-mouth. You can pole over to the shore now, constable ; we've done with this part of the business."

The constable obeyed the order and soon Sir Clinton rejoined the Inspector on the bank.

" It's likely to be a troublesome business," the Chief Constable admitted as his subordinate came up. " The bottom's very irregular and the chances are that the grapnel will stick, two times out of three. However, the sooner we get to work, the better."

He considered for a moment or two.

" Tack a light line to the grapnel as well as the rope. Get the raft out past the cave and let a constable pitch the grapnel in there. Then when you've dragged, or if the grapnel sticks, he can pull the hook back again with the light line and start afresh alongside the place where he made the last cast. But it's likely to be a slow business, as you say."

The Inspector agreed and set his constables to work at once. Sir Clinton withdrew to a little distance, sat down on a small hillock from which he could oversee the dragging operations, and patiently awaited the start of the search. His eyes, wandering with apparent incuriosity over the group at the water's edge, noted with approval that Armadale was wasting no time.

Having made his instructions clear, the Inspector came over to where the Chief Constable was posted.

" Sit down, Inspector," Sir Clinton invited. " This may take all day, you know, and it's as cheap sitting as standing."

When the Inspector had seated himself, the Chief Constable turned to him with a question.

" You've seen to it that no one has gone up on to the terrace ? "

Inspector Armadale nodded affirmatively.

" No one's been up on top," he explained, " I'd like to go and have a look round myself ; but since you were so clear about it, I haven't gone."

" Don't go," Sir Clinton reiterated his order. " I've a sound reason for letting no one up there."

He glanced for a moment at the group of constables.

" Another thing, Inspector," he continued. " There's no secrecy about that matter. In fact, it might be useful if you'd let it leak out to the public that no one has been up above there and that no one will be allowed to go until I give the word. Spread it round, you understand ? "

Slightly mystified, apparently, the Inspector acquiesced.

" Do you see your way through the case, Sir Clinton ? " he demanded. " You've given me the facts, but we'll need a good deal more, it seems to me."

Sir Clinton pulled out his cigarette-case and thoughtfully began to smoke before answering the question. When he spoke again, his reply was an indirect one.

" There's an old jurist's saying that I always keep

in mind," he said. " It helps to clarify one's ideas in a case :

> Quis, quid, ubi, quibus auxiliis, cur, quomodo, quando ?

That puts our whole business into a nutshell." He glanced at the Inspector's face. " Your Latin's as feeble as my own, perhaps ? There's an English equivalent :

> What was the crime, who did it, when was it done, and where,
> How done, and with what motive, who in the deed did share ?

How many of these questions can you answer now, offhand, Inspector ? The rest of them will tell you what you've still got to ferret out."

Inspector Armadale pulled out a notebook and pencil.

" Would you mind repeating it, Sir Clinton ? I'd see through it better if I had it down in black and white."

The Chief Constable repeated the doggerel and Armadale jotted it down under his dictation.

" That seems fairly searching," he admitted, re-reading it as he spoke.

" Quite enough for present purposes. Now, Inspector, how much do you really know ? I mean, how many answers can you give ? There are only seven questions in all. Take them one by one and let's hear your answers."

" It's a pretty stiff catechism," said the Inspector, looking again at his notebook. " I'll have a try, though, if you give me time to think over it."

Sir Clinton smiled at the qualification.

"Think it over, then, Inspector," he said. "I'll just go and set them to work with the dragging. They seem to be ready to make a start."

He rose and walked down to the group at the edge of the pool.

"You know what's wanted?" he asked. "Well, suppose we make a start. Get the raft out to about ten yards or so beyond the cave-mouth and begin by flinging the grapnel in as near the cliff-edge as you can. Then work gradually outwards. If it sticks, try again very slightly off the line of the last cast."

He watched one or two attempts which gave no result and then turned back to the hillock again.

"Well, Inspector?" he demanded as he sat down and turned his eyes on the group engaged with the dragging operations. "What do you make of it?"

Inspector Armadale looked up from his notebook.

"That's a sound little rhyme," he admitted. "It let's you see what you don't know and what you do know."

Sir Clinton suppressed a smile successfully.

"Or what you think you know, perhaps, Inspector?"

"Well, if you like to put it that way, sir. But some things I think one can be sure of."

Sir Clinton's face showed nothing of his views on this question.

"Let's begin at the beginning," he suggested. "'What was the crime?'"

"That's clear enough," the Inspector affirmed with-

108

out hesitation. " These three electrotypes have been stolen. That's the crime."

Sir Clinton seemed to be engrossed in the dragging which was going on methodically below them.

" You think so ? " he said at length. " H'm ! I'm not so sure."

Inspector Armadale corrected himself.

" I meant that I'd charge the man with stealing the replicas. You couldn't charge him with anything else, since nothing else is missing. At least, that's what you told me. He wanted the real medallions, but he didn't pull that off."

Sir Clinton refused to be drawn. He resorted to one of his indirect replies.

" ' What was the crime ? ' " he repeated. " Now, I'll put a case to you, Inspector. Suppose that you saw two men in the distance and that you could make out that one of them was struggling and the second man was beating him on the head. What crime would you call that ? Assault and battery ? "

" I suppose so," Armadale admitted.

" But suppose, further, that when you reached them you found the victim dead of his injuries, what would you call the crime then ? "

" Murder, I suppose."

" So your view of the crime would depend upon the stage at which you witnessed it, eh ? That's just my position in this Ravensthorpe affair. You've been looking at it from yesterday's standpoint, and you call it a theft of three replicas. But I wonder what you'll call it when we know the whole of the facts."

The Inspector declined to follow his chief to this extent.

" All the evidence we've got, so far, points to theft, sir. I've no fresh data that would let me put a new name to it."

" Then you regard it as a completed crime which has partly failed in its object ? "

The Inspector gave his acquiescence with a nod.

" You think it's something else, Sir Clinton ? " he inquired.

The Chief Constable refused to be explicit.

" You've got all the evidence, Inspector. Do you really think a gang would take the trouble to steal replicas when they could just as easily have taken the three originals—that's the point. The replicas have no intrinsic value beyond the gold in them, and that can't be worth more than twenty or thirty pounds at the very outside. A mediocre haul for a smart gang, isn't it ? Hardly Trade Union wages, I should think."

" It seems queer at first sight, sir," he admitted, " but I think I can account for that all right when you come to the rest of your rhyme."

Sir Clinton showed his interest.

" Then let's go on," he suggested. " The next question is : ' Who did it ? ' What's your answer to that, Inspector ? "

" To my mind, there seems to be only one possible thief."

Sir Clinton pricked up his ears.

" You mean it was a single-handed job ? Who was the man, then ? "

" Foxton Polegate," asserted the Inspector.

He watched Sir Clinton's face narrowly as he brought out the name, but the Chief Constable might have been wearing a mask for all the change there was in his features as he listened to the Inspector's suggestion. As if he felt that he had overstepped the bounds of prudence, Armadale added hastily :

" I said ' possible thief,' sir. I don't claim to be able to bring it home to him yet."

" But you think it might even be ' probable ' instead of only ' possible,' Inspector ? Let's hear the evidence, please."

Inspector Armadale turned over the leaves of his notebook until he reached some entries which he had previously made.

" First of all, sir, Polegate must have known the value of these medallions—the originals, I mean. Second, he learned that they would be on show last night ; and he knew where they'd be placed in the museum. Third, it was after Polegate came by this knowledge that the practical joke was planned. Fourth, who suggested the sham burglary ? Polegate. Then fifth, who gave himself the job of actually taking the medallions ? Polegate again. Sixth, where was Polegate immediately after the robbery ? We've only his own word for it that he was strolling about, having a smoke. He might have been elsewhere, easily enough. Seventh, he was dressed up as a Harlequin when you saw him : but he might quite easily have slipped on a white jacket and a pair of Pierrot's trousers over his Harlequin costume. He could disguise himself as a

111

Pierrot in a couple of ticks and come out as a Harlequin again just as quick. So he might quite well have been the man in white that they were all busy chasing last night. Eighth, he knows the ground thoroughly and could give strangers the slip easily enough at the end of the chase. And, ninth, he didn't appear when you wanted him last night. He only turned up when he'd had plenty of time to get home again, even if he'd been the man in white. That's a set of nine points that need looking into. *Prima facie*, there's a case for suspicion, if there's no more. And there isn't anything like so strong a case against anyone else, Sir Clinton."

" Well, let's take the rest of the first line," said the Chief Constable, without offering any criticism of the Inspector's statement of the case. " ' When was it done, and where ? ' "

" At 11.45 p.m. and in the museum," retorted Armadale. " That's beyond dispute. It's the clearest thing in the whole evidence."

" I should be inclined to put it at 11.44 p.m. at the latest, or perhaps 11.43 p.m.," said Sir Clinton, with an air of fastidiousness.

The Inspector looked at him suspiciously, evidently feeling that he was being laughed at for his display of accuracy.

" I go by Miss Rainhill's evidence," he declared. " She was the only one who had her eye on her watch, and she said she pulled out the switch at 11.45 precisely."

" I go by the evidence of Polegate and young Chacewater," said Sir Clinton, with a faint parody of the

Inspector's manner. " They were taken by surprise when the light went out, although they expected it to be extinguished at 11.45 p.m."

" Oh, have it your own way, sir, if you lay any stress on the point," conceded the Inspector. " Make it 11.44 or 11.45 ; it's all the same, so far as I'm concerned."

Armadale seemed slightly ruffled by his chief's method of approaching the subject. Sir Clinton turned to another side of the matter.

" I suppose you say the crime has been committed in the museum ? " he inquired.

The Inspector looked at him suspiciously.

" You're trying to pull my leg, sir. Of course, it was committed in the museum."

Sir Clinton's tone became apologetic.

" I keep forgetting that we're not talking about the same thing, perhaps. Of course, the theft of the replicas was committed in the museum. We're quite in agreement there."

He threw away his cigarette, selected a fresh one, and lighted it before continuing.

" And on that basis, I suppose there's no mystery about the next query in the rhyme : ' How done ? ' "

" None whatever, in my mind," the Inspector affirmed. " Polegate could take what he wanted, once the light was out."

Sir Clinton did not dispute this point.

" Of course," he said. " And now for the next query : ' With what motive ? ' Where do you stand in that matter, Inspector ? "

113

But here Armadale evidently felt himself on sure ground.

"Polegate's a rackety young fool, sir. This is where local knowledge comes in. He's got no common sense—always playing practical jokes. He's been steadily muddling away the money his father left him. I shouldn't be surprised if he's hard up. That's the motive."

"And you think he'd steal from his oldest friends ?"

"Every man has his price," retorted the Inspector, bluntly. "Put on the screw hard enough in the way of temptation, and any man'll fall for it."

"Rather a hard saying that, Inspector ; and perhaps a trifle too sweeping." Sir Clinton turned on Armadale suddenly. "What would be *your* price, now, if I asked you to hush up this case against young Polegate ? Put a figure on it, will you ?"

Armadale flushed angrily at the suggestion ; then, seeing that he had been trapped, he laughed awkwardly.

"Nobody knows even their own price till it's put on the table, Sir Clinton," he countered, with a certain acuteness.

The Chief Constable turned away from the subject.

"You're depending on there being a fair chance of Polegate getting away with the medallions without being suspected. But when young Chacewater and Miss Rainhill were in the scheme as well as Polegate, suspicion was sure to light on him when the medallions vanished. The other two were certain to tell what they knew about the business."

Inspector Armadale glanced once more at his note-book in order to refresh his memory of the rhyme.

" That really comes under the final head : ' Who in the deed did share ? ' " he pointed out.

" Pass along to the next caravan, then, if you wish," Sir Clinton suggested. " What animals have you in the final cage ? "

The Inspector seemed to deprecate his flippancy.

" It's been very cleverly done," he said, seriously. " You objected that suspicion was bound to fall on young Polegate ; and so it would have done, if he hadn't covered his tracks so neatly. He's set everyone on the hunt for a gang at work, or at least for an outside criminal. Now I believe it was a one-man show from the start, worked from the inside. Polegate planned the practical joke—that gave him his chance. Then he forced himself forward as the fellow who was to do the actual stealing—and that let him get his hands on the medallions while young Chacewater held the keeper up for him. Without the hold-up of the keeper, the thing was a wash-out. The joke helped young Polegate to enlist innocent assistance."

" But still suspicion would attach to him," Sir Clinton objected.

" Yes, except for a false trail," the Inspector agreed. " But he laid a false trail. Instead of waiting for the switch to be pulled out, he fired his shot from the bay, extinguished the light and then rushed out of the bay and went for the medallions."

" Well ? " said Sir Clinton in an encouraging tone.

" When he'd smashed the glass of the case, he took

out the whole six medallions, and not merely three of them as he told you he'd done."

" And then ? "

" He pocketed the replicas and stuck the real things under the case with plasticine. Then he continued the false trail by bolting out of the house. He was the man in white. When he got clear of the people who were chasing him, he came back to the house again, ready to play his part as an innocent practical joker. And he had his tale ready, of how someone was beside him at the case, wearing a Pierrot costume. That stamped the notion of an outside gang on everybody's mind. Both sets of medallions had gone. He —the innocent practical joker—could have produced the replicas from his pocket and sworn they were all that the gang had left in the case by the time he got to it."

" And . . . ? "

" And then, a few days later, he'd have managed to get into the museum on some excuse—he's a friend of the family—and he'd have had no difficulty in taking the real medallions from under the case where he'd left them. He'd have to take the chance that they'd been overlooked. The false trail would help in that. He'd hardly expect a close search of the museum after the man in white had got clear away. And by running the business on these lines, he'd avoid any chance of being caught with the stuff actually in his pocket at any time."

" But in that case, why did he hand over the real things to me like a lamb as soon as I challenged him ? "

The inspector was ready for this.

" Because as soon as he came into the museum last night, he found that you apparently knew everything —or a good deal more than he'd counted on. Anyhow, he didn't know how much you knew ; and he felt he'd got into a tight corner. He just let the whole thing slide and made up his mind to get out before things got too hot. So he pretended that so far as he was con- cerned, the practical joke was the thing ; and he gave up the real medallions and kept the replicas in his pocket."

" Why ? He might as well have given up the lot."

" No," the Inspector contradicted. " He'd got to keep the false trail going, for otherwise there would have been awkward questions as to why he diverged from the prearranged programme. I mean the shoot- ing out of the light, the lies about the man in white, and so forth. So he stuck to the replicas and made out that there was an outsider mixed up in the affair. But thanks to the practical joke, the outsider had missed the real stuff ; and Polegate was really the saviour of the Leonardo set."

Sir Clinton seemed to be pondering over Armadale's version of the affair. At last he gave his own view.

" A jury wouldn't look at that evidence," he pointed out.

" I don't suppose they would," Armadale admitted. " But there may be more to come yet."

" I expect so," Sir Clinton agreed.

He rose as he spoke, and, followed by the Inspector, went down to the edge of the lakelet.

" No luck yet ? " he inquired.

" None, sir. It's a very difficult bottom to work a grapnel over. It sticks three times out of four."

Sir Clinton watched the line of the drag which they were making.

" It'll take a while to cover the ground at this rate," he commented, noting the smallness of the area they had searched up to that moment.

As he turned away from the water-side, he noticed Cecil Chacewater approaching round the edge of the lakelet, and leaving the Inspector to superintend the dragging, he walked over to meet the newcomer. As he came near, he could see that Cecil's face was sullen and downcast.

" 'Morning, Sir Clinton. I heard you were here, so I came across to say good-bye before I clear out."

Sir Clinton could hardly pretend astonishment in view of what he knew about the state of affairs at Ravensthorpe ; but he did not conceal his regret at the news.

" There was a row-royal between Maurice and me this morning," Cecil explained, gloomily. " Of course this medallion business gave him his chance, and he jumped in with both feet, you know. He abused me like a fish-wife and finally gave me permission to do anything except stay at Ravensthorpe after to-night. So I'm off."

" I wish you hadn't got mixed up with that silly practical joke," Sir Clinton said in some concern. " I can't forgive that young blighter for luring you into it."

Cecil's resentment against his brother was evidently

too deep to let him look on the matter from this point of view.

" If it hadn't been that, it would have been something else. Any excuse would have served his turn, you know. He'd have flung me out sooner or later—probably sooner. I've felt for long enough that he was itching to clear me off the premises. Foxy's little show only precipitated things. The root of the trouble was there long before."

" Well, it's a sad business." Sir Clinton saw that it was useless to dwell on the subject. " You're going up to town ? Any address you can give me ? "

" I'll probably put up with a man for a day or two. He's been inviting me to his place once or twice lately, but I've never been able to fit it in ; so I may as well take him at his word now. I've got to look round for something to do, you know."

" If you want someone to speak for you, Cecil, refer them to me when you apply for anything. And, by the way, if you happen to run short, you know my address. A letter will always find me."

Cecil thanked him rather awkwardly.

" I hope it won't come to that," he wound up. " Something may turn up sooner than one hopes."

Sir Clinton thought it well to change the subject again.

" By the way, Cecil," he asked, " do you know anything about this man Foss ? What sort of person is he ? "

It seemed an unfortunate topic. Cecil's manner was anything but gracious as he replied :

119

" Foss ?   Oh, you know what sort of a fellow he is already.   A damned eavesdropper on his hosts and a beggar with a tongue hinged in the middle so that he can talk with both ends at once.   I'd like to wring his neck for him !   What do they call the breed that runs off and splits to the police ?   Copper's narks, isn't it ?"

" It wasn't exactly that side of him that I wanted to hear about, Cecil.   I'm quite fully acquainted with his informative temperament already.   What I want to know is the sort of man he is socially and so forth."

Cecil curbed his vexation with an effort.

" Oh, he seems to have decent enough manners—a bit Yankee, perhaps, in some things.   He must do well enough out of this agent business of his, acting for Kessock and the like, you know.   He arrived here with a big car, a chauffeur, and a man.   Except for his infernal tale-bearing, I can't say he's anything out of the ordinary."

Sir Clinton, apparently feeling that he had struck the wrong vein in the conversational strata, contented himself with a nod of comprehension and let Cecil choose his own subject for the next stage in their talk. He was somewhat surprised when it came.

" Have you heard the latest from the village ? " Cecil demanded.

Sir Clinton shook his head.

" I've had very little time to collect local gossip this morning, Cecil.   I've been busy getting things started for this bit of work in the lake, you see."

" If you'd been down in Hincheldene village you could hardly have missed it.   I went down this morning to get some tobacco and I found the whole place buzzing with it. That was before I'd seen Maurice, luckily."

"Suppose you tell me what it is," Sir Clinton suggested, drily.

"Do you remember my telling you about the family spectre, the White Man ?" Cecil asked. "Well, it seems that the village drunkard, old Groby, was taking a short cut through our woods last night—or rather this morning, for he's a bit of a late going-to-rooster— and he got the shock of his life in one of the glades. He swears he saw the White Man stealing about from tree to tree. By his way of it, he was near enough to see the thing clearly—all white, even the face. What a lark ! "

"You seem to take your family spectre a bit lightly, Cecil. What's the cream of the jest ? "

Cecil's face took on a vindictive expression.

"Oh, it gave me a chance of getting home on Maurice, after he'd given me the key of the street. I told him all about it and I rubbed in the old story. You know what I mean ? The White Man never appears except when the head of the family's on his last legs. Maurice didn't like it a bit. He looked a bit squeamish over it ; and I came away leaving that sticking in his gills."

Sir Clinton hardly concealed his distaste for this kind of thing.

"You flatter yourself, I expect. Maurice is hardly likely to waste any thought over superstitions of that sort."

121

Cecil's expression still showed a tinge of malice.

"You'd wonder," he said. "It's all very well for you to sneer at these affairs ; but it looks a bit different when you yourself happen to be the object of them, I guess. It's easy to say 'Superstition' in a high-minded way ; but if there's a one per cent. chance that the superstition's going to hit you personally, then, you know, it rankles a bit. Anything to give pain is my motto where Maurice is concerned."

Quite oblivious of Sir Clinton's rather disgusted expression, he laughed softly to himself for a moment or two.

"And the funniest thing in the whole affair," he went on, "is that I know all about this White Man. Can't you guess what it was ? "

Sir Clinton shook his head.

"Why, don't you. see ? " Cecil demanded, still laughing. "What old Groby came across must obviously have been Maurice himself in his white Pierrot dress, coming back from the burglar-hunt ! That's what makes it so damned funny. Fancy Maurice getting the creeps on account of himself ! It's as good a joke as I've heard for a while."

He laughed harshly.

"You don't seem to see it. Well, well. Perhaps you're right. And now I must be getting back to the house. I've a lot of stuff to collect before I go off."

He shook hands with Sir Clinton and moved off towards Ravensthorpe. The Chief Constable gazed after him for a moment or two.

"That young man's in a most unpleasant frame of

mind," he commented to himself. " He's obviously quite off his normal balance when he'd make a point of that kind of thing. I can't say I take much stock in brotherly love ; but this is really overdoing the business. Both of them seem to have taken leave of ordinary feelings. It's just as well they're parting, perhaps."

Rather moodily he retraced his steps to where the Inspector was directing the operations by the bank of the lakelet ; but by the time he reached the group his face had taken on its normal expression.

" Fishing still poor ? " he demanded, as he came up.

" Nothing so far, sir," the Inspector confessed. " These rocks are the very deuce to work amongst. I've been running the grapnel over the same track two or three times, just in case we miss the thing the first shot. We've had no luck at all—unless you count this as a valuable find : a bit of limestone or something like that."

He kicked a shapeless mass of white stone as he spoke. Sir Clinton stooped over it : a dripping mass about the size of a man's fist. The Inspector watched him as he examined it ; but Sir Clinton's face suggested neither interest nor satisfaction.

" Might be a bit of marble that got swept over the top when they were putting up the balustrade in the old days," the Inspector hazarded.

Sir Clinton looked at it again and shook his head.

" I doubt it," he said. " However, since it's the only thing you've fished up, you'd better keep it, Inspector. One never knows what may be useful. I might make a paper-weight out of it as a souvenir."

The Inspector failed to see the point of the joke, but he laughed as politely as he could.

" Very well, Sir Clinton, I'll see that it's put aside."

He glanced over the Chief Constable's shoulder.

" Here's Mr Clifton coming, sir."

Sir Clinton turned round to find that Michael Clifton had approached while he was engaged with the dragging operations. Leaving the group by the bank, he walked slowly to meet the advancing figure.

" Good morning, Mr Clifton. Come up to see how we're getting on, I suppose. There's nothing to report, I'm afraid."

" Drawn blank ? " Michael inquired, needlessly. " There ought to be something there, all the same."

" It may have been only a stone," Sir Clinton pointed out. " You heard a splash ; that's all we have to go on. And a stone would make that as well as anything else."

" That's true," Michael admitted. " None of us saw the thing hit the water, so we've no notion what it was like. It might have been a stone for all we can tell. But why should the fellow pitch a brick into the water ? That's what puzzles me."

Before Sir Clinton could reply, a shout came from the bank, and the Inspector waved to them to come down.

" We've got something, sir," he called, as they drew nearer.

Followed by Michael, Sir Clinton hurried up to the group at the water's edge. The Inspector was kneeling down, carefully disentangling the grapnel from something white. At last he rose and held out his capture. Michael gave an exclamation.

" A white jacket ! "

A little further shaking of the material showed that it was a complete white Pierrot costume, except for the cap and shoes. The Inspector spread it out on the grass to dry, after holding the jacket outspread in the air so that they could gauge its size by comparison with his own body.

" That's what I've been hoping to get hold of, Inspector," Sir Clinton said. " I doubt if you'll find much more in the pool. But perhaps you'd better go on dragging for a while yet. Something else might turn up."

He examined the costume carefully ; but it was quite evident that there were no identifying marks on it. During the inspection, Michael showed signs of impatience ; and as soon as he could he unostentatiously drew Sir Clinton away from the group.

" Come up here, Mr Clifton," the Chief Constable suggested, as he turned towards the hillock he had chosen earlier in the morning. " We can keep an eye on things from this place."

He sat down and Michael, after a glance to see that they were out of earshot of the dragging party, followed his example.

" What do you make of that ? " he demanded eagerly.

Sir Clinton seemed to have little desire to discuss the matter.

" Let's be quite clear on one point before we begin," he reminded Michael. " I'm a Chief Constable, not a broadcasting station. My business is to collect information, not to throw it abroad before the proper time comes. You understand ? "

Rather dashed, Michael admitted the justice of this.

" I'm a public servant, Mr Clifton," Sir Clinton pointed out, his manner taking the edge off the directness of his remarks, " and I get my information officially. Obviously it wouldn't be playing the game if I scattered that information around before the public service has had the use of it."

" I see that well enough," Michael protested. " All I asked was what your own views are."

Sir Clinton smiled and there was a touch of mischief in his eye as he replied.

" Seeing that my conclusions are based on the evidence—at least I like to think so, you know— they're obviously part and parcel of my official knowledge. Hence I don't divulge them till the right moment comes."

He paused to let this sink in, then added lightly :

" That's a most useful principle, I find. One often makes mistakes, and of course one never divulges them either, until the right time comes. It's curious, but I've never been able yet to satisfy myself that the right time has come in any case of the sort."

Michael smiled in his turn ; and Sir Clinton went on :

" But there's no reason why you shouldn't draw your own conclusions and give me the benefit of them. I'm not too proud to be helped, you know."

For a moment Michael kept silence, as if considering what his next move should be. Sir Clinton had given

him what might have looked like a snub ; but Michael
had acuteness enough to tell him that the matter was
one of principle with the Chief Constable and not
merely a pretext devised on the spur of the moment to
suppress inconvenient curiosity.

"It just occurred to me," he confessed, " that there's
a possible explanation of that thing they've fished up.
Do you remember that I found Maurice in the Fairy
House up above there "—he indicated the cliff-top
with a gesture—" and when I left him there he was
still wearing a white costume like this one ? "

" So you told us last night," Sir Clinton confirmed.

" Now when Maurice turned up in the museum
later on," Michael continued, " he was wearing
ordinary evening clothes. He'd got rid of the
Pierrot dress in the meantime."

" That's true," Sir Clinton agreed.

" Isn't it possible," Michael went on, " that after I
left him, Maurice got over his troubles, whatever they
were, and pitched his disguise over the edge here.
This may quite well be it."

" Rather a rum proceeding, surely," was Sir Clinton's comment. " Can you suggest any earthly reason
why he should do a thing like that ? "

" I can't," Michael admitted, frankly. " But the
whole affair last night seemed to have neither rhyme
nor reason in it ; and after swallowing the escape of
that beggar we were after, I'm almost prepared for
anything in this neighbourhood. I just put the
matter before you. I can't fake up any likely explanation to account for it."

Sir Clinton seemed to be reflecting before he spoke again.

" To tell you the truth, I was rather disappointed with the result of that drag. Quite obviously—this isn't official information, for you can see it with your own eyes—quite obviously that Pierrot costume must have been wrapped round some weight or other, or it wouldn't have sunk to the bottom. And in the dragging the weight fell out. I could make a guess at what the weight was ; but I wish we'd fished it up. It doesn't matter much, really ; but one likes to get everything one can."

Michael, unable to guess what lay behind this, kept silent in the hope that there was more to come ; but the Chief Constable swung off to a fresh subject.

" Did you take a careful note of the costumes of the gang who helped you in the attempt to round the beggar up ? Could you make a list of them if it became necessary ? "

Michael considered for the best part of a minute before answering.

" Some of them I could remember easily enough ; but not all, I'm sure. It was a bit confused, you know ; and some of the crew turned up pretty late, when all my attention was focused on the final round-up. I really couldn't guarantee to give you an accurate list."

Sir Clinton's nod indicated approval.

" That's what I like," he said. " I'd rather have a definite No than a faked-up list that might mean nothing at all. But there's one point that's really

important. Did you notice, among your assistants,
anybody in white like the man you were hunting ? "

Michael apparently had no need to pause before
replying.

" No," he said definitely, " I saw nobody of that
sort. I suppose you mean Maurice. He certainly
wasn't in the cordon when it went into the spinney or
when it came out on the terrace. I'm absolutely sure
of my ground there. But of course he may have been
one of the late-comers. Almost as soon as we got to
the terrace we had to sprint off down to the lake side,
you see ; and he might quite well have been a bit slow
in the chase and have reached the top only after we'd
come down here."

" That's all I wanted to know," said Sir Clinton,
with a finality which prevented any angling for further
information.

Michael evidently had no desire to outstay his
welcome, for in a few minutes he rose to his feet.

" I think I'll go over to Ravensthorpe now," he said.
" I suppose you're not going to leave here for a
while ? "

The words recalled to Sir Clinton the fact that he
had not yet congratulated Michael on his engagement.
He hastened to repair the oversight.

" I was looking for you at the dance last night," he
explained, after Michael had thanked him, " but before
I got hold of you, this burglary business cropped up,
and I've had hardly a minute to spare since then. By
the way, if you're going over to the house, you might
tell Joan that I shall probably have to pay them a visit

shortly, but I'll ring up and let them know when I'm coming."

Michael nodded and turned away, skirting the lake-let on his way to Ravensthorpe. Sir Clinton sauntered over to the waterside and watched the dragging operations which were still going on. When he made his way back to the hillock again, Inspector Armadale followed him.

" There's another point that occurred to me, sir," he explained. " I think you told me that Polegate was wearing a Harlequin's costume last night ? "

" That's correct," Sir Clinton confirmed. " And what then ? "

" One difficulty I've had," the Inspector went on, was to explain how the fellow in white got away from them all so neatly. I think I see now how it was done."

Sir Clinton made no effort to conceal his interest.

" Yes, Inspector ? "

Armadale obviously took this as complimentary.

" This is how I figure it out, sir. Polegate had a white jacket and Pierrot trousers on over his Harlequin costume. At the end of the chase he bolted into the spinney and out on to the terrace above here. That gave him a breathing-space. It took Mr Clifton a minute or two to organize his cordon ; and during that time the thief was hidden from them by the trees."

" That's obviously true," Sir Clinton admitted. " If he did change his costume, it must have been at that moment."

" I expect he had a weight of some sort ready on the terrace," the Inspector continued. " When he'd stripped off his jacket and trousers, he wrapped them round the weight and pitched them over into the pool. That would make the splash they all heard."

" And after that ? "

The Inspector was evidently delighted with his idea.

" That leaves us with Polegate in Harlequin dress on the terrace, with a minute or two to spare before the cordon was ready to move forward into the spinney."

" Admitted."

" Do you remember the camouflaged ships in the War, Sir Clinton ? "

" I sailed in one, if that's what you mean."

" Well, you know what they were like : all sorts of cock-eyed streaks and colours mixed up in a regular tangle to destroy their real outlines. And what's a Harlequin's costume ? Isn't it the very same thing ? "

Sir Clinton confirmed this with an historical allusion.

" You're quite correct, Inspector. As a matter of fact, the Harlequin's dress was originally designed to represent Invisibility. Nobody except Columbine was supposed to be able to see Harlequin, you know."

Inspector Armadale hurried to his conclusion.

" What was to hinder Polegate, during that breathing-space, getting back into the spinney ? It was a moonlight night. You know what the spinney would be like under a full moon : it would be all dappled with spots of moonlight coming through the trees. And against a setting of that sort the Harlequin costume would be next door to invisible. He'd only have to stand still in some chequered spot and no one would detect him. They were all hunting for a man dressed in white. None of them noticed him. None of them saw him, I guess."

Much to the Inspector's surprise, Sir Clinton shook his head.

" I'd be prepared to bet pretty heavily that someone saw him," he affirmed.

The Inspector looked at his Chief for a moment, obviously taken aback.

" You think someone saw him ? "

Then a flood of light from a fresh angle in his mind seemed to illuminate the question.

" You mean he had a confederate in the cordon ? Someone who let him through and kept it dark ? I never thought of that ! You had me beaten there, Sir Clinton. And of course, now I see it, that's the simplest solution of the whole affair. If we can get a list of the people in the cordon, we'll be able to pick out the confederate before long."

Sir Clinton damped his enthusiasm slightly.

" It won't be so easy to get that list, Inspector. Remember the confusion of the whole business : the hurry, the effect of moonlight, the masks, the costumes, and all the rest of it. You may be able to put a list together ; but you'll have some difficulty yourself in believing that you've tracked down every possible person who was in the line. And if you miss one . . ."

" He may be the man, you mean ? Well, there's no harm in trying. I'll turn a sergeant on to gather all the news he can get."

" It'll be a good test of his capacity, then, even if nothing else comes out of it," Sir Clinton certified, carelessly.

CHAPTER VIII

THE MURDER IN THE MUSEUM

SIR CLINTON cut short the shrill ringing of his desk telephone by picking up the receiver.

" The Chief Constable speaking," he informed his inquirer.

Michael Clifton's voice sounded over the wire.

" Can you come up to Ravensthorpe at once, Sir Clinton, or send Inspector Armadale ? There's a bad business here. Mr Foss has been murdered. I've taken care that no one has got off the premises ; and I've seen to it that his body has been left as it was found."

Sir Clinton glanced at his wrist-watch.

" I'll drive across as soon as possible. See that things are left undisturbed, please. And collect all the people who can give any evidence, so that we needn't waste time hunting for them. Good-bye."

He shifted the switch of his telephone and spoke again.

" Is Inspector Armadale here just now ? " he asked the constable who answered his call. " Tell him I wish to see him in my room immediately."

While waiting for Armadale, Sir Clinton had a few moments in which to consider the information he had just received.

" This looks like Part II of the Ravensthorpe affair," he reflected. " Foss's only connection with

Ravensthorpe was the business of these Medusa Medallions. First one has the theft of the replicas ; now comes the murder of this American agent. It's highly improbable that two things like that could be completely independent."

His cogitation was interrupted by the entry of Armadale, and in a few words Sir Clinton gave him the fresh information which had come to hand.

" We'll go up there at once in my car, Inspector. Get the necessary things together, please. Don't forget the big camera. We may need it. And the constable who does photography for us had better come along also."

Inspector Armadale wasted no time. In a very few minutes they were on the road. As he drove, Sir Clinton was silent ; and Armadale's attempt to extract further information from him was a complete failure.

" You know as much as I do, Inspector," the Chief Constable pointed out. " Let's keep clear of any preconceived ideas until we see how the land lies up yonder."

When they reached Ravensthorpe, they found Michael Clifton waiting for them at the door.

" There are only two people who seem to know anything definite about things," he replied to the Chief Constable's first inquiry. " Joan's one of them, but she really knows nothing to speak of. The other witness is Foss's man—Marden's his name. Will you have a look at the body first of all, and then see Joan and this fellow ? "

Sir Clinton nodded his acquiescence and the party

followed Michael to the museum. Mold, the keeper, was again on guard at the door of the room, and Sir Clinton made a gesture of recognition as he passed in, followed by Armadale.

A cursory glance showed Foss's body lying in one of the bays formed by the show-cases round the wall. The Inspector went forward, knelt down, and held a pocket-mirror to the dead man's lips.

" Quite dead, sir," he reported after a short time.

" The police surgeon will be here shortly," Sir Clinton intimated. " If he's dead, we can postpone the examination of the body for a short time. Everything's to be left as it is until we come back. Turn the constable on to photograph the body's position in case we need it, though I don't think we shall. Now where's Miss Chacewater? We'd better get her version of the affair first. Then we can question the valet."

Without being acutely sensitive to atmosphere, Michael Clifton could not help noticing a fresh characteristic which had come into the Chief Constable's manner. This was not the Sir Clinton with whom he was acquainted : the old friend of the Chacewater family, with his faintly whimsical outlook on things. Instead, Michael was now confronted by the head of the police in the district, engaged in a piece of official work and carrying it through in a methodical fashion, as though nothing mattered but the end in view.

Followed by the two officials, Michael led the way to the room where Joan was waiting. The Chief Constable wasted no time in unnecessary talk. In fact, he plunged straight into business in a manner which suggested more than a touch of callousness. Only later on did Michael realize that in this, perhaps, Sir Clinton displayed more tact than was apparent at the moment. By his manner, he suggested that a murder was merely an event like any other—rather uncommon, perhaps, but not a thing which called for any particular excitement ; and this almost indifferent attitude tended to relax Joan's overstrained nerves.

" You didn't see the crime actually committed, of course ? "

Joan shook her head.

" Shall I begin at the beginning ? " she asked.

Sir Clinton, by a gesture, invited her to sit down. He took a chair himself and pulled out a notebook. Inspector Armadale copied him in this. Michael remained standing near Joan's chair, as though to lend her his moral support.

After thinking for a moment or two, Joan began her story.

" Some time after lunch, I was sitting on the terrace with Mr Foss. I forget what we were talking about—nothing of any importance. Soon after that, Maurice came out of the house and sat down. I was surprised to see him, for he'd arranged to play golf this afternoon. But he'd sprained his right wrist badly after lunch, it seems, and had 'phoned to put off his match. He sat nursing his wrist, and we began to speak of one thing and another. Then, I remember, Mr Foss somehow turned the talk on to some of the things we have. It was mostly about Japanese things that they spoke ;

136

and Mr Foss seemed chiefly interested in some of the weapons my father had collected. I remember they talked about a Sukesada sword we have and about the Muramasa short sword. Mr Foss said that he would like to see them some time. He thought that Mr Kessock would be interested to hear about them."

She broke off and seemed to be trying to remember the transitions of the conversation. Sir Clinton waited patiently ; but at last she evidently found herself unable to recall any details of the next stage in the talk.

" I can't remember how it came up. It was just general talk about things in our collection and things Mr Foss had seen elsewhere, but finally they got on to the Medusa Medallions somehow. Mr Foss was telling Maurice how tantalizing it was to buy these things and pass them on to collectors when he'd like to keep them for himself if only he could afford it. Then it came out that he always took a rubbing of all the coins and medals he came across. I remember he made some little joke about his ' poor man's collection ' or something like that. I forget exactly how it came about, but either he asked Maurice to let him have another look at the Leonardo medallions or Maurice volunteered to let him take rubbings there and then. I can't recall the exact way in which the suggestion was made. I wasn't paying much attention at the time."

She looked up to see if Sir Clinton showed any sign of annoyance at incomplete information ; but his face betrayed neither dissatisfaction nor approval. Inspector Armadale, though following the evidence keenly and making frequent notes, seemed to think that very little of her information was to the point.

" Then," Joan went on, " I remember Mr Foss getting up from his chair and saying : ' If you'll wait a moment, I'll get the things.' And he went away and left Maurice and me together. I said : ' What's he gone for ? ' And Maurice said : ' Some paper to take rubbings of the medallions and some stuff he uses for that, dubbin or something.' In a few minutes, Mr Foss came back again with some sheets of paper and some black stuff in his hand. I was interested in seeing how he did his rubbing or whatever you call it, so I went with them to the museum."

" And then ? " Sir Clinton prompted. As they were evidently coming near the moment of the murder in Joan's narrative, it was clear that he wished to leave her no time to think of the crime itself.

" We went into the museum. Since that night of the masked ball, Maurice has removed most of the smaller articles of value from the cases and put them into the safe; so in order to get the medallions he had to open the safe. It's a combination lock, you know ; and as I knew Maurice wouldn't like us to be at his elbow while he was setting the combination, I took Mr Foss under my wing and led him over to where the Sukesada sword is hung on the wall. We looked at it for a few moments. I remember taking it out of its sheath to show the blade to Mr Foss. Then I heard Maurice slamming the door of the safe ; and when we went into the bay where it is, Maurice was there with the Leonardo medallions in his hand."

"One moment," Sir Clinton interrupted. "You said it was a combination lock on the safe. Do you happen to know the combination?"

Joan shook her head.

"Maurice is the only one who knows that. He never told it to any of us."

Sir Clinton invited her to continue.

"Maurice handed Mr Foss one of the medallions and Mr Foss took it over to the big central case—the one with the flat top. Then he began to take a rubbing of the medallion with his paper and black stuff. He didn't seem quite satisfied with his first attempt, so he had a second try at it. As we were watching him, he seemed to prick up his ears, and then he said : 'There's someone calling for you, Miss Chacewater.' I couldn't hear anything myself ; but he explained that the voice was pretty far off. He had extra good hearing, I remember he said. He seemed very positive about it, so I went off to see what it was all about."

"Was that the last time you saw him?"

"Yes," said Joan, but she had obviously more to tell.

"And then?"

"As I was going away from the museum door, I met Mr Foss's man, Marden. He had a small brown-paper parcel in his hand. He stopped me and asked me if I knew where Mr Foss was. Something about the parcel, I gathered, though I didn't stop to listen to him. I told him Mr Foss was in the museum ; and I went on to see if I could find who was calling. I searched about and came across Mr Clifton ; but I didn't hear anyone calling my name.   Mr Foss must have been mistaken."

"And then ? "

Michael Clifton evidently thought it unnecessary that Joan should bear the whole burden of giving evidence.   At this point he broke in.

"Miss Chacewater and I were together in the winter-garden when I heard a shout of 'Murder !'   I didn't recognize the voice at the time.   I left Miss Chacewater where she was and made my way as quick as I could towards the voice.   It came from the museum, so I hurried there.   I found Foss on the floor with a dagger of some sort in his chest.   He was gone, so far as I could see, before I came on the scene at all.   The man Marden was in the room, tying up his hand.   It was bleeding badly and he said he'd cut it on the glass of a case.   I kept him under my eye till I could get a couple of keepers ; and then I rang you up at the station."

"What had become of Mr Chacewater ? " Sir Clinton asked, without showing that he attached more than a casual interest to the question.

"That's the puzzle," Michael admitted.   "I didn't see him anywhere in the museum at the moment and I've been hunting for him everywhere since then : but he's not turned up.   He may have gone out into the grounds, of course, and left Foss alone in the museum ; and possibly he had got out of earshot before the cry of 'Murder !' was raised by the valet.   I don't know."

Sir Clinton saw that the Inspector wished to ask a question, but he silenced him by a glance.

" One more point, and we're done, I think," he said, turning to Joan. " Can you give me a rough idea of the time when the cry of ' Murder ! ' was raised ? I mean, how long was it after you had left the museum yourself ? "

Joan thought for a few seconds.

" It took me three or four minutes before I came across Mr Clifton, and we were together—how long would you say, Michael ?—before we heard the shout ? "

" Not more than five minutes," Michael suggested.

" That's about it," Joan confirmed. " That would make it about eight or nine minutes, roughly, between the time I left the museum and the time we heard the shout."

" About that," Michael agreed.

Sir Clinton rose and closed his notebook.

" That's all you have to tell us ? Everything that bears on the matter, so far as you know ? "

Joan paused for a moment or two before replying.

" That's all that I can remember," she said at last, after an evident effort to recall any fresh details. " I can't think of anything else that would be of use."

" You've no idea where your brother is ? "

" None at all," Joan answered. Then a thought seemed to strike her. " You don't think Maurice had anything to do with this ? " she demanded, anxiously.

" He'll turn up shortly to speak for himself, I've no doubt," Sir Clinton said, as though to reassure her. " Now that's all we need just now, so far as you're concerned. I'm going to take Mr Clifton away for a few minutes, but he'll be back again almost immediately."

With a reassuring smile, the Chief Constable excused himself and led the way to the door, followed by Michael and the Inspector. As soon as he was out of the room, he turned to Michael.

" You're quite sure that Mr Chacewater wasn't in the museum when you reached it ? "

Michael considered carefully before replying.

" I don't see how he could have been. I glanced into all the bays ; and you know there isn't cover enough for a cat in the place."

" Was the safe door open or shut, did you notice ? "

Michael again reflected before replying.

" Shut, I'm almost certain."

Sir Clinton in his turn seemed to reflect for a moment or two.

" We'll have a look at this fellow Marden, now, I think, Inspector, if you'll bring him along to the museum. We'd better hear his tale on the spot. It'll save explanations about the positions of things."

Inspector Armadale departed on his quest while Michael and the Chief Constable made their way to the scene of the crime. Suddenly Sir Clinton turned and confronted Michael.

" Have you any notion whatever as to where Maurice has gone ? I want the truth."

Michael was manifestly taken aback by the direct demand.

" I haven't a notion," he declared. " He wasn't in

the museum when I got there, so far as I know. You can put me on my oath over that, if you like."

The Chief Constable scanned his face keenly, but made no comment on his statement. He led the way to the museum ; and they had hardly passed through the door before Inspector Armadale returned with the valet.

Marden appeared to be a man of about thirty years of age. Sir Clinton noticed that he carried himself well and did not seem to have lost his head in the excitement of the past hour. When he spoke, it was without any appreciable accent ; and he seemed to take pains to be perfectly clear in his evidence. Sir Clinton, by an almost imperceptible gesture, handed over the examination of the valet to the Inspector. Armadale pulled out his notebook once more.

" What's your name ? " he demanded.

" Thomas Marden."

" How long have you been in Mr Foss's service ? "

" Since he arrived here from America, about three months ago."

" How did he come to engage you ? "

" Advertisement."

" You knew nothing about him before that ? "

" Nothing."

" Where was he living then ? "

" At 474a Gunner's Mansions, S.W. It's a service flat."

" He still has that flat ? "

" Yes."

" How did he spend his time ? "

The valet seemed astonished by the question.

" I don't know.   None of my business."

Inspector Armadale was not to be turned aside.

" You must have known whether he stayed in the flat or went out regularly at fixed times."

Marden seemed to see what was wanted.

" You mean, did he go out to an office every day ? No, he came and went just when it suited him."

" Had he much correspondence ? "

" Letters ?   Just about what one might expect."

The Inspector looked up gloomily.   So far, he had not got much to go upon.

" What do you mean by : ' Just what one might expect ? ' "

" He got some letters every day, sometimes one or two, sometimes half a dozen.   Just what one might expect."

" Have you any idea whether they were business letters or merely private correspondence ? "

Marden seemed annoyed by the question.

" How should I know ? " he demanded, stiffly. " It's not my business to pry into my employer's affairs."

" It's your business to read the addresses on the envelopes to see that the postman hasn't left wrong letters.   Did you notice nothing when you did that ? Were the addresses mainly typewritten or written by hand ? "

" He got bills and advertisements with the address typewritten—like most of us.   And one or two letters came addressed by hand."

144

" Did you notice the stamps ? "

" Some were American, of course."

" So it comes to this," Inspector Armadale concluded, " he was not carrying on a big business from the flat ; most of his letters were ordinary bills and so forth ; but he had some private correspondence as well ; and part of his correspondence was with America ? Why couldn't you tell us that straight off, instead of having it dragged out of you ? "

The valet was quite unruffled by the Inspector's tone.

" I hadn't put two and two together the way you do. They were just letters to me. I didn't think anything about them."

Inspector Armadale showed no appreciation of this indirect tribute to his powers.

" Had he many visitors ? "

" Not at the flat. He may have met his friends in the restaurant downstairs for all I know."

" Do you remember any visitors at the flat ? "

" No."

The Inspector seemed to recollect something he had missed.

" Did he get any telegrams ? "

" Yes."

" Frequently ? "

" Fairly often."

" You've no idea of the contents of these wires ? "

Marden obviously took offence at this.

" You asked me before if I pried into his affairs ; and I told you I didn't."

" How often did these wires arrive ? " the Inspector demanded, taking no notice of Marden's annoyance.

" Perhaps once or twice a week."

" Did he bet ? " the Inspector inquired, as though it had just struck him that the telegrams might thus be explained.

" I know nothing about that."

Armadale went off on a fresh tack.

" Did he seem to be well off for money ? "

" He paid me regularly, if that's what you mean."

" He had a car and a chauffeur, hadn't he ? "

" Yes."

" Were they his own or simply hired ? "

" I don't know.   Not my business."

" The Gunner's Mansions flats are expensive ? "

" They get the name of it.   I don't know what he paid."

" You don't seem to have had much curiosity, Marden."

" I'm not paid for being curious."

The Inspector put down his pencil and reflected for a moment or two.

" Have you any idea of his address in America ? "

" Not my business."

" Did he write many letters ? "

" I couldn't say.   None of my business."

" You can at least say whether he gave you any to post."

" He didn't."

" Have you anything else you can tell us about him ? "

Marden seemed to think carefully before he replied.
" All his clothes were split new."

" Anything else ? "

" He carried a revolver—I mean an automatic."

" What size was it ? "

" About that length."

The valet indicated the length approximately with his hands, and winced slightly as he moved the bandaged one.

" H'm ! A ·38 or a ·45," Armadale commented. " Too big for a ·22, anyway."

He took up his pencil again.

" Now come to this afternoon. Begin at lunch-time and go on."

Marden reflected for a moment, as though testing his memory.

" I'd better begin before lunch. Mr Foss came to me with a parcel in his hand and asked me to take it over to Hincheldene post office. He wanted it regis-tered. He offered to let me take the car if I wished ; but I preferred to walk over. I like the fresh air."

" And then ? " demanded the Inspector with an unconscious plagiarism of his Chief.

" Immediately after lunch, I set out and walked through the grounds towards Hincheldene village. I didn't hurry. It was a nice afternoon for a walk. By and by I met a keeper, and he told me I couldn't go any farther in that direction. He'd orders to turn back anyone, he said. I talked to him for a minute or two, and explained where I was going ; and I pulled the parcel out of my pocket as a guarantee of good faith.

He didn't know me, you see. And when I got the parcel out, I noticed the label quite by chance."

" Ah, you do look at addresses after all ! " interjected the Inspector.

" Quite by chance," Marden went on, without taking any notice of the thrust. " And I saw that Mr Foss had made a mistake."

" How did you know that," Inspector Armadale demanded, with the air of a cat pouncing on a mouse. " You said you'd taken no interest in his correspondence and yet you knew this parcel was directed to a wrong address. Curious, isn't it ? "

Marden did not even permit himself to smile as he discomfited the Inspector.

" He'd left out the name of the town. An obvious oversight when he was writing the label."

" Well, go on," growled the Inspector, evidently displeased at losing his score.

" As soon as I saw that, I knew it was no good taking the thing to the post office as it was. So I asked the keeper a question or two about the shortest way to Hincheldene without getting on to the barred ground. Then I turned and came home again, intending to ask Mr Foss to complete the address on the parcel."

" What time was it when you reached here again ? "

Marden considered for a while.

" I couldn't say precisely. Sometime round about half-past three or a bit later. I didn't look at the time."

" What did you do then ? "

" I hunted about for Mr Foss, but he didn't seem to be in the house. At last, when I was just giving it up, I met Miss Chacewater coming away from this room, and she told me that Mr Foss was inside. She went away, and I came to the door. It was half-open and I could hear voices inside : Mr Foss and Mr Chacewater from the sound. I thought they'd soon be coming out and that I'd get Mr Foss as he passed me ; so I waited, instead of interrupting them."

" How long did you wait ? "

" Only a minute or two, so far as I can remember."

" You could hear them talking ? "

" I could hear the sound of their voices. I couldn't hear what they said. There's an echo or something in this room and all I heard was the tone they were speaking in."

" What sort of tone do you mean ? "

Marden paused as though searching for an adjective.

" It seemed to me an angry tone. They raised their voices."

" As if they were quarrelling ? "

" Like that. And then I heard Mr Chacewater say : ' So that's what you're after ? ' Then I heard what sounded like a scuffle and a gasp. I was taken aback, of course. Who wouldn't be ? I stood stock still with the parcel in my hand for a moment or two. Then I got my head back and I pushed open the door and rushed into the room."

" Be careful here," Sir Clinton interrupted. " Don't try to force your memory. Tell us exactly what comes back into your mind."

Marden nodded.

" When I got into the room here," he went on,

149

" the first thing I saw was Mr Chacewater. He had his back to me and was just turning the corner here."

Marden walked across and indicated the end of the bay beyond the one which contained the safe, the last recess in the room at the end opposite from the door.

" He went round this corner in a hurry. That's the last I saw of him."

Marden's face betrayed his amazement even at the recollection.

" Never mind that just now," said Sir Clinton. " Tell us what you did yourself."

" I couldn't see Mr Foss at the first glance ; but when I got near the corner where I'd seen Mr Chacewater, I saw Mr Foss lying on the ground. I thought he'd slipped or something ; and I went over to give him a hand up. Then I saw a big knife or a dagger through his chest and some blood on his mouth. As I was hurrying over to his side, I slipped on the parquet —it's very slippery—and down I came. I put out my hand to save myself and my fist broke the glass in one of these cases. When I got up again, my hand was streaming with blood. It's a nasty gash. So I pulled out my handkerchief and wrapped it round my hand before I did anything else. It was simply gushing with blood and I thought of it first of all."

Marden held up his roughly swathed hand in proof.

" I got to my feet again and went over to Mr Foss. By that time he was either dead or next door to it. He didn't move. I didn't touch him, for I saw well enough he was done for. Then I went to the door and shouted ' Murder ! ' as hard as I could. Then while

I was shouting, it struck me as queer that Mr Chacewater had disappeared."

" It didn't occur to you that he might have slipped out of the room while your back was turned—when you were busy over Mr Foss ? " demanded Inspector Armadale in a hostile tone.

Marden shook his head.

" It didn't occur to me at all, because I knew it hadn't happened. No one could have got out of the room without my seeing him."

" Go on with your story, please," Sir Clinton requested.

" There's nothing more to tell. I kept shouting ' Murder ! ' and I searched the room here while I was doing it. I found nothing."

" Was the safe door closed when you saw it first ? " Sir Clinton inquired.

" Yes, it was. I thought perhaps Mr Chacewater might be inside, with the door pulled to ; so I tried the handle. It was locked."

Sir Clinton put a further inquiry.

" You heard only two voices in the room before you burst in ? "

A new light seemed to be thrown by this question across Marden's mind.

" I heard only two people speaking : Mr Foss and Mr Chacewater ; but of course I couldn't swear that only two people were in the room. That's what you meant, isn't it ? "

Inspector Armadale caught the drift of the inquiry.

" I suppose if one man can disappear in a mysterious

way, there's nothing against two men vanishing in the same way," he hazarded. " So all you can really tell us is that Mr Foss and Mr Chacewater were here at any rate, and possibly there were other people as well ?"

" I couldn't swear to anyone except these two," Marden was careful to state.

" Another point," Sir Clinton went on. " Have you any idea whether Mr Foss came into contact with a person or persons outside the house during his stay here ? I mean people known to him before he came to Ravensthorpe ? "

" I couldn't say."

" None of your business, I suppose ? " Inspector Armadale put in, with an obvious sneer.

" None of my business, as you say," Marden returned, equably. " I wasn't engaged as a detective."

" Well, this question falls into your department," Sir Clinton intervened, as Armadale showed signs of losing his temper. " What costume was Mr Foss wearing on the night of the masked ball ? You must know that."

Marden replied without hesitation.

" He was got up as a cow-puncher. He hired the costume from London when he heard about the fancy dress. It was a pair of cow-boy trousers, big heavy things with fringes on them ; a leather belt with a pistol-holster on it ; a coloured shirt ; a neck-cloth ; and a flappy cow-boy hat."

" Rather a clumsy rig-out, then ? "

Marden seemed to find difficulty in repressing a smile.

152

" It was as much as he could do to walk at all, until he got accustomed to the things. He told me it gave him a good excuse for not dancing. He wasn't a dancing man, he said."

" He carried a revolver, you say. Did you ever see any sign that he was afraid of anything of this sort happening to him ? "

" I don't understand. How could I know what he was afraid of or what he wasn't ? It was none of my business."

Sir Clinton's smile took the edge off Marden's reply.

" Oh, I think one might make a guess," he said, " if one kept one's eyes open. A terrified man would give himself away somehow or other."

" Then either he wasn't afraid or else I don't keep my eyes open. I saw nothing of the sort."

Sir Clinton reflected for a moment or two. He glanced at Armadale.

" Any more questions you'd like to put ? No ? Then that will do, Marden. Of course there'll be an inquest and your evidence will be required at it. You can stay on here until you're needed. I'll see Miss Chacewater about it. But for the present you've given us all the help you can ? "

" Unless you've any more questions you want to ask," Marden suggested.

Sir Clinton shook his head.

" No, I think I've got all I need for the present, thanks. I may want you again later on, of course."

Marden waited for nothing further, but left the room pursued by a slightly vindictive glance from

Inspector Armadale. When he had disappeared, Sir Clinton turned to Michael Clifton.

" Hadn't you better go back to Joan, now ? She must be rather nervous after this shock."

Michael came to himself with a slight start when the Chief Constable addressed him. Hitherto his rôle had been purely that of a spectator ; and he had been so wrapped up in it that it came as a faint surprise to find himself directly addressed. Throughout the proceedings he had been semi-hypnotized by the deadly matter-of-fact way in which the police were going about their work. When he had first heard of the murder, he had felt as though something unheard-of had invaded Ravensthorpe. Of course murders did take place : one read about them in the newspapers. But the idea that murder could actually be done in his own familiar environment had come to him with more than a slight shock. The normal course of things seemed suddenly diverted.

But during the last ten minutes he had been a witness of the beginning of the police investigation ; and the invincible impression of ordinariness had begun to replace the earlier nightmare quality in his mind. Here were a couple of men going about the business as though it were of no more tragic character than a search for a lost dog. It was part of their work to hunt out a solution of the affair. They were no more excited over it than a chess-player looking for the key-move in a problem. The cool, dispassionate way in which the Chief Constable had handled the affair seemed to strike a fresh note and to efface the suggestions of the macabre side of things which had been Michael's first impression of the matter. The Dance of Death retreated gradually into the background in the face of all the minute questionings about letters, and visits, and parcels—these commonplace things of everyday life.

" If I can be of no use here," he said, " I think I'd better go."

He hesitated for a moment as a fresh thought struck him.

" By the way, how much of this is confidential ? "

Sir Clinton looked at him with an expressionless face.

" I think I may leave that to your discretion. It's not for broadcasting, at any rate."

" What about Maurice ? " Michael persisted.

" I'd leave Maurice out of it as far as possible," said Sir Clinton, in obvious dismissal. " Now, Inspector, I think we'd better have a look at the late Mr Foss."

Michael retreated from the room as they turned towards the body on the floor.

" Leave Maurice out of it ! " he thought, as he walked at a snail's pace towards the room where he had left Joan. " That's a nice bit of advice ! If you leave Maurice out of it, there seems to be nothing left in it. Now what the devil am I to say to her ? If I say nothing, she'll jump to the worst conclusion ; and if I say anything at all, she'll jump to the same."

CHAPTER IX

THE MURAMASA SWORD

As the door closed behind Michael Clifton, the Chief Constable turned to the Inspector.

"Now we can get to business, Inspector. Let's have a look round the place at leisure, and perhaps the surgeon will turn up before we reach the body itself."

Followed by Armadale, he stepped over to the bay containing the corpse of Foss and began methodically to inspect the surroundings.

"This must have been the case that Marden slipped against when he cut his hand," the Inspector pointed out. "There's a big hole in the glass and some blood on the broken edges of the gap."

"Oh, yes, there's blood enough to suit most people," Sir Clinton admitted, with a glance towards the shattered case. But he seemed less interested in the glass than in the floor surface ; for he moved slowly to and fro, evidently trying to place himself so that the sunlight from the window was reflected up to him from the parquet. After a moment or two, he seemed satisfied.

"That part of Marden's story seems true enough. He did slip here. If you come across, you'll see a line where the polish of the parquet has been taken off by some hard part of his shoe. You won't be able to spot it unless you make a mirror of the floor."

The Inspector in his turn moved over and satisfied himself of the existence of the faint mark.

" That confirms part of his story," he admitted, grudgingly. " There's a lot of blood about, quite apart from the stuff from the body. One might make something out of that."

" Suppose we try," Sir Clinton suggested. " Assume that he cut his hand here on the glass. He'd be all asprawl on the floor ; and the first thing he'd do would be to put his hands down to help himself up. That would account for these biggish patches here, under the case. Then a foot or so away you see those round marks of droplets with tiny splashes radiating from them with a fair regularity all round. These must have been made by drops falling from his hand while he stood still—no doubt while he was feeling with the other hand for his handkerchief to stanch the bleeding."

The Inspector indicated his agreement.

" After he'd got it fixed up, one might expect him to go over and look at Foss. He'd gone down on the floor, you remember, while he was hurrying to Foss's assistance."

" There's no sign of that," Armadale hastened to point out. " I can't see any blood-drops round about the body."

" Oh, don't be in too much of a hurry, Inspector. Perhaps they fell in the pool of Foss's own blood or, more probably, his handkerchief soaked up any blood that flowed just then."

Sir Clinton, still with his eyes on the ground, began to cast about in search of further traces.

" Ah, here are a couple of drops at the end of the bay. Have a look at them, Inspector."

Armadale knelt down and examined the clots.

" Made on his way to the door, probably," he suggested.

" They might have been, if he was swinging his arm as one does when one walks freely ; but one doesn't usually swing the arm when there's a fresh wound in the hand, I think. These aren't round blobs like the others ; they're elongated, and all the splashing from them is at one end—the end towards the safe. His hand, when they were made, was moving towards the safe's bay, whatever his body was doing."

Sir Clinton made a rough measurement of the distance between the two drops.

" If they'd been nearer together or further apart, then each of them might have been made while his arm was going backwards in its natural swing while he was walking towards the door. But the distance between them won't fit that. You'll see at once if you try walking over the ground yourself, Inspector ; for you're just about Marden's height and your stride must be nearly the same as his."

" He said something about going to the safe and trying the handle," the Inspector admitted, grudgingly. " So far, his tale's got some support."

Sir Clinton smiled covertly at Armadale's obvious desire to pick holes in the valet's narrative.

" Well, let's find out how it happened," Sir Clinton suggested. " He evidently passed this bay and went on towards the next one, where the safe is. We'll follow his example."

They turned the corner of the show-case and stepped over to the safe door.

" There's a trace of blood on the handle, true enough," the Inspector admitted. " But I'm not sure he told the truth about why he came to the safe."

Sir Clinton inspected the smear of blood on the handle, but he seemed to attach very little importance to it.

" I suppose one mustn't jump to conclusions and assume that everything's all above-board," he conceded. " But even if we keep open minds, wouldn't it be the most natural thing in the world for Marden to try the safe door ? Remember what had happened according to his story. Mr Chacewater was in the room, for Marden saw him with his own eyes. Mr Chacewater turned the corner of a bay—the one next this ; and then Marden lost him for good. If you'd been in Marden's place, wouldn't you have searched about, and then, finding no trace of the missing man, wouldn't you have jumped to the conclusion that he might be hidden in the safe ? And wouldn't you have given the handle a pull, just to make sure the safe was really locked and that Mr Chacewater wasn't hiding inside it ? "

" I suppose so," conceded the Inspector, evidently dissatisfied.

" I expect his tale isn't complete, of course. He could hardly give every detail. It would be a bit suspicious if he had, I think. If his tale had been

159

absolutely complete in every detail, I'd be inclined to suspect a previously prepared recitation rather than an account of the facts. In a case of this sort, one could hardly expect a water-tight narrative, could one ? "

He continued his examination of the floor ; but there seemed to be no other blood-stains of any importance.

" Now let's have a glance at the body," he suggested. " We needn't shift it till the surgeon comes ; but we can see what's to be seen without altering its position in the meanwhile."

The Inspector was the first to reach the spot, and as he knelt down beside the corpse he gave an exclamation of surprise.

" Here's an automatic pistol, sir. It's lying almost under the body, but I can see the muzzle. It looks like a ·38 calibre."

" Leave it there. We'll get at it later."

Sir Clinton examined the body itself. The cause of death seemed obvious enough, for the weapon still remained in the wound. A glance at it set the Chief Constable's eye ranging over the museum cases. He retreated from the bay and searched for a time until he found what he was looking for : an empty sheath in an unlocked case. Without touching the sheath, he scanned the Japanese inscription on its surface.

" So that's the thing ? "

The Inspector had come across to his side and stood looking at the sheath.

" So the thing's one of the specimens ? " he asked.

" Yes. Don't touch it, Inspector. We may as

well see whose finger-prints are on it, though it's quite on the cards that it's been handled by other people lately as well as the murderer. It's rather a show specimen, you see—one of Muramasa's making. This was the sword they were discussing when they were out on the terrace. Muramasa's weapons have the name of being unlucky ; and this one seems to bear out the legend.''

The Inspector looked at the sheath with apparent care, but his thoughts seemed to be elsewhere.

" Nobody could have got away from here through the windows," he observed, rather irrelevantly. " They're all barred outside, and the catches are fast on the sashes."

Evidently Sir Clinton had noticed this in the course of his previous search, for he gave a tacit assent to the Inspector's statement without even glancing up at the windows.

" Here are the sheets of rubbing-paper that Foss was using," the Inspector went on, picking them up as he spoke. " They'll have his finger-prints on them, so I'll stow them away. We might need them. One never knows."

" We can get actual prints from the body if we need them," Sir Clinton pointed out. " You don't suppose it's a suicide case, do you ? "

The Inspector was too wary to throw himself open to attack. He contented himself with putting the papers away carefully in his pocket-book.

" Finger-prints will be useful, though," Sir Clinton went on. " At the earliest possible moment, Inspector, I want you to get prints from the fingers of every-one in the house. Start with Miss Chacewater. She'll agree to let you take her's without any trouble ; and after that you can go on to Mr Clifford and so down the scale. We've no authority for insisting, of course ; but you can make a note if anyone objects. I expect you'll get the lot without difficulty."

At this moment Mold opened the door to admit the police surgeon ; and Sir Clinton broke off in order to explain the state of affairs to him. Dr Greenlaw was a business-like person who wasted no time. While Sir Clinton was speaking, he knelt down beside the corpse and made a cursory examination of it. When he rose to his feet again, he seemed satisfied.

" That sword appears to have entered the thorax between the fifth and sixth ribs," he pointed out. " It's pierced the left lung, evidently ; you notice the blood-foam on his lips ? And most probably it's penetrated right into the heart as well. It looks as if it had ; but of course I'll need to carry out a P.M. before I can give you exact details."

" I suppose we can take out the sword before we shift the body ? " asked the Inspector. " We want to examine it before anyone else touches it."

" Certainly," Greenlaw replied. " You can see for yourselves what happened. He was struck from the front by a right-handed man—a fairly heavy blow, I should judge from the depth to which that sword has buried itself. There's no sign of a twist in the wound, which looks as though he went down under it at once. Quite possibly the base of the skull may have been fractured on the floor by the force of his fall. We'll see when we come to the P.M. But in any case that wound alone would be quite sufficient to cause almost immediate death. It's a blade almost as broad as a bayonet, as you can see. I'll go into the whole thing carefully when I can make a thorough examination. You'll have him sent down to the mortuary, of course?"

" As soon as we've finished our work here."

" Good. I'll make a note or two now, if you don't mind. Then I'll leave you to get on. As things are, there's nothing there which you couldn't see for yourselves."

He took out a pocket-book and began to jot down his notes.

" Just a moment, doctor," Sir Clinton interposed. " I've got a patient for you here. I'd like you to have a look at his hand and bandage up some cuts before you go."

Greenlaw nodded in agreement and went on with his note-taking.

" Now, Inspector," Sir Clinton continued, " we'd better get this sword out. Be sure to take all the care you can not to rub out any finger-prints."

Armadale obeyed, and after some cautious man-œuvres he succeeded in withdrawing the weapon, which he laid carefully on the top of the central show-case.

" Now we can have a look at him," Sir Clinton said. " You don't mind our shifting the position of the body, doctor ? "

Greenlaw closed his notebook and prepared to assist them if necessary.

" Begin with the contents of his pockets, Inspector,"
Sir Clinton suggested.

" The blade's gone clean through his left breast
pocket," the Inspector pointed out.   He felt the outside of the pocket gingerly with his fingers.

" Nothing there except his handkerchief, so far as I
can feel.   It's all soaked with his blood.   I'll leave
that to the last.   I want to keep my hands clean while
I go over the rest."

He wiped his finger-tips carefully on his own handkerchief and continued his search.

" Right-hand breast pocket : a note-case."

He drew it out and handed it to Sir Clinton, who
opened it and counted the contents.

" Three hundred and fifty-seven pounds in notes,"
he announced at length.   " That's a fair sum to be
carrying about with one.   Ten visiting cards : ' J. B.
Foss,' with no address."

He crossed over to the central case and put down the
note-case thoughtfully.

" The left-hand waistcoat pockets are saturated
with blood," Armadale continued.   " I'll leave them
over for the present.   Top right-hand waistcoat
pocket, empty.   Lower right-hand waistcoat pocket :
a small penknife and a tooth-pick.   Not much blood
here ; he was lying slightly on his left side and it must
have flowed in that direction, I suppose.   Right-hand
jacket pocket, outside : nothing.   I'll take the trousers
now.   Right-hand pocket : key-ring and a purse."

He handed them to Sir Clinton, who examined them
in turn before putting them on the central case.

"Only keys of suit-cases here," the Chief Constable reported. "We haven't come across the latch-key of his flat, if you notice."

He counted the contents of the purse.

"Eight and sixpence and one ten-shilling note."

The Inspector proceeded with his examination.

"Here's something funny! He's got a smallish pocket over his hip, just below the trouser button. That's unusual. But it's empty," he added, after an eager search.

"Let me look at that," Sir Clinton demanded.

He stooped down and inspected the pocket closely, then stood up and passed his hand across the corresponding spot on his own clothes. As he did so, Armadale noticed a peculiar expression pass across the Chief Constable's face, as though some new idea had dawned upon him and had cleared up a difficulty. But Sir Clinton divulged nothing of what was passing in his mind.

"Make quite sure it's empty," he said.

Armadale turned the little pocket inside out.

"There's nothing there," he pointed out. "It wouldn't hold much—it's hardly bigger than a ticket pocket."

He looked at the pocket again, evidently puzzled by the importance which the Chief Constable attached to it.

"It's a silly place to have a pocket," he said at last. "It's not like the old-fashioned fob. That was kept tight shut by the pressure of your body. This thing's mouth is loose and it's simply a gift to a pickpocket."

"I think we'll probably find another of the same

kind on the other side," Sir Clinton contented himself with saying. "Let's get on with the rest of them."

Armadale turned the body slightly and put his hand into the hip pocket.

"It's empty, too," he announced. "It's a very loose pocket with no flap on it. I expect he carried his pistol there and he had the pocket built for easy handling of his gun."

He looked at the ·38 automatic which had been disclosed as he turned the body.

"That wouldn't have fitted into the little pocket," he pointed out. "The pistol's far too big for the opening."

Sir Clinton nodded his agreement with this view.

"He didn't use it for his pistol. Now, the left-hand pockets, please. You can wash your hands as soon as you've gone through them."

Inspector Armadale stolidly continued his investigation.

"Left-hand breast pocket in jacket," he announced. "Nothing but his handkerchief, saturated with blood."

He handed it to Sir Clinton, who inspected it carefully before putting it with the rest of the collection.

"No marks on it, either initials or laundry-mark," he said. "Evidently been bought and used without marking."

"Ticket pocket, empty," the Inspector went on, withdrawing his fingers from it. "Top left waistcoat pocket : a self-filling Swan pen and a metal holder for same. Lower left waistcoat pocket : an amber cigarette-holder. Not much to go on there."

He turned to the trousers.

" Left-hand trouser pocket : five coppers."

Handing them over, he proceeded.

" Your notion's quite right, sir. There's another of these side pockets here. But it's empty like the other one."

Instead of replying, Sir Clinton gingerly picked up the automatic pistol from the floor and placed it along with the other objects on the central case.

" You'd better examine that for finger-prints, Inspector," he suggested. " I leave you to make the arrangements about taking the body down to the mortuary. The sooner the better. Now, doctor, we'll get your patient for you, if the Inspector will be good enough to bring him to the lavatory near by, where you can get his wounds patched up."

Inspector Armadale soon produced Marden, who seemed rather surprised at being summoned again.

" It's all right, Marden," Sir Clinton assured him. " It merely struck me that when there was a doctor on the premises you ought to have these cuts of yours properly fixed up."

Dr Greenlaw speedily removed the temporary bandage which the valet had improvised.

" I'll need to put some stitches into this," he said, as the extent of the injury became evident. " Luckily these glass cuts are clean-edged. You'll hardly see the scar after a time."

Sir Clinton inspected the wounds sympathetically.

" You've made a bit of a mess of your hand, Marden," he commented. " It's just as well I thought of getting Dr Greenlaw to look after you."

167

Marden seemed to have been looking for an opening.
" I'm glad you called me up again, sir," he explained.
"I've just thought of two other points about this
affair."

" Yes ? "

While the doctor was cleaning and disinfecting the
wounds, Marden addressed himself to the Chief
Constable.

" I forgot to say, sir, that when I got back to the
house I found Mr Foss's car waiting for him. I said
a word or two to the chauffeur as I passed. It only
struck me afterwards that this might be important. I
forgot about it at the time."

" Quite right to tell us," Sir Clinton confirmed.

" The second thing was what the chauffeur told me.
He'd been ordered to wait for Mr Foss, it seems ; and
he got the idea that Mr Foss was leaving Ravensthorpe
this afternoon for good. I was surprised by that ;
for I'd heard nothing about it from Mr Foss."

He flinched slightly with the smart of his wounds, as
Greenlaw washed them carefully.

Sir Clinton seemed to be struck by a fresh idea.

" Before the doctor bandages you up, would you
mind if we took your finger-prints, Marden ? I'm
asking everyone to let us take theirs, and this seems to
be the best chance we shall have of getting yours, you
see ? Of course, if you object, I've no power to insist
on it."

" I've no objections, sir. Why should I have ? "

" Then you might take impressions of the lot,
Inspector," Sir Clinton suggested. " Don't spend too

much time over it. We must get the bandages on this hand as quick as possible."

Inspector Armadale hurried away for his outfit and soon set to work to take the valet's finger-prints. While he was thus engaged a fresh suggestion seemed to occur to Sir Clinton.

" By the way, Marden, you have that parcel which Mr Foss sent to the post ? "

" I can give you it in a moment, sir, once the doctor has finished with my hand."

" Very good. I'd like to see it."

The Chief Constable waited patiently until Marden's hand was completely bandaged ; then he dispatched the valet for the parcel. When it was forthcoming, he dismissed Marden again. The doctor took his leave, and Armadale was left alone with Sir Clinton.

" Now let's see what Foss was sending off, Inspector."

Cutting the string, Sir Clinton unwrapped the paper and disclosed a small cardboard box. Inside, on a layer of cotton-wool, was a wrist-watch. Further search failed to bring to light any enclosed note.

" I suppose he was sending it to be cleaned," the Inspector hazarded. " Probably he wrote a letter by the same post."

" Let's have a look at it, Inspector. Be careful not to mark it with your fingers."

Sir Clinton took the watch up and examined it closely.

" It looks fairly new to need repair."

He held it to his ear.

" It's going. Not much sign of damage there."

169

"Perhaps it needed regulating," Armadale suggested.

"Perhaps," Sir Clinton's tone was non-committal. "Take a note of the time as compared with your own watch, Inspector; and just check whether it's going fast or slow in a few hours. Try it for finger-prints along with the rest of the stuff."

He replaced it gently in its bed of cotton-wool and closed the box, taking care not to finger the cardboard.

"Now, if you'll send for the chauffeur, we may get something from him."

But the chauffeur proved a most unsatisfactory witness. He admitted that Foss had ordered him to bring round the car at 3.15 and wait for further orders; but he was unable to give any clear account of the talk he had with his employer when the order was given.

"I can't remember what he said exactly; but I got the notion he was leaving here to-day. I'm dead sure of that; for I packed up my own stuff and had it ready to go off at a moment's notice. It's on the grid of the car now. I was so taken aback that I haven't thought of unpacking it."

Sir Clinton could get nothing further out of the man, and he was eventually dismissed.

"Now we'll have a run over the late Mr Foss's goods," the Chief Constable proposed, when they had dismissed the chauffeur.

But the search of Foss's bedroom yielded at first nothing of much interest.

"This doesn't look as if that chauffeur had been telling the truth," Armadale pointed out, when they found all Foss's clothes arranged quite normally in

170

wardrobe and drawers. " Foss himself had made no preparations for moving, that's evident. I'll see that chauffeur again and go into the matter more carefully."

" You might as well," Sir Clinton concurred. " But I doubt if you'll get him to shift from his story. He seemed to be very clear about the main point, though he was weak in details."

They subjected all Foss's belongings to a careful scrutiny.

" No name marked on any of the linen ; no tags on any of the suits ; no labels inside the jacket pockets," Inspector Armadale pointed out. " He seems to have been very anxious not to advertise his identity. And no papers of any sort. It looks a bit queer, doesn't it ? "

As he spoke, he noticed a small leather case standing in a corner.

" Hullo, here's an attaché case. Perhaps his papers are in it."

He crossed over and picked up the case, but as he did so an expression of surprise crossed his face.

" This thing's as heavy as lead ! It must weigh ten or twelve pounds at least ! "

" It's not an attaché case," Sir Clinton pointed out. " Look at the ends of it."

Armadale turned the case round in his hand. At the upper part of one end the leather had been cut away, disclosing a small ebonite disc rather more than an inch in diameter and pierced with a pattern of tiny holes. At the opposite end of the case there were two small holes side by side and a larger one above ; and examination showed brass sockets inside which seemed meant for the reception of plugs.

" You'd better get his keys, Inspector. Probably the key of this thing will be on the ring."

With his curiosity raised to an acute pitch, Armadale went off in search of the key-ring ; and was soon back again with it in his hand.

" Now we'll see what it is," he said, as he turned the key in the case's lock and pressed the opening spring.

The lifting of the lid disclosed a wooden casing fitted with a couple of hinged doors, an open recess in which were two levers, and a hinged metal plate, on which was an inscription. Armadale read it aloud uncomprehendingly :

" ' Marconi Otophone. Inst. No. S/O 1164.' What the deuce is this ? "

Sir Clinton put out his hand and lifted the hinged metal plate, disclosing below two wireless valves in their sockets.

" Some wireless gadget," the Inspector ejaculated. " Now what could he possibly have wanted with a thing like that ? "

Sir Clinton examined the instrument with interest, then he closed the case.

" We'll take this along with us, Inspector."

Then, with a sudden change of mind, he contradicted himself.

" No, we'll leave it here for the present. That will be much better."

Somewhat mystified by this change of intention, the

Inspector agreed. Sir Clinton's manner did not invite questions.

" I think we had better see Miss Chacewater again. There are one or two questions I'd like to put to her, Inspector ; and you had better be there."

In a minute or two, Joan was found, with Michael Clifton in attendance. Sir Clinton did not think it worth while to sit down.

" Just a couple of points I want to ask about. First of all, is there any record of the combination which opens the lock of the safe in the museum ? "

Joan shook her head.

" Maurice was the only one of us who knew it. My father did leave a note of it ; but I remember that Maurice destroyed that. He specially wished to keep it to himself."

" Another point," Sir Clinton went on. " Did Foss know, on the night of the burglary, which of the rows contained the real medallions and which row the replicas were in ? "

Joan reflected for a moment or two before replying.

" He must have known. Maurice had shown him the things once at least, if not oftener ; and I know there was no secret as to which were the real things and which were the counterfeits."

Sir Clinton seemed satisfied with this information.

" One last thing," he continued. " I suppose you could show me where your brother keeps his correspondence. We must get hold of Kessock's address and notify him about Foss's death ; and there seems no way of doing it as quick as this one. If the papers aren't locked up, perhaps I could see them now ? "

It appeared that the letters were available and Sir Clinton turned them over rapidly.

" Fifth Avenue ? That's satisfactory."

He put the papers back in their place.

" There's just one thing more. I'm going to put a constable on guard at the door of the museum for a while—day and night for a day or two, perhaps. You won't mind ? "

" Certainly not. Do as you wish."

Sir Clinton acknowledged the permission. Then, as though struck by an after-thought, he inquired :

" Have you Cecil's address ? "

Joan shook her head.

" He said he'd let me know where he was staying, but he hasn't written. Perhaps he hasn't settled down yet. He may be staying at an hotel for a day or two."

" Please ring me up as soon as he sends word."

Joan promised to do this, and Sir Clinton continued :

" By the way, Inspector Armadale wishes to take the finger-prints of everyone in the house. Would you mind setting an example and having yours taken along with the rest ? If you do it, then it will be easier for us to get the others. They won't be suspicious when they hear that it's a general inquisition."

Both Joan and Michael consented without ado.

" The Inspector will be with you in a moment or two," Sir Clinton said, as he took his leave. " Just a word with you, Inspector."

Armadale followed him from the room.

174

"Now, Inspector, there's a lot for you to do yet. First of all, get these finger-prints. Then telephone to London and get Kessock's business address. As soon as you get it, let me know."

"But you got his address from the correspondence, sir, surely. It's in Fifth Avenue."

"I want his other address—his office in New York, you understand?"

"His office will be shut by now, if you're going to cable," the Inspector pointed out, thoughtlessly.

"No, it won't. You forget that their time is some hours behind ours. We'll catch him in office hours if you hurry. Then when you've done that, get Foss's face photographed; and arrange for a constable and reliefs to be posted at the museum door till further orders. The museum door is to be left open and the light is to be left burning at night, so that he can keep his eye on things."

Inspector Armadale jotted some notes in his pocket-book. As he closed this, he seemed to think of something.

"There's just one thing, sir. You want to get into the safe? Couldn't we get the number of the lock combination from the makers? They must know it."

Sir Clinton shook his head.

"Unfortunately the safe has no maker's name-plate on it, Inspector. I looked at the time we examined it. It's a fairly old pattern, though, I noticed; and if it hasn't got a balanced fence arbour, I think I can guarantee to find the combination of it with a little assistance."

175

Armadale looked rather blank.

" I thought these things were too stiff to tackle," he said.

Sir Clinton suppressed a smile.

" You ought to read Edgar Allan Poe, Inspector. ' Human ingenuity cannot concoct a cipher which human ingenuity cannot resolve,' was a dictum of his. If I'm not mistaken about that safe, I think I could guarantee to open it in less than ten minutes. The resources of science, and all that, you know. But I think it would be better to wait a while and see if Mr Chacewater turns up to open it for us himself."

" But perhaps Mr Chacewater's body is inside it now," the Inspector suggested. " There may have been a double murder, for all we know."

" In that case, we shall find him when we open it," Sir Clinton assured him lightly. " If he's inside, he'll hardly be likely to shift his quarters."

CHAPTER X

THE SHOT IN THE CLEARING

WHEN Sir Clinton reached his office on the morning after the murder at Ravensthorpe, he found Inspector Armadale awaiting him with a number of exhibits.

" I've brought everything that seemed worth while," Armadale explained. " I thought you might care to look at some of the things again, although you've seen them already."

" That's very good of you, Inspector. I should like to see some of them, as a matter of fact. Now suppose we begin with the finger-prints. They might suggest a few fresh ideas."

" They seem to suggest more notions than I have room for in my head," the Inspector confessed ruefully. " It's a most tangled case, to my mind."

" Then let's start with the finger-prints," the Chief Constable proposed. " At least they'll settle some points, I hope."

Armadale unwrapped a large brown-paper parcel.

" I got the lot without any difficulty ; and last night we photographed them all and enlarged the pictures. They're all here."

" You took Foss's ones, I suppose ? "

" Yes, and I managed to find some of Maurice Chacewater's too."

" That's pretty sharp work," Sir Clinton complimented his subordinate. " How did you manage to make sure they were his ? "

" I asked for his set of razors, sir, and took them from the blades. He'd left prints here and there of his finger and thumb either on the blade or on the handle. Of course I couldn't get anything else very sharp ; but these are quite enough for the purpose, as you'll see."

He laid out three enlarged photographs on the desk before Sir Clinton ; then, below each of the first two, he put down a second print.

" This first print," he said, pointing to it, " represents the finger-prints we found on the automatic pistol. You can see that it's the arch pattern on the thumb. Now here "—he indicated the companion print—" is Foss's thumb-print ; and if you look at it, you'll see almost at a glance that it's identical with the print on the pistol. They're identical. I've measured them. And there are no other prints except Foss's on the pistol."

" Good," said Sir Clinton. " ' And that, said John, is that.' We know where we are so far as the pistol's concerned. Pass along, please."

" I've examined the pistol," the Inspector continued. " It's fully loaded in the magazine and has an extra cartridge in the barrel ; but it hasn't been fired recently so far as I can see."

" Now for the next pair of prints," Sir Clinton suggested.

" This represents the thumb-print from the sword, or whatever you call it," said the Inspector. " Also

178

prints of the two middle fingers of the right hand, found on the weapon. The second print of the pair shows identical finger-prints from a different source. The thumb-prints in the two cases are not exactly alike, because you get only the edge of the thumb marked in the grip on a sword, whereas the other specimen gives a full imprint. But I think you'll find they're the same. I've measured them, too. You can see that the thumb pattern is a loop type, quite different from Foss's prints ; and there's a trace of a tiny scar at the edge of the thumb in both these prints. I'd like you to compare them carefully, sir."

Sir Clinton took up the two prints and scanned them with care, comparing the images point by point.

" There's no mistake possible," he said. " The two sets are identical, so far as I can see ; and the scar on the thumb is a clinching bit of evidence."

" You admit they're from the same hand ? " asked the Inspector, with a peculiar look at Sir Clinton.

" Undoubtedly. Now whose are the second set ? "

The Inspector continued to look at his superior with something out of the common in his expression.

" The second set of prints came from Maurice Chacewater's razors," he said.

The Chief Constable's lips set tightly and a touch of grimness showed in his face.

" I see we shall have to be quite clear about this, Inspector," he said, bluntly. " By the look of you, you seemed to think I'd be taken aback by this evidence, because Mr Chacewater is a friend of mine. I was taken aback—naturally enough. But if you think it's going to make any difference to the conduct of this case—and I seemed to see something of the sort in your face—you can put that out of your mind once for all. The business of the police is to get hold of the murderer, whoever he may be. Friendship doesn't come into these affairs, Inspector. So kindly don't suspect me of anything of that kind in future. You know what I mean ; I needn't put it into words."

Without giving Armadale time for a reply, he picked up the last print.

" What's this ? "

" It's the set of prints I took from the valet's fingers," the Inspector hastened to explain. " It corresponds to nothing I've found anywhere else. You can see it's a whorl type on the thumb."

Sir Clinton examined the print for a moment or two, then put it down.

" What about the box and the wrist-watch?" he asked.

Inspector Armadale's face showed that here he was puzzled.

" There's nothing on either of them—not a recent mark of any description. And yet the man who packed them up must have fingered both things."

" With gloves on, evidently."

" But why gloves ? " the Inspector demanded.

" Why gloves ? " Sir Clinton echoed, rather sarcastically. " To avoid leaving finger-prints, of course. That's obvious."

" But why avoid leaving finger-prints on a thing that you're sending to a jeweller for repair ? "

" Think it over, Inspector. I won't insult you by

180

telling you my solution. Let's take another point. Have you the watch itself here ? "

The Inspector produced it and handed it over. Sir Clinton took out a pocket-knife and opened the back of the case.

" No use," he announced, after examining the back cover carefully. " It's never been repaired. There are no reference marks scratched on the inside of the back as there usually are when a watch has gone back to the watch-makers. If there had been, we might have found out something about Foss in that way, by getting hold of the watch-makers. By the way, have you timed this thing as I asked you to do ? "

" It's running on time," Armadale answered. " It hasn't varied a rap in the last twelve hours."

" A practically new watch ; running to time ; never needed repair so far ; dispatched by post with no finger-marks of the dispatcher : surely you can see what that means ? "

Inspector Armadale shook his head.

" It might be a secret message," he hazarded, though without much confidence. " I mean a prearranged code."

" So it might," Sir Clinton agreed. " The only thing against that in my mind is that I'm perfectly sure that it wasn't."

Armadale looked sulky.

" I'm hardly clever enough to follow you, sir, I'm afraid."

Sir Clinton's expression grew momentarily stern ; but the shade passed from his face almost instantly.

" This is one of these cases, Inspector, where I think that two heads are better than one. Now if I tell you what's in my mind, it might tempt you to look at things exactly as I do ; and then we'd have lost the advantage of having two brains at work on the business independently. We're more likely to be usefully employed if we pool the facts and keep our interpretations separate from each other."

The tone of the Chief Constable's voice went a good way towards soothing the Inspector's ruffled feelings, the more so since he saw the weight of Sir Clinton's reasoning.

" I'm sorry, sir. I quite see your point now."

Sir Clinton had the knack of leaving no ill-feelings in his subordinates. By an almost imperceptible change of manner, he dismissed the whole matter and restored cordiality again.

" Let's get back to the pure facts, Inspector. Each of us must look at them in his own way ; but we can at least examine some of them without biasing each other. Did you get any more information out of that chauffeur ? "

Inspector Armadale seemed glad enough to forget the slight friction between himself and his Chief, as the tone of his voice showed when he replied.

" I could get nothing out of him at all, sir. He seems a stupid sort of fellow. But it was quite clear that somehow or other he'd picked up the idea that Foss meant to leave Ravensthorpe for good yesterday afternoon. He stuck to that definitely ; and the packing up of his traps shows that he believed it."

" We can take it, then, that Foss gave reason for the man thinking that he was going away. Put your own interpretation on that, Inspector ; but you needn't tell me what you make of it."

The Inspector's smile showed that ill-feeling had gone.

" Very well, Sir Clinton. And I'll admit that I had my suspicions of the valet. He seems to have a clear bill now in the matter of the finger-prints on the weapon. Perhaps I was a bit rough on the man ; but he annoyed me—a cheeky fellow."

" Oh, don't let's use hard words about him," Sir Clinton suggested chaffingly. " Let's call him cool, simply."

" Well, his finger-prints weren't on the handle of the sword, anyhow," the Inspector admitted.

" I hardly expected them to be," was all the comment Sir Clinton saw fit to make. " Now what about friend Foss ? By the way, I don't mind saying that I still think these two affairs at Ravensthorpe are interconnected. And one thing's clear at any rate : Foss wasn't the man in white. You remember he was wearing a cow-boy costume according to the valet's evidence ; and we found that costume in his wardrobe, which confirms Marden."

The Inspector seemed to be taking a leaf out of Sir Clinton's book. He refrained from either acquiescing in or contradicting the Chief Constable's statement that the two cases were linked.

" Foss had more ready money in his pocket than most people carry ; he was in a position to clear out of Ravensthorpe at any moment without needing to go back to his flat or even to a bank. I think these facts are plain enough," he pointed out. " And they fit in with the chauffeur's evidence, such as it is."

" And he had no latch-key of his flat with him," Sir Clinton supplemented. " Of course it was a service flat and he may have left the key behind him instead of carrying it with him. One could find that out if it were worth while."

" There's a good deal that needs explaining about Foss," the Inspector observed. " I've got his photograph here, taken from the body yesterday."

He produced it as he spoke.

" Send a copy to Scotland Yard, Inspector, please, and ask if they have any information about him. Considering everything, it's quite likely we might learn something. You might send his finger-prints also, to see if they have them indexed there."

" I'll send Marden's too, when I'm at it," the Inspector volunteered, " and the chauffeur's. We might as well be complete when we're at it."

Sir Clinton indicated his agreement without saying anything. He changed the subject when he next spoke.

" We've agreed to pool the facts, Inspector, and I've got a contribution—two contributions in fact—towards the common stock. Here's the first."

He laid a telegraph form on the desk before Armadale, and the Inspector read the wording :

Have no agent named Foss am not negotiating for Leonardo medallions. Kessock.

" Well, that's a bit of a surprise ! " ejaculated the

Inspector. " It was obvious that there was something fishy ; but I hadn't imagined it was as fishy as all that. Kessock knows nothing about him, then ? "

" My cable was fairly explicit. It's clear that friend Foss had no authority from Kessock."

" But what about all that correspondence between Maurice Chacewater and Kessock that we saw ? "

" Forgeries, so far as the Kessock letters were concerned, obviously. One of Kessock's household must have been in league with Foss and intercepted Maurice Chacewater's letters. Then replies were forged and dispatched. I've cabled Kessock about it this morning, so as to get the news in at once. The confederate may hear of Foss's murder through the newspapers in four or five days when our papers get across there. He might bolt when he got the news. I've given Kessock a chance to forestall that if he wants to."

" That puts a new light on things, certainly," Armadale said when he had considered the new facts. " Foss was a wrong 'un masquerading here for some purpose or other—the medallions, probably. That fits in with all the unmarked linen and the rest of it. But why was he murdered ? "

Sir Clinton disregarded the question.

" I've got another fact to contribute," he went on. " You remember that Marconi Otophone in Foss's room ? I've made some inquiries about it. It's a thing they make for the use of deaf people—a modern substitute for the ear-trumpet."

The Inspector made a gesture of bewilderment.

" But Foss wasn't deaf ! He admitted to you that

he had good enough hearing, when he was telling you about overhearing Foxton Polegate in the winter-garden."

" That's quite true," Sir Clinton rejoined. " But he evidently needed an Otophone for all that."

The Inspector pondered for a few moments before speaking.

" It beats me," he said at last.

Sir Clinton dismissed the subject without further discussion.

" Now what about Maurice Chacewater ? " he inquired. " There's no great difficulty in suggesting *how* he disappeared from the museum. It's common talk hereabout that Ravensthorpe has secret passages ; and one of them may end up in the wall of the museum."

It was the turn of Armadale to contribute a fresh fact.

" He didn't appear at any local station yesterday or this morning ; and he didn't use a motor of any sort that I've been able to trace. I've had men on that job and it's been thoroughly done."

" Congratulations, Inspector."

" If he hasn't got away, then he must be somewhere in the neighbourhood still."·

" I should say that was indisputable, if not certain," commented Sir Clinton, with a return of his faintly chaffing manner. " A man can only be in one place at once, if you follow me. And if he's not there, then he must be here."

" Yes. But where is ' here,' in this particular case ? " inquired Armadale, following his Chief's mood. " I expect he's hiding somewhere around.

It's what anyone might do if they found themselves up
to the hilt in a case of murder "—he paused for an instant—" or manslaughter, and got into a panic over it."

Sir Clinton ignored the Inspector's last sentence.

" I wish I could get into touch with Cecil Chacewater. He ought to be at home just now. He's the
only man in the family now, and he ought to take charge
of things up there."

" You haven't got his address yet, sir ? "

" Not yet."

Sir Clinton put the subject aside.

" Now, Inspector, let me remind you of what's
wanted :

> What was the crime, who did it, when was it done, and where,
> How done, and with what motive, who in the deed did share ?

You put it down as murder ? "

" Or manslaughter," corrected Armadale. " And
we know When, How, and Where, at any rate."

" Do we ? " Sir Clinton rejoined. " Speak for
yourself. I'm not so sure about When and Where
yet, and How is still a dark mystery so far as I'm concerned. I mean," he added, " so far as legal proof goes."

The Inspector was about to say something further
when a knock at the door was heard and a constable
appeared in answer to Sir Clinton's summons.

" The Ravensthorpe head keeper wants to see you,
Sir Clinton, if you can spare him a moment. He says
it's important."

The Chief Constable ordered the keeper to be
admitted.

" Well, Mold, what's your trouble ? " he inquired, when the man appeared.

" It's this way, Sir Clinton," Mold began. " Seein' the queer sort o' things we've seen lately, it seemed to me that maybe another queer thing that's happened might be important. So I thought it over, and I made bold to come and tell you about it."

He seemed to lose confidence a little at this point ; but Sir Clinton encouraged him by a show of interest.

" Last night," he went on, " I was goin' through the wood at the back o' the house—about eleven o'clock it was, as near as I can make it. At the back o' the house there's a strip of woodland, then a little bit of a clearin', and then the rest of the wood. I'd come out o' the bigger bit o' the wood and got most o' the way across the clearin' when it happened. I can tell you just where it was, for I was passin' the old ruin there— the Knight's Tower they call it."

He paused for a moment or two, evidently finding continuous narrative rather a strain.

" The moon was well up by that time. It's just past the full these days ; and the place was as clear as day. Everythin' was quiet, except an old owl that lives in a hollow tree up by there. I could hear the swish of my feet in the grass and mighty little else ; for the grass was dewy and made a lot o' noise with my stepping through it. Well, as I was goin' along, all of a sudden I heard a shot. It sounded close by me ; an' I turned at once. There's a poachin' chap that's given me a lot o' trouble, an' I didn't put it past him to think he might be tryin' to give me a scare. But when I

turned round there was nothin' to be seen. There
was nothin' there at all ; an' yet that shot had come
from quite close by."

" Did it sound like the report of a shot-gun ? " Sir
Clinton asked.

Mold seemed to be in a difficulty.

" Shot-gun sounds I know fairly well. 'T weren't
from a shot-gun. More like a pistol-shot it sounded,
when I'd had time to think over it. An' yet it weren't
altogether like a pistol-shot, neither. That's a sharp
sound. This was more booming-like, if you understand me."

" I'm afraid I don't quite see it yet, Mold," Sir
Clinton admitted. " I know how difficult it is to
describe sounds, though. Have another try. Did it
remind you of anything ? "

A light seemed to flicker for a moment in Mold's
memory.

" I know ! " he exclaimed. " It was like this. I've
got it ! Did you ever stand at the door of our Morris-
tube range in the village while there was firin' goin' on
inside ? Well, this was somethin' like that, only more
so. I mean as if they'd fired somethin' a bit heavier
than a miniature rifle. That's it ! That's just how it
sounded."

He was evidently relieved by having found what he
considered an apt simile.

" What happened after that ? " Sir Clinton
demanded.

" When I saw nobody near me I'll admit I felt a bit
funny. Here was a shot comin', so it seemed, out o'

the empty air, with nothin' to account for it.   Straight
away, I'll admit, sir, I began thinkin' of that Black
Man that little Jennie Hitchin has been spreadin' the
story about lately . . ."

Sir Clinton pricked up his ears.

" We'll hear about the Black Man later on, Mold, if
you please.   Tell us what you did at that moment."

" Well, sir, I searched about.   The moon was clear
of clouds and the place was just an open glade.   The
shot had come from quite near by, as I said.   But when
I hunted I could find nothing.   There wasn't a track
in the dew on the grass.   My own tracks showed up in
the moonlight as clear as clear.   There wasn't anyone
hiding in the old ruin ; I went through and around it
twice.   There wasn't a sound ; for the shot had
frightened the owl.   I found nothing.   And yet I'd
take my oath that shot was fired not more than ten or
a dozen yards away from me."

" Did you hear any whistle of shot or a bullet ? "

" No, sir."

" H'm !   That's the whole story ?   Now, tell us
about this Black Man you mentioned."

Mold seemed rather ashamed.

" Oh, that's just child's chatter, Sir Clinton.   I
oughtn't to have mentioned it."

" I'm quite willing to listen to ' child's chatter,'
Mold, if it happens to be unusual."

Mold evidently decided to take the plunge, though
obviously he regretted having mentioned the matter
at all.

" This Jennie Hitchin's a child that lives with her

grandmother on the estate. The girl's there at night in case anything goes wrong with the old woman. Old Mrs. Hitchin was taken ill one night lately, about the middle of the night. Pretty bad she seemed ; and Jennie had to dress and go off for the doctor in a hurry. That took her through the woods—it's a short cut that way and the moonlight was bright. An' as she was goin' along . . ."

" What night was this," Sir Clinton interrupted.

The keeper thought for a moment or two.

" Now I come to think of it," he said, " 't was the night of that robbery up at Ravensthorpe. So it was. An' as Jennie was goin' along through the woods she saw—so she says—a Black Man slippin' about from tree to tree."

" A man in dark clothes ? "

" No, sir. If I understood rightly, 't was a black man. I mean a naked man with a black skin, black all over."

" Did he molest the child ? "

" No, sir. He seemed to be tryin' to keep out of her road if anythin'. But o' course it gave her a start. She took and ran—and small blame to her, I think. She's only eleven or so, an' it gave her a dreadful fright. An' of course next day this tale was all over the country-side. I wonder you didn't hear it yourself, sir."

" It's news to me, Mold, I'm afraid. Even the police can't know everything, you see. Now before you go I want something more from you. That night when you were on guard in the museum, you remem-

191

ber. Do you recall seeing anyone there at any time during the evening dressed in cow-boy clothes ? You know, the kind of thing in the Wild West films."

Mold pondered for a time, evidently racking his memory.

" No, sir. I remember nobody like that. I think I'd have recalled it if I had. I'm rather keen on films about cow-boys myself, and if I'd seen a cow-boy I'd have had a good look at him, just out o' curiosity."

Sir Clinton had apparently got all he needed from Mold just then ; and he sent him away quite reassured that his visit had not been wasted.

" What do you make of all that, Inspector ? " he inquired with a faintly quizzical expression on his face, as soon as the door had closed behind the keeper.

Armadale shook his head. Then, seeing a chance of scoring, he smiled openly.

" I was to keep my ideas to myself, you remember, Sir Clinton."

The Chief Constable gave him smile for smile.

" That arrangement must be especially useful when you've no ideas at all, Inspector."

Armadale took the thrust with good humour.

" Give me time to think, Sir Clinton. You know I've only a slow mind, and perhaps this isn't one of my bright days."

Before Sir Clinton could retort the desk telephone rang and the Chief Constable lifted the receiver.

" Yes, I am . . . Thanks very much. I'll take down the address if you'll read it to me."

He jotted something down on a sheet of paper.

" Thanks. Good-bye, Joan."

He flicked the note over to Armadale.

" Would you mind seeing if we can get on to that house by 'phone, Inspector? Hunt up the London Directory for it."

" It's Cecil Chacewater's address ? " said Armadale, glancing at the slip.

" Yes. The man he's staying with may be on the 'phone."

In a few minutes the Inspector came back with the number and Sir Clinton rang up. After a short talk he put down the receiver and turned to Armadale.

" He says he can't come to-day. You heard me explaining that we want that secret passage opened, if there is one. But he doesn't seem to think there's any hurry. He has some business which will keep him till to-morrow."

" I heard you tell him that his brother's disappeared," the Inspector commented. " I'd have thought that would have brought him back quick enough."

" It hasn't, evidently," was all that Sir Clinton thought it necessary to say. There seemed to be no reason for admitting the Inspector into the secret of the Ravensthorpe quarrels.

CHAPTER XI

UNDERGROUND RAVENSTHORPE

WHEN Inspector Armadale presented himself at the Chief Constable's office next morning he found Sir Clinton still faithful to his proposed policy of pooling all the facts of the case.

" I've just been in communication with the coroner," Sir Clinton explained. " I've pointed out to him that possibly we may have further evidence for the inquest on Foss ; and I suggested that he might confine himself to formalities as far as possible and then adjourn for a day or two. It means keeping Marden and the chauffeur here for a little longer ; but they can stay at Ravensthorpe. Miss Chacewater has no objections to that. She agreed at once when I asked her."

" The jury will have enough before them to bring in a verdict of murder against someone unknown," the Inspector pointed out. " Do you want to make it more definite while we're in the middle of the case ? "

Sir Clinton made a non-committal gesture as he replied :

" Let's give ourselves the chance, at least, of putting a name on the criminal. If we don't succeed there's no harm done. Now here's another point. I've had a telephone message from Scotland Yard. They've nothing on record corresponding to the finger-prints of Marden or the chauffeur. Foss was a wrong 'un. They've identified his finger-prints ; and his photo-

graph seems to have been easily recognizable by some
of the Yard people who had dealings with him before.
He went by the name of Cocoa Tom among his inti-
mates ; but his real name was Thomas Pailton.   He'd
been convicted a couple of times, though not recently."

" What was his line ? " the Inspector inquired.

" Confidence trick in one form or another, they say.
Very plausible tongue, apparently."

" Did they say anything more about him ? " asked
the Inspector.   " Anything about working with a gang
usually, or something like that ?   If he did, then we
might get a clue or two from his associates."

" He usually played a lone hand, it seems," Sir
Clinton answered.   " Apparently he used to be on the
Halls—the cheaper kind.   ' The Wonderful Wizard
of Woz ' he called himself then.   But somehow he
made the business too hot for him and cleared out into
swindling."

" Ah ! "   Armadale evidently saw something which
had not occurred to him before.   " Those pockets of
his—the ones that puzzled me.   They might have
been useful to a man who could do a bit of sleight of
hand.   I never thought of that at the time."

He looked accusingly at Sir Clinton, who laughed at
the expression in the Inspector's eyes.

" Of course I admit I saw the use of the pockets
almost at once," he said.   " But that's not a breach of
our bargain, Inspector.   The facts are all that we are
pooling, remember ;   and the fact that Foss had
these peculiar pockets was as well known to you as to
myself.   This notion about sleight of hand is an inter-

pretation of the facts, remember ; and we weren't to share our inferences."

" I knew pretty well at the time that you'd spotted something," Armadale contented himself with saying. " But since you put it in that way I'll admit you were quite justified in keeping it to yourself as special information, sir. I take it that it's a race between us now ; and the one that hits on the solution first is the winner. I don't mind."

" Then there's one other bit of information needed to bring us level. I've just had a message over the 'phone from Mr Cecil Chacewater. It appears he's just got home again ; came by the first train in the morning from town, apparently. He's waiting for us now, so we'd better go up to Ravensthorpe. I have an idea that he may be able to throw some light on his brother's disappearance. At least he may be able to show us how that disappearing trick was done ; and that would always be a step forward."

When they reached Ravensthorpe Cecil was awaiting them. The Inspector noticed that he seemed tired and had a weary look in his eyes.

" Been out on the spree," was Armadale's silent inference ; for the Inspector was inclined to take a low view of humanity in general, and he put his own interpretation on Cecil's looks.

Sir Clinton, in a few rapid sentences, apprised Cecil of the facts of the case.

" I'd heard some of that before, you know," Cecil admitted. " Maurice's disappearance seems to have caused a bit of a stir. I can't say he's greatly missed for the sake of his personality ; but naturally it's disturbing to have a brother mislaid about the place."

" Very irksome, of course," agreed Sir Clinton, with a faint parody of Cecil's detached air.

Cecil seemed to think that the conversation had come to a deadlock, since the Chief Constable made no effort to continue.

" Well, what about it ? " he demanded. " I haven't got Maurice concealed anywhere about my person, you know."

He elaborately felt in an empty jacket pocket, ending by turning it inside out.

" No," he pointed out, " he isn't there. In fact, I'm almost certain I haven't got him anywhere in this suit."

Cecil's studied insolence seemed to escape Sir Clinton's notice.

" There was a celebrated historical character who said something of the same sort once upon a time. ' Am I my brother's keeper ? ' you remember that ? "

" Good old Cain ? So he did. And his name begins with a C, just like mine, too ! Any other points of resemblance you'd like to suggest ? "

" Not just now," Sir Clinton responded. " Information would be more to the purpose at present. Let's go along to the museum, please. There are one or two points which need to be cleared up as soon as possible."

Cecil made no open demur ; but his manner continued to be obviously hostile as they made their way along the passages. At the museum door the constable on guard stood aside in order to let them pass in.

"Wait a moment," Sir Clinton ordered, as his companions were about to enter the room. "I want to try an experiment before we go any further."

He turned to Cecil.

"Will you go across and stand in front of the case in which the Muramasa sword used to be kept? You'll find the sheath still in the case. And you, Inspector, go to the spot where we found Foss's body."

When they had obeyed him he swung the door round on its hinges until it was almost closed, and then looked through the remaining opening.

"Say a few words in an ordinary tone, Inspector. A string of addresses or something of that sort."

"William Jones, Park Place, Amersley Royal," began the Inspector, obediently ; "Henry Blenkinsop, 18 Skeening Road, Hinchley ; John Orran Gordon, 88 Bolsover Lane . . ."

"That will be enough, thanks. I can hear you quite well. Now lower your voice a trifle and say 'Muramasa,' 'Japanese,' and 'sword,' please. And mix them into the middle of some more addresses."

The Inspector's tone as he spoke showed plainly that he was a trifle bewildered by his instructions.

"Fred Hall, Muramasa, Endelmere ; Harry Bell, 15 Elm Japanese Avenue, Stonyton ; J. Hickey, sword, The Cottage, Apperley . . . Will that do?"

"Quite well, Inspector. Many thanks. Think I'm mad? All I wanted was to find out how much a man in this position could see and hear. Contributions to the pool. First, I can see the case where the

Muramasa sword used to lie. Second, I can hear quite plainly what you're saying. The slight echo in the room doesn't hinder that."

He swung the door open and came into the museum.

" Now, Cecil," he said—and the Inspector noticed that all sign of lightness had gone out of his tone, " you know that Maurice disappeared rather mysteriously from this room ? He was in it with Foss ; there was a man at the door ; Foss was murdered in that bay over there ; and Maurice didn't leave the room by the door. How did he leave ? "

" How should I know ? " demanded Cecil, sullenly. " You'd better ask him when he turns up again. I'm not Maurice's nursemaid."

Sir Clinton's eyes grew hard.

" I'll put it plainer for you. I've reason to believe that there's an entrance to a secret passage somewhere in that bay beyond the safe. It's the only way in which Maurice could have left this room. You'll have to show it to us."

" Indeed ! " Cecil's voice betrayed nothing but contempt for the suggestion.

" It's for your own benefit that I make the proposal," Sir Clinton pointed out. " Refuse if you like. But if you do I've a search-warrant in my pocket and I mean to find that entrance even if I have to root out most of the panelling and gut the room. You won't avert the discovery by this attitude of yours. You'll merely make the whole business public. It would be far more sensible to recognize the inevitable and show us the place yourself. I don't want to damage things any more than is necesary. But if I'm put to it I'll be thorough, I warn you."

Cecil favoured the Chief Constable with an angry look ; but the expression on Sir Clinton's face convinced him that it was useless to offer any further opposition.

" Very well," he snarled. " I'll open the thing, since I must."

Sir Clinton took no notice of his anger.

" So long as you open it the rest doesn't matter. I've no desire to pry into things that don't concern me. I don't wish to know how the panel opens. Inspector, I think we'll turn our backs while Mr Chacewater works the mechanism."

They faced about. Cecil took a few steps into the bay. There was a sharp snap ; and when they turned round again a door gaped in the panelling at the end of the room.

" Quite so," said Sir Clinton. " Most ingenious."

His voice had regained its normal easy tone ; and now he seemed anxious to smooth over the ill-feeling which had come to so acute a pitch in the last few minutes.

" Will you go first, Cecil, and show us the way ? I expect it's difficult for a stranger. I've brought an electric torch. Here, you'd better take it."

Now that he had failed in his attempt, Cecil seemed to recover his temper again. He took the torch from the Chief Constable and, pressing the spring to light it, stepped through the open panel.

" I think we'll lock the museum door before we go

down," Sir Clinton suggested. " There's no need to expose this entrance to anyone who happens to come in."

He walked across the museum, turned the key in the lock, and then rejoined his companions.

" Now, Cecil, if you please."

Cecil Chacewater led the way ; Sir Clinton motioned to the Inspector to follow him, and brought up the rear himself.

" Look out, here," Cecil warned them. " There's a flight of steps almost at once."

They made their way down a spiral staircase which seemed to lead deep into the foundations of Ravensthorpe. At last it came to an end, and a narrow tunnel gaped before them.

" Nothing here, you see," Cecil pointed out, flashing the torch in various directions. " This passage is the only outlet."

He led the way into the tunnel, followed by the Inspector. Sir Clinton lagged behind them for a moment or two, and then showed no signs of haste, so that they had to pause in order to let him catch up.

The tunnel led them in a straight line for a time, then bent in a fresh direction.

" It's getting narrower," the Inspector pointed out.

" It gets narrower still before you're done with it," Cecil vouchsafed in reply.

As the passage turned again Sir Clinton halted.

" I'd like to have a look at these walls," he said.

Cecil turned back and threw the light of the torch over the sides and roof of the tunnel.

" It's very old masonry," he pointed out.

201

Sir Clinton nodded.

" This is a bit of old Ravensthorpe, I suppose ? "

" It's older than the modern parts of the building," Cecil agreed. He seemed to have overcome his ill-humour and to be making the best of things.

" Let's push on, then," Sir Clinton suggested. " I've seen all I wanted to see, thanks."

As they proceeded, the tunnel walls drew nearer together and the roof grew lower. Before long the passage was barely large enough to let them walk along it without brushing the stones on either side.

" Wait a moment," Sir Clinton suggested, as they reached a fresh turning.   " Inspector, would you mind making a rough measurement of the dimensions here ?"

Somewhat mystified, Inspector Armadale did as he was bidden, entering the figures up in his notebook while Cecil stood back, evidently equally puzzled by these manœuvres.

" Thanks, that will do nicely," Sir Clinton assured him when the task had been completed.   " Suppose we continue ? "

Cecil advanced a few steps.   Then a thought seemed to strike him.

" It gets narrower farther on.   We'll have to go on hands and knees, and there won't be room to pass one another.   Perhaps one of you should go first with the torch.   There's nothing in the road."

Sir Clinton agreed to this.

" I'll go first, then.   You can follow on, Inspector."

Inspector Armadale looked suspicious at this suggestion.

"He might get away back and shut us in," he murmured in Sir Clinton's ear.

The Chief Constable took the simplest way of reassuring the Inspector.

"That's an ingenious bit of mechanism in the panel, up above," he said to Cecil. "I had a glance at it as I passed, since it's all in plain sight. From this side, you've only to lift a bar to open it, haven't you?"

"That's so," Cecil confirmed.

Armadale was evidently satisfied by the information which Sir Clinton had thus conveyed to him indirectly. He squeezed himself against the wall and allowed the Chief Constable to come up to the head of the party. Sir Clinton threw his light down the passage in front of them.

"It looks like all-fours, now," he commented, as the lamp revealed a steadily diminishing tunnel. "We may as well begin now and save ourselves the chance of knocking our heads against the roof."

Suiting the action to the word, he got down on hands and knees and began to creep along the passage.

"At least we may be thankful it's dry," he pointed out.

The tunnel grew still smaller until they found more than a little difficulty in making their way along it.

"Have we much farther to go?" asked the Inspector, who seemed to have little liking for the business.

"The end's round the next corner," Cecil explained.

They soon reached the last bend in the passage, and as he turned it Sir Clinton found himself at the entrance to a tiny space. The roof was even lower than that of the tunnel, and the floor area was hardly

203

more than a dozen square feet. A stone slab, raised a few inches from the ground, seemed like a bed fitted into a niche.

" A bit wet in this part," Sir Clinton remarked. " If I'd known that we were in for this sort of thing I think I'd have put on an old suit this morning. Mind your knees on the floor, Inspector. It's fairly moist."

He climbed into the niche, which was no bigger than the bunk of a steamer, and began to examine his surroundings with his torch. Inspector Armadale, taking advantage of the space thus made clear, crept into the tiny chamber.

" This place looks as if it had been washed out, lately," he said, examining the smooth flagstones which formed the floor. He turned his attention to the roof, evidently in search of dripping water ; but he could find none, though the walls were moist.

Suddenly Sir Clinton bent forward and brought his lamp near something on the side of the niche.

The Inspector, seeing something in the patch of light, craned forward to look also, and as he did so he seemed to recognize what he saw.

" Why, that's . . ." he ejaculated.

Sir Clinton's lamp went out abruptly, and Inspector Armadale felt his arm gripped warningly in the darkness.

" Sorry," the Chief Constable apologized. " My finger must have shifted the switch on the torch. Out of the way, Inspector, please. There's nothing more to be seen here."

Inspector Armadale wriggled back into the passage

again as Sir Clinton made a movement as though to
come out of his perch in the recess.

" So this is where Maurice got to when he left the
museum ? " the Chief Constable said, reflectively.
" Well, he isn't here now, that's plain.   We'll need to
look elsewhere, Inspector, according to your scheme.
If he wasn't elsewhere he was to be here.   But as he
isn't here he's obviously elsewhere.   And now I think
we'll make our way up to the museum again.   Wait a
moment !   We've got to get back into that passage
with our heads in the right direction.   Once we're into
the tunnel there won't be room to turn round."

It took some manœuvring to arrange this, for the
tiny chamber was a tight fit for even three men ; but
at last they succeeded in getting back into the tunnel
in a position which permitted them to creep forwards
instead of backwards.   They finally accomplished the
long journey without incident, and emerged through
the gaping panel into the museum once more.

" Now we'll turn our backs again, Inspector, and
let Mr Chacewater close the panel."

Again the sharp click notified them that they could
turn round.   The panelling seemed completely solid.

" There are just a couple of points I'd like to know
about," Sir Clinton said, turning to Cecil. " You don't
know the combination that opens the safe over there,
I believe ? "

Cecil Chacewater seemed both surprised and relieved
to hear this question.

" No," he said.   " Maurice kept the combination
to himself."

Sir Clinton nodded as though he had expected this answer.

" Just another point," he continued. " You may not be able to remember this. At any time after you and Foxton Polegate had planned that practical joke of yours, did Foss ask you the time ? "

Cecil was obviously completely taken aback by this query.

" Did he ask me the time ? Not that I know of. I can't remember his ever doing that. Wait a bit, though. No, he didn't."

Sir Clinton seemed disappointed for a moment. Then, evidently, a fresh idea occurred to him.

" On the night of the masked ball, did anyone ask you the time ? "

Cecil considered for a moment or two.

" Now I come to think of it, a fellow dressed as a cow-boy came up and said his watch had stopped."

" Ah ! I thought so," was all Sir Clinton replied, much to the vexation of Inspector Armadale.

" By the way," the Chief Constable went on, " I'd rather like to get to the top of one of those turrets up above." He made a gesture indicating the roof. " There's a stair, isn't there ? "

Armadale had difficulty in concealing his surprise at this unexpected demand. Cecil Chacewater made no difficulties, but led them upstairs and opened the door of the entrance to a turret. When they reached an open space at the summit, Sir Clinton leaned on the parapet and gazed over the surrounding country with interest. As the space was restricted, Cecil remained within the turret, at the top of the stair ; but the Inspector joined his Chief on the platform.

" Splendid view, isn't it, Inspector ? "

" Yes, sir. Very fine."

Armadale was evidently puzzled by this turn of affairs. He could not see why Sir Clinton should have come up to admire the view instead of getting on with the investigation. The Chief Constable did not seem to notice his subordinate's perplexity.

" There's Hincheldene," Sir Clinton pointed out. " With a decent pair of glasses one could read the time on the clock-tower on a clear day. These woods round about give a restful look to things. Soothing, that greenery. Ah ! Just follow my finger, Inspector. See that white thing over yonder ? That's one of these Fairy Houses."

He searched here and there in the landscape for a moment.

" There's another of them, just where you see that stream running across the opening between the two spinneys—yonder. And there's a third one, not far off that ruined tower. See it ? I wonder if we could pick up any more. They seem to be thick enough on the ground. Yes, see that one in the glade over there ? Not see it ? Look at that grey cottage with the creeper on it ; two o'clock ; three fingers. See it now ? "

" I can't quite make it out, sir," the Inspector confessed.

He seemed bored by Sir Clinton's insistence on the matter ; but he held up his hand and tried to discover the object. After a moment or two he gave up the attempt and, turning round, he noticed his Chief slipping a small compass into his pocket.

" Quite worth seeing, that view," Sir Clinton remarked, imperturbably, as he made his way towards the turret stair. " Thanks very much, Cecil. I don't think we need trouble you any more for the present ; but I'd like to see your sister, if she's available. I want to ask her a question."

Cecil Chacewater went in search of Joan, and after a few minutes she met them at the foot of the stair.

" There's just one point that occurred to me since you told us about that interview you and Maurice had with Foss before you went to the museum. You were sitting on the terrace, weren't you ? "

" Yes," Joan confirmed.

" Then you must have seen Foss's car drive up when it came to wait at the front door for him ? "

" I remember seeing it come up just before we went to the museum. I didn't say anything about it before. It didn't seem to matter much."

" That was quite natural," Sir Clinton reassured her. " In fact, I'm not sure that it matters much even yet. I'm just trying for any evidence I can get. Tell me anything whatever that you noticed, no matter whether it seems important or not."

Joan thought for almost a minute before replying.

" I did notice the chauffeur putting the hood up, and I wondered what on earth he was doing that for on a blazing day."

" Anything else ? "

" He had his tool-kit out and seemed to be going to do some repair or other."

" At the moment when he'd brought the car round for Foss ? " demanded the Inspector, rather incredulously. " Surely he'd have everything spick and span before he left the garage ? "

" You'd better ask him about it himself, Inspector," said Joan, tartly. " I'm merely telling what I saw ; and I saw that plain enough. Besides, he may have known he'd plenty of time. Mr Foss was going away with us and obviously he wasn't in a hurry to use the car."

Sir Clinton ignored the Inspector's interruption.

" I've got my own car at the door," he observed. " Perhaps you could go out on to the terrace and direct me while I bring it into the same position as you saw Foss's car that afternoon."

Joan agreed ; and they went down together.

" Now," said Sir Clinton as he started the engine, " would you mind directing me ? "

Joan, from the terrace, indicated how he was to manœuvre until he had brought his own car into a position as near as possible to that occupied by Foss's car on the afternoon of the murder.

" That's as near as I can get it," she said at last.

Sir Clinton turned in his seat and scanned the front of Ravensthorpe.

" What window is this that I'm opposite ? " he inquired.

" That's the window of the museum," Joan explained. " But you can't see into the room, can you ? You're too low down there."

"Nothing more than the tops of the cases," Sir Clinton said. "You'd better get aboard, Inspector. There's nothing more to do here."

He waved good-bye to Joan as Armadale stepped into the car, and then drove down the avenue. The Inspector said nothing until they had passed out of the Ravensthorpe grounds and were on the high road again. Then he turned eagerly to the Chief Constable.

"That was a splash of blood you found on the wall of the underground room, wasn't it ? I recognized it at once."

"Don't get excited about it, Inspector," said Sir Clinton, soothingly. "Of course it was blood ; but we needn't shout about it from the house-tops, need we ? "

Armadale thought he detected a tacit reproof for his exclamation at the time the discovery was made.

"You covered up that word or two of mine very neatly, sir," he admitted frankly. "I was startled when I saw that spot of blood on the wall, and I nearly blurted it out. Silly of me to do it, I suppose. But you managed to smother it up with that bungling with your lamp before I'd given anything away. I'd no notion you wanted to keep the thing quiet."

"No harm done," Sir Clinton reassured him. "But be careful another time. One needn't show all one's cards."

"You certainly don't," Armadale retorted.

"Well, you have all the facts, Inspector. What more do you expect ? "

Armadale thought it best to change the subject.

"That water that we saw down there," he went on. "That never leaked in through the roof. The masonry overhead was as tight as a drum and there wasn't a sign of drip-marks anywhere. That water came from somewhere else. Someone had been washing up in that cellar. There had been more blood there—lot's of it ; and they'd washed it away. That tiny patch was a bit they'd overlooked. Isn't that so, sir ?"

"That's an inference and not a fact, Inspector," Sir Clinton pointed out, with an expression approaching to a grin on his face. "I don't say you're wrong. In fact, I'm sure you're right. But only facts are supposed to go into the common stock, remember."

"Very good, sir."

But the Inspector had something in reserve.

"I'll give you a fact now," he said with ill-suppressed triumph. "As you came away, you happened to ask Mr Chacewater if he'd come home by the first train this morning."

"Yes."

"And he said he did ?"

"Yes."

"Well," said Armadale, with a tinge of derision in his voice, "he took you in, there ; but he didn't come over me with that tale. He didn't come by the first train ; he wasn't in it ! And what's more, he didn't come by train to our station at all, for I happened to make inquiries. I knew you were anxious for him to come back, and I thought I'd ask whether he'd come."

"That's very interesting," said Sir Clinton.

He made no further remark until they reached the police station. Then, as they got out of the car, he turned to the Inspector.

" Care to see me do a little map-drawing, Inspector ? It might amuse you."

CHAPTER XII

CHUCHUNDRA'S BODY

SIR CLINTON'S map-drawing, however, was destined to be postponed. Hardly had they entered his office when the telephone bell rang. After a few moments' conversation he put down the receiver and turned to Armadale.

"That's Mold, the keeper. He's found Maurice Chacewater's body. He's telephoning from his own cottage, so I told him to wait there and we'll go up in the car. The body's in the woods and we'll save time by getting Mold to guide us to it instead of hunting round for the place."

It did not take long to reach the head keeper's cottage, where they found Mold in a state of perturbation.

"Where is this body?" Sir Clinton demanded, cutting short Mold's rather confused attempts to explain matters. "Take us to it first of all and then I'll ask what I want to know."

Under the keeper's guidance they made their way through the woods, and at last emerged into a small clearing in the centre of which rose a few ruined walls.

"This is what they call the Knight's Tower," Armadale explained.

Sir Clinton nodded.

"I expected something of the sort. Now, Mold, where's Mr Chacewater's body?"

The keeper led them round the Tower, and as they turned the corner of a wall they came upon the body stretched at full length on the grass.

" The turf's short," said Armadale, with some disappointment. "There's no track on it round about here."

" That's true," said Sir Clinton. " We'll have to do without that help."

He walked over to where Maurice Chacewater was lying. The body was on its back ; and a glance at the head was enough to show that life must be extinct.

" It's not pretty," Sir Clinton said as he pulled out his handkerchief and covered the dead face. " Shot at close range, evidently. I don't wonder you were a bit upset, Mold."

He glanced round the little glade, then turned again to the keeper.

" When did you find him ? " he demanded.

" Just before I rang you up, sir. As soon as I came across him, I ran off to my cottage and telephoned to you."

" When were you over this ground last ?—before you found him, I mean."

" Just before dusk, last night, sir. He wasn't there, then."

" You're sure ? "

" Certain, sir. I couldn't have missed seeing him."

" You haven't touched the body ? "

Mold shuddered slightly.

" No, sir. I went off at once and rang you up."

" You met no one hereabouts this morning ? "

" No, sir."

" And you saw no one last night, either ? "

" No, sir."

" It was somewhere round about here, wasn't it, that you heard that mysterious shot you told us about ?"

" Yes, sir. I was just here at the time."

Mold walked about twenty yards past the tower, to show the exact position. Sir Clinton studied the lie of the land for a moment.

" H'm ! Have you any questions you want to ask, Inspector ? "

Armadale considered for a moment or two.

" You're sure you haven't moved this body in any way ? " he demanded.

" I never put a finger on it," Mold asserted.

" And it's lying just as it was when you saw it first ? " Armadale pursued.

" As near as I can remember," Mold replied, cautiously. " I didn't wait long after I saw it. I went off almost at once to ring up the police."

Armadale seemed to have got all the information he expected. Sir Clinton, seeing that no more questions were to come, turned to the keeper.

" Go off to the house and tell Mr Cecil Chacewater that his brother's found and that he's to come here at once. You needn't say anything about the matter to anyone else. They'll hear soon enough. And when you've done that, ring up the police station and tell them to send up a sergeant and a couple of constables to me here. Hurry, now."

Mold went without a word. Sir Clinton waited till he was out of earshot and then glanced at Armadale.

" One thing stares you in the face," the Inspector said in answer to the look. " He wasn't shot here. That wound would mean any amount of blood ; and there's hardly any blood on the grass."

Sir Clinton's face showed his agreement. He looked down at the body.

" He's lying on his back now ; but after he was shot he lay on his left side till *rigor mortis* set in," he pointed out.

The Inspector examined the body carefully.

" I think I see how you get that," he said. " This left arm's off the ground a trifle. If he'd been shot here and fell in this position, the arm would have relaxed and followed the lie of the ground. Is that it ? "

" Yes, that and the hypostases. You see the marks on the left side of the face."

" A dead man doesn't shift himself," the Inspector observed with an oracular air. " Someone else must have had a motive for dragging him about."

" Here's a revolver," Sir Clinton pointed out, picking it up gingerly to avoid marking it with finger-prints. " You can see, later on, if anything's to be made out from it."

He put the revolver carefully down on a part of the ruined wall near at hand and then returned to the body.

" To judge by the *rigor mortis*," he said, after making a test, " he must have been dead for a good while—a dozen hours or more."

" What about that shot that the keeper said he heard ? " queried Armadale.

" The time might fit well enough. But *rigor mortis*

216

is no real criterion, you know, Inspector. It varies too much from case to case."

Inspector Armadale pulled out a small magnifying glass and examined the dead man's hand carefully.

" Those were his finger-prints on that Japanese sword right enough, sir," he pointed out. " You can see that tiny scar on the thumb quite plainly if you look."

He held out the glass, and Sir Clinton inspected the right thumb of the body minutely.

" I didn't doubt it from the evidence you had before, Inspector ; but this certainly clinches it. The scar's quite clear."

" Shall I go through the pockets now ? " Armadale asked.

" You may as well," Sir Clinton agreed.

Inspector Armadale began by putting his fingers into the body's waistcoat pocket. As he did so his face showed his surprise.

" Hullo ! Here's something ! "

He pulled out the object and held it up for Sir Clinton's inspection.

" One of the Leonardo medallions," Sir Clinton said, as soon as he had identified the thing. " Let me have a closer look at it, Inspector."

He examined the edge with care.

" This seems to be the genuine article, Inspector. I can't see any hole in the edge, which they told me was drilled to distinguish the replicas from the real thing. No, there's no mark of any sort here."

He handed it back to the Inspector, who examined

it in his turn. Sir Clinton took it back when the Inspector had done with it, and placed it in his pocket.

" I think, Inspector, we'll say nothing about this find for the present. I've an idea it may be a useful thing to have up our sleeve before we've done. By the way, do you still connect Foxton Polegate with this case ? "

Armadale looked the Chief Constable in the eye as he replied.

" I'm more inclined to connect Cecil Chacewater with it, just now, sir. Look at the facts. It's been common talk that there was ill-feeling between those two brothers. Servants talk ; and other people repeat it. And the business that ended in the final row between the two of them was centred in these Leonardo medallions. That's worth thinking over. Then, again, Cecil Chacewater disappeared for a short while. You couldn't get in touch with him. And it was just at that time that queer things began to happen here at Ravensthorpe. Where was he then ? It seems a bit suggestive, doesn't it ? And where was he last night ? If you looked at him this morning, you couldn't help seeing he'd spent a queer night, wherever he spent it. That was the night when this body was brought here from wherever the shooting was done. And when you asked Cecil Chacewater how he'd come home, he said he'd arrived by the first train this morning. That was a lie. He didn't come by that train. He'd been here before that."

To the Inspector's amazement and disgust Sir Clinton laughed unaffectedly at this exposition.

"It's nothing to laugh at, sir. You can't deny these things. I don't say they prove anything ; but you can't brush them aside merely by laughing at them. They've got to be explained. And until they've been explained in some satisfactory way things will look very fishy."

Sir Clinton recovered his serious mask.

"Perhaps I laughed a little too soon, Inspector. I apologize. I'm not absolutely certain of my ground ; I quite admit that. But I'll just give you one hint. Sometimes one case looks as if it were two independent affairs. Sometimes two independent affairs get inter-locked and look like one case. Now just think that over carefully. It's perhaps got the germ of some-thing in it, if you care to fish it out."

"Half of what you've said already sounds like riddles to me, sir," Armadale protested, fretfully. "I'm never sure when you're serious and when you're pulling my leg."

Sir Clinton was saved from the embarrassment of a reply by the arrival of Cecil Chacewater. He nodded curtly to the two officials as he came up. The Inspector stepped forward to meet him.

"I'd like to put one or two questions to you, Mr Chacewater," he said, ignoring the look on Sir Clinton's face.

Cecil looked Armadale up and down before replying.

"Well, go on," he said, shortly.

"First of all, Mr Chacewater," the Inspector began, "I want to know when you last saw your brother alive."

Cecil replied without the slightest hesitation :

219

" On the morning I left Ravensthorpe.   We'd had a disagreement and I left the house."

" That was the last time you saw him ? "

" No.   I see him now."

The Inspector looked up angrily from his notebook.

" You're giving the impression of quibbling, Mr Chacewater."

" I'm answering your questions, Inspector, to the best of my ability."

Armadale tried a fresh cast.

" Where did you go when you left Ravensthorpe ? "

" To London."

" You've been in London, then, until this morning? "

Cecil paused for a moment or two before answering.

" May I ask, Inspector, whether you're bringing any charge against me ? If you are, then I believe you ought to caution me.   If you aren't, then I don't propose to answer your questions.   Now, what are you going to do about it ? "

Armadale was hardly prepared for this move.

" I think you're injudicious, Mr Chacewater," he said in a tone which he was evidently striving not to make threatening.   " I know you didn't arrive by the first train this morning, though you told us you did. Your position's rather an awkward one, if you think about it."

" You can't bluff me, Inspector," Cecil returned. " Make your charge, and I'll know how to answer it. If you won't make a charge, I don't propose to help you with a fishing inquiry."

The Inspector glanced at Sir Clinton's face, and on

it he read quite plainly the Chief Constable's disapproval of his proceedings. He decided to go no further for the moment. Sir Clinton intervened to make the situation less strained.

" Would you mind looking at him, Cecil, and formally identifying him ? "

Cecil came forward rather reluctantly, knelt down beside his brother's body, examined the clothes, and finally, removing the handkerchief, gazed for a moment or two at the shattered face. The shot had entered the right side of the head and had done enough damage to show that it had been fired almost in contact with the skin.

Cecil replaced the handkerchief and rose to his feet. For a few moments he stood looking down at the body. Then he turned away.

" That's my brother, undoubtedly."

Then, as if speaking to himself, he added in a regretful tone :

" Poor old Chuchundra ! "

To the Inspector's amazement Sir Clinton started a little at the word.

" Was that a nickname, Cecil ? "

Cecil looked up, and the Inspector could see that he was more than a little moved.

" We used to call him that when we were kids."

Sir Clinton's next question left the Inspector still further bemused.

" Out of *The Jungle Book* by any chance ? "

Cecil seemed to see the drift of the inquiry, for he replied at once :

221

" Yes. *Rikki-tikki-tavi,* you know."

" I was almost certain of it," said Sir Clinton. " I can put a name to the trouble, I think. It begins with A."

Cecil reflected for a moment before replying.

" Yes. You're right. It does begin with A."

" That saves a lot of bother," said Sir Clinton, thankfully. " I was just going to fish in a fresh direction to get that bit of information. I'm quite satisfied now."

Cecil seemed to pay little attention to the Chief Constable's last remark. His eyes went round to the shattered thing that had been his brother.

" I'd no notion it was as bad as all this," he said, more to himself than to the others. " If I'd known, I wouldn't have been so bitter about things."

The sergeant and constables appeared at the edge of the clearing.

" Seen all you want to see, Inspector ? " asked Sir Clinton. " Then in that case we can leave the body in charge of the sergeant. I see they've got a stretcher with them. They can take it down to Ravensthorpe."

Armadale rapidly gave the necessary orders to his subordinates.

" Now, Inspector, I think we'll go over to Ravensthorpe ourselves. I want to see that chauffeur again. Something's occurred to me."

As the three men walked through the belt of woodland Sir Clinton turned to Cecil.

" There's one point I'd like to have cleared up. Do you know if Maurice had any visitors in the last three

222

months or so—people who wanted to see the collection ? "

Cecil reflected for a time before he could recall the facts.

" Now you mention it, I remember hearing Maurice say something about a fellow—a Yankee—who was writing a book on Leonardo. That chap certainly came here one day and Maurice showed him the stuff. The medallions were what he chiefly wanted to look at, of course."

" You didn't see him ? "

" No. None of us saw him except Maurice."

Sir Clinton made no comment ; and they walked on in silence till they came to the house. Inspector Armadale was by this time completely at sea.

" Find that chauffeur, Inspector, please ; and bring him along. I've got one or two points which need clearing up."

When the chauffeur arrived it was evident that Armadale had not been mistaken when he described him as stupid-looking. Information had to be dragged out of him by minute questioning.

" Your name's Brackley, isn't it ? " Sir Clinton began.

" Yes, sir. Joe Brackley."

" Now, Brackley, don't be in a hurry with your replies. I want you to think carefully. First of all, on the day that Mr Foss was murdered, he ordered you to bring the car round to the front door."

" Yes, sir. I was to wait for him if he wasn't there."

223

" You pulled up the car here, didn't you ? "

Sir Clinton indicated the position in front of the house.

" Yes, sir.   It was there or thereabouts."

" Then you put up the hood ? "

" Yes, sir."

" What possessed you to do that on a sunny day ? "

" One of the fastenings was a bit loose and I wanted to make it right before going out."

" You didn't think of doing that in the garage ? "

" I didn't notice it, sir, until I'd brought the car round.   My eye happened to fall on it.   And just then I saw Mr Foss going off into the house with some people.   He didn't seem in a hurry, so I thought I'd just time to make the repair before he came out."

" You got on to the running-board to reach the hood, didn't you ? "

" Yes, sir."

" Which running-board ?   The one nearest the house ? "

" No, sir.   The other one."

" So you could see the front of the house as you were working ? "

" Yes, sir."

" Did you see anything—anything whatever— while you were at work ?   You must have raised your eyes occasionally."

" I could see the window opposite me."

" By and by, I think, Marden, the valet, came up and spoke to you ? "

" Yes, sir, he did.   He'd been going to the post, he

said, but there had been some mistake or other and he'd
come back."

" He left you and went into the house ? "

" Yes, sir."

" After that, did you see Marden again—I mean
within, say, twenty minutes or so ? "

" Yes, sir."

" Where did you see him, if you can remember ? "

" Up there, sir, at that window.   He was talking to
Mr Foss."

" When you were up on the running-board, you
could just see into the room ? "

" Yes, sir."

" What happened after that ? "

" I finished the repair; so I came down off the
running-board and let down the hood again."

" Anything else you can remember, Brackley ? "

" No, sir."

" Very well.   That will do.   By the way, Inspector,"
Sir Clinton turned round, preventing the Inspector
from making any comments while the chauffeur was
standing by.   " I'd clean forgotten the patrolling of
the place up yonder.   I've never found time to go up
there ; but it's really a bit out of date now.   I think
we can dispense with the patrol after to-night.   And
the same holds for that guard on the museum.   There's
no need for either of them."

" Very good, sir," Armadale responded, mechanically.

The Inspector was engaged in condemning his own
stupidity.   Why had he not seen the possibilities

involved in that repair of the hood ?   With the extra foot of elevation of course the chauffeur could see further into the museum than a man standing on the ground.   And here was the damning evidence that Marden's story was a lie.   And the Inspector had missed it.   He almost gritted his teeth in vexation as he thought of it.   The keystone of the case : and the Chief Constable had taken it under his nose !

Sir Clinton turned to Cecil as the chauffeur retired.

" I shall be here about one o'clock in the morning, Cecil," he said, lowering his voice.   " I want you to be on the watch and let me in without anyone getting wind of my visit.   Can you manage it ? "

" Easily enough."

" Very well.   I'll be at the door at one o'clock sharp.   But remember, it's an absolutely hush-hush affair.   There must be no noise of any sort."

" I'll see to that," Cecil assured him.

Sir Clinton turned to the Inspector.

" Now I think we'll go across to where we left my car."

On the way to the police station Sir Clinton's manner did not encourage conversation ; but as they got out of the car he turned to Armadale.

" Map-drawing's a bit late in the day now, Inspector ; but we may as well carry on for the sake of completeness."

He led the way to his office, took a ruler and protractor from his desk, and set to work on a sheet of paper.

" Take this point as the museum," he said.   " This

line represents the beginning of the tunnel. I took the bearing that time when I lagged behind you. At the next turn—this one here—I made a pretence of examining the walls and took the bearing as we were standing there. I got the third bearing when I asked you to measure the dimensions of the tunnel. As it has turned out, secrecy wasn't really necessary ; but it seemed just as well to keep the survey to ourselves. I got the distances by pacing, except the last bit. There I had to estimate it, since we were crawling on all fours ; but I think I got it near enough."

" And you carried all the figures in your memory ? "

" Yes. I've a fairly good memory when I'm put to it."

" You must have," said Armadale, frankly.

" Now," Sir Clinton went on. " By drawing in these lines we get the position of that underground room. It's here, you see. The next thing is to find out where it lies, relative to the ground surface. I had a fair notion ; so when I got to the top of the turret I took the bearing of the Knight's Tower. I'll just rule it in. You see the two lines cut quite near the cell. My notion is that there's a second entrance into that tunnel from that ruined tower. In the old days it may have been a secret road into the outpost tower when a siege was going on."

" I see what you're getting at now," Armadale interrupted. " You mean that Maurice Chacewater's body was in the cell and that it was shifted from there up the other secret passage—the one we didn't see—and left alongside the tower this morning ? "

227

" Something of that sort."

" And now we've got to find who killed Maurice Chacewater down there, underground ? "

" There's nothing in that, Inspector. He killed himself. It's a fairly plain case of suicide."

" But why did he commit suicide ? "

Sir Clinton appeared suddenly smitten with deafness. He ignored the Inspector's last inquiry completely.

" I shall want you to-night, Inspector. Come to my house at about half-past twelve. And you had better wear rubber-soled boots or tennis shoes if you have them. We'll go up to Ravensthorpe in my car."

" You're going to arrest Marden, sir ? "

" No," was Sir Clinton's reply, which took the Inspector completely aback. " I'm not going to arrest anybody. I'm going to show you what Foss was going to do with his otophone ; that's all."

CHAPTER XIII

THE OTOPHONE

Punctually at half-past twelve the Inspector arrived at Sir Clinton's house. The Chief Constable's first glance was at the feet of his subordinate.

"Tennis shoes ? That's right. Now, Inspector, I want you to understand clearly that silence is absolutely essential when we get to work. We'll need to take a leaf out of the book of the *Pirates of Penzance :*

> With cat-like tread
> Upon our prey we steal.

That's our model, if you please. The car's outside. We'll go at once."

As preparations for an important raid, these remarks seemed to Armadale hardly adequate ; but as Sir Clinton showed no desire to amplify them, the Inspector was left to puzzle over the immediate future without assistance. The hint about the otophone had roused his curiosity.

"Foss's hearing was quite normal," he said to himself, turning the evidence over in his mind. "He heard that conversation in the winter-garden quite clearly enough. So quite evidently one couldn't call him deaf. And yet he was dragging an otophone about with him. I don't see it."

The Chief Constable pulled up the car in the avenue at a considerable distance from the house.

"Change here for Ravensthorpe," he explained, opening the door beside him. " I can't take the motor nearer for fear of the engine's noise giving us away."

He glanced at the illuminated clock on the dashboard.

"We're in nice time," he commented. " Come along, Inspector ; and the less said the better."

They reached the door of Ravensthorpe exactly at one o'clock. Cecil was waiting for them on the threshold.

"Switch off those lights," Sir Clinton said in a whisper, pointing to the hall lights which Cecil had left burning. " We mustn't give the show away if we can help it. Someone might be looking out of a window and be tempted to come down and turn them out. You're supposed to be in bed, aren't you ? "

Cecil nodded without speaking, and, crossing the hall, he extinguished the lamps. Sir Clinton pulled an electric torch from his pocket.

"There's a staircase giving access to the servant's quarters, isn't there ? "

Cecil confirmed this, and Sir Clinton turned to the Inspector.

"Which of your men is on duty at the museum door to-night ? "

"Froggatt," the Inspector answered.

"We'll go along to him," said Sir Clinton. " I want you, Cecil, to take the constable and post him at the bottom of that stair. Here's the flash-lamp."

Froggatt was surprised to see the party.

"Now, Froggatt," the Chief Constable directed.

" You're to go with Mr Chacewater. He'll show you where to stand. All you have to do is to stick to your post there until you're relieved. It'll only be a matter of ten minutes or so. Don't make the slightest sound unless anything goes wrong. Your business is to prevent anyone getting down the stair. There'll be no trouble. If you see anyone, just shout : ' Who's there ? ' That'll be quite enough."

The Inspector and Sir Clinton waited on the threshold of the museum until Cecil came back.

" Very convenient having these museum lights on all night," Sir Clinton remarked. " We don't need to muddle about with the flash-lamp. Now just wait here for a moment, and don't speak a word. I'm going upstairs."

He ascended to the first floor, entered Foss's room and picked up the otophone, with which he returned to his companions.

" Now we can get to work," he whispered, leading the way into the museum. " Just lock that door behind us, Inspector."

Followed by the other two he stepped across the museum to the bay containing the safe. There he put the otophone on the floor and opened the case of the instrument. From one compartment he took an ear-phone with its head-band. A moment's search revealed the position of the connection, and he plugged the ear-phone wire into place in sockets let into the outside of the attaché case. A little further examination revealed a stud beside the leather handle, and this Sir Clinton pressed.

"That should start the thing," he commented.

He lifted the hinged metal plate slightly and peered into the cavity which contained the valves.

"That seems all right," he said, as his eye caught the faint glow of the dull emitters.

Shutting down the plate again, the Chief Constable put his finger into the compartment from which he had taken the ear-phone, pressed a concealed spring, and pulled up the floor of the compartment.

"This is the microphone," he explained, drawing out a thick ebonite disk mounted on the false bottom of the compartment. "It's attached to a longish wire so that you can take it out and put it on a table while the case with the valves and batteries lies on the floor out of the way. Now we'll tune up."

He brought microphone and ear-phone together, when a faint musical note made itself heard. Then he handed the microphone to Cecil.

"Hold that tight against the safe door, Cecil. Get the base in contact with the metal of the safe and keep the microphone face downwards. It's essential to hold it absolutely steady, for the slightest vibration will put me off."

He fitted on the head-band and moved the two tiny levers of the otophone until the adjustment of the instrument seemed to satisfy him. Then, very cautiously, he began to work the mechanism of the combination lock. For some time he seemed unable to get what he wanted; but suddenly he made a slight gesture of triumph.

"It's an old pattern, as I thought. There's no

balanced fence arbour. This is going to be an easy business."

Easy or not, it took him nearly a quarter of an hour to accomplish his task ; for at times he obviously went astray in the work.

" Try to keep your feet still," he said. " Every movement you make is magnified up to the noise of a pocket avalanche."

At last the thing was done. The safe door swung open. Sir Clinton took off the head-band, received the microphone from Cecil, and packed it away in the case of the otophone along with the ear-phone.

" You'd better jot down the number of the combination, Cecil," he suggested. " It's on the dial at present."

While Cecil was busy with this, the Chief Constable switched off the otophone and put it in a place of safety.

" Now we'll see what's inside the safe," he said.

He swung the door full open and disclosed a cavity more like a strong-room than a safe.

" Have you any idea where the medallions were usually kept ? " he inquired.

Cecil went over to one of the shelves and searched rapidly.

" Why, there are only two of them here ! " he exclaimed in dismay.

" Hush ! " Sir Clinton warned him sharply. " Don't make a row. Have a good look at the things."

Cecil picked up the medallions and scanned them minutely. His face showed his amazement as he turned from one to another.

" These are the replicas ! Where have the genuine Leonardos gone ? "

" Never mind that for the present. Put these things back again. I'm going to close the safe. We mustn't risk talking too much here ; and the sooner we're gone the better."

He picked up the otophone and led the way out of the museum.

" You might bring Froggatt back to his post here," he said. " We don't need him at the stair any longer. I must go upstairs again for a moment with this machine."

Cecil piloted Froggatt back to his original post just as the Chief Constable rejoined them.

" I don't want to talk here," Sir Clinton said to Cecil. " Get a coat and walk with us down to the car. We've done our work for the night."

The Chief Constable waited until they were well away from the house before beginning his explanation.

" That otophone is—as I expect you saw—simply a microphone for picking up sound, plus a two-valve amplifier for magnifying it. The sounds that reach the microphone are amplified by the valve set to any extent, within limits, that you like to set it for. You can make the crumpling of a piece of paper sound like a small thunderstorm if you choose ; and it's especially sensitive to clicks and sounds of that sort. The mere involuntary shifting of your feet on that parquet floor made a lot of disturbance.

" Now in the older type of combination locks, if the dial was carefully manipulated, a person with sharp

234

hearing might just be able to detect a faint click when a tumbler fell into place in the course of a circuit ; and by making a note of the state of the dial corresponding to each click the combination could finally be discovered. In the modern patterns of locks this has been got round. They've introduced a thing called a balanced fence arbour, which is lifted away from the tumblers as soon as the lock spindle is revolved ; so in this new pattern there's no clicking such as the older locks give."

" I see now," said the Inspector. " That's an old pattern lock ; and you were using the otophone to magnify the sound of the clicks ? "

" Exactly," Sir Clinton agreed. " It made the thing mere child's play. Each click sounded like a whip-crack, almost."

" So that's why Foss brought the otophone along ? He meant to pick the lock of the safe and get the medallions out of it ? "

" That was one possibility, of course," Sir Clinton said, with a grave face. " But I shouldn't like to say that it was the only possibility."

He smoked for a few moments in silence, then he turned to Cecil.

" Now I've a piece of work for you to do ; and I want you to do it convincingly. First thing to-morrow morning you're to find some way of spreading the news that you've recovered all the genuine medallions and that they're in the safe. Don't give any details ; but see that the yarn gets well abroad."

" But all the real medallions are gone ! " said Cecil

in disgust. "And whoever's got them must know they're gone."

"There's nothing like a good authoritative lie for shaking confidence," Sir Clinton observed, mildly. "That's your share in the business. You'd better mention it at breakfast time to as many people as you can ; and you can telephone the glad news to me, with the door of the telephone box open so that anyone can hear it. Yell as loud as you please, or louder if possible. It won't hurt me at the other end. In any case, see that the happy tidings wash the most distant shores."

"Well, since you say so, I'll do it. But it's sure to be found out, you know, sooner or later."

"All I want is a single day's run of it. My impression is that, if things go well, I'll have the whole Ravensthorpe affair cleared up by this time to-morrow. But I don't promise that as a certainty."

"And this yarn is part of your scheme ? "

"I'm setting a trap," Sir Clinton assured them. "And that lie is the bait I'm offering."

As they reached the car, he added :

"See that your constable doesn't say a word about this affair to-night—to anyone. That's important, Inspector."

CHAPTER XIV

THE SECOND CHASE IN THE WOODS

"I'VE made all the necessary arrangements, sir," Inspector Armadale reported to the Chief Constable on the following evening. "A dozen constables —two with rubber-soled shoes—and a couple of sergeants. They're to be at the Ravensthorpe gate immediately it's dark enough. The sergeants have the instructions ; the constables don't even know where they're going when they leave here."

"That's correct," Sir Clinton confirmed. "Let's see. That's fourteen altogether. Less two, twelve. Plus you and myself, fourteen. I think we'll add to our number. Nothing like being on the safe side. Mr Chacewater's personally interested in the affair ; I think we'll take him in also. And Mr Clifton might reasonably claim some share in the business. That makes sixteen. You're detaching two constables to watch that lakelet. Well, surely fourteen of us ought to be able to pick up the scoundrel without difficulty."

"You're sure that he'll make for the terrace over the pool, sir ? "

"Nothing's sure in this world, Inspector. But I think there's a fair chance that he'll make in that direction. And if he doesn't, why, then, we can run him down wherever he goes."

"If he goes up there, we'll have him," the Inspector affirmed. "There'll be no amateur bungling this time, like the last affair. I'll see to that myself. He won't slip through a constabulary cordon as he did when he'd only a lot of excited youngsters to deal with."

" I leave that part of the business entirely in your hands, Inspector," the Chief Constable assured him.

" What I can't see," the Inspector continued, with a faint querulousness in his tone, " is why you're going about the thing in this elaborate way. Why not arrest him straight off and be done with it ? "

" Because there's one little party that you've omitted to take into your calculations, Inspector—and that's the jury. Suspicion's not good enough for us at this stage. Criminal trials aren't conducted on romantic lines. Everything's got to be proved up to the hilt. Frankly, in this case, you've been scattering your suspicions over a fairly wide field, haven't you ? "

" It's our business to be suspicious of everybody," the Inspector pleaded in extenuation.

" Oh, within limits, within limits, Inspector. You started by suspecting Foxton Polegate ; then you branched off to Marden ; after that you hovered a bit round Maurice Chacewater ; and at the end you were hot on Cecil Chacewater's heels. There's too much of the smart reader of detective stories about that. He suspects about six of the characters without having any real proof at all ; and then when the criminal turns up clearly in the last chapter he says : ' Well, that fellow was on my list of suspects.' That style of thing's no use in real criminal work, where you've got to produce evidence and not merely some vague suspicions."

" You're a bit hard, sir," the Inspector protested.

238

"Well, you criticized my methods, remember. If I were to arrest the fellow just now, I doubt if I could convince a jury of his guilt. And they'd be quite right. It's their business to be sceptical and insist on definite proof. It's that proof that I expect to get out of to-night's work."

"It will be very instructive for me, sir," Inspector Armadale commented, with heavy irony.

"You take things too seriously," Sir Clinton retorted, with an evident double meaning in the phrase. "What you need, Inspector, is a touch of fantasy. You'll get a taste of it to-night, perhaps, unless my calculations go far astray. Now I'm going to ring up Mr Chacewater and make arrangements for to-night."

And with that he dismissed the Inspector.

Armadale retired with a grave face; but when he closed the door behind him his expression changed considerably.

"There he was, pulling my leg again, confound him!" he reflected. "A touch of fantasy, indeed! What's he getting at now? And the worst of it is I haven't got to the bottom of the business yet myself. He's been quite straight in giving me all the facts. I'm sure of that. But they seem to me just a jumble. They don't fit together anyhow. And yet he's not the bluffing kind; he's got it all fixed up in his mind; I'm sure of that, whether he's right or wrong. Well, we'll see before many hours are over."

And with reflections like these Inspector Armadale had to content himself until nightfall.

As they drove up to the Ravensthorpe gates the Inspector found Sir Clinton in one of his uncommunicative moods. He seemed abstracted, and even, as the Inspector noted with faint malice, a little anxious about the business before them. When they reached the gates they found the constabulary squad awaiting them. Sir Clinton got out of the car, after running it a little way up the avenue.

" Now, the first thing you've got to remember," he said, addressing the squad, " is that in no circumstances are you to make the slightest noise until you hear my second whistle. You know what you're to do ? Get up behind the house at the end opposite to the servants' wing and stay there till you get my signal. Then you're to come out and chase the man whom the Inspector will show you. You're not to try to catch him. Keep a hundred yards behind him all the time ; but don't lose sight of him. The Inspector will give you instructions after you've chased for a while. Now which of you are the two with tennis shoes ? "

Two constables stepped out of the ranks. Sir Clinton took them aside and gave them some special instructions.

" Now, you'd better get to your places," he said, turning to the squad again. Remember, not a sound. I'm afraid you'll have a long wait, but we must take things as they come."

As the squad was led off into the night, he moved over to where the Inspector was standing.

" I want something out of the car," he said. The Inspector followed him and waited while Sir Clinton switched off the headlights and the tail lamp. The Chief Constable felt in a locker and handed something to Armadale.

"A pair of night-glasses, Inspector. You'll need them. And that's the lot. We'd better get to our position. There's no saying when the fellow may begin his work."

Rather to the mystification of the Inspector, Sir Clinton struck across the grass instead of following the avenue up to the house. After a fairly long walk they halted under a large tree.

"A touch of fantasy was what I recommended to you, Inspector. I think a little tree-climbing is indicated. Sling these glasses round your neck as I'm doing and follow on."

"Quite mad!" was the Inspector's involuntary comment to himself. "I suppose, once we get up there, he'll come down again and tell me I needed exercise."

He followed the Chief Constable, however; and was at last directed to a branch on which he could find a safe seat.

"Think I'm demented, Inspector?" Sir Clinton demanded with the accuracy of a thought-reader. "It's not quite so bad as that, you'll be glad to hear. Turn your glasses through that rift in the leaves. I was at special pains to cut it yesterday evening, in preparation for you. What do you see?"

The Inspector focused his glasses and scanned the scene visible through the fissure in the foliage.

"The front of Ravensthorpe," he answered.

" Some windows ? "

" Yes."

" Well, one of them's the window of the museum ; and this happens to be one of the few points from which you can see right into the room. If the lights were on there, you'd find that we're looking squarely on to the door of the safe."

With this help the Inspector was able to pick out the window which evidently he was expected to watch.

" It'll be a slow business," Sir Clinton said in a bored tone. " But one of us has got to keep an eye on that window for the next hour or two at least. We can take it in turn."

They settled down to their vigil, which proved to be a prolonged one. The Inspector found his perch upon the branch anything but comfortable ; and it grew more wearisome as the time slipped past.

" Fantasy ! " he commented bitterly to himself as he shifted his position for the twentieth time. " Cramp's more likely."

But at last their tenacity was rewarded. It was during one of the Inspector's spells of watching. Suddenly the dark rectangle of the window flashed into momentary illumination and faded again.

" There he is ! " exclaimed the Inspector. " He's carrying a flash-lamp."

Sir Clinton lifted his glasses and examined the place in his turn.

" I can see him moving about in the room," the Inspector reported excitedly. " Now he's going over towards the safe. Can you see him, sir ? "

" Fairly well. What do you make of him ? "

The Inspector studied his quarry intently for a while.

" That's the otophone, isn't it, sir ? I can't see his face ; it seems as if he'd blackened it. . . . No, he's wearing a big mask. It looks like . . ."

His voice rose sharply.

" It's Marden ! I recognize that water-proof of his ; I could swear to it anywhere."

" That's quite correct, Inspector. Now I think we'll get down from this tree as quick as we can and I'll blow my whistle. That ought to startle him. And I've arranged for that to be the signal for a considerable amount of noise in the house, which ought to give the effect we want."

He slipped lightly down the branches, waited for the slower-moving Inspector, and then blew a single shrill blast on his whistle.

" That's roused them," he said, with satisfaction, as some lights flashed up in windows on the front of Ravensthorpe. " I guess that amount of stir about the place will flush our friend without any trouble."

He gazed through his glasses at the main door.

" There he goes, Inspector ! "

A dark figure emerged suddenly on the threshold, hesitated for a moment, and then ran down the steps. Armadale instinctively started forward ; but the cool voice of the Chief Constable recalled him.

" There's no hurry, Inspector ! You'd better hang your glasses on the tree here. They'll only hamper you in running."

Hurriedly the Inspector obeyed ; and Sir Clinton

leisurely hung up his own pair. Armadale turned again and followed the burglar with his eyes.

" He's making for the old quarry, sir."

" So I see," Sir Clinton assured him. " I want the fellow to have a good start, remember. I don't wish him to be pressed. Now we may as well get the chase organized."

Followed by the Inspector, he hurried towards the front of Ravensthorpe.

" I think that's a fair start to give him," he estimated aloud. Then, lifting his whistle, he blew a second blast.

Almost immediately the figures of Cecil Chacewater and Michael Clifton emerged from the main door, while a few seconds later the police squad rounded the corner of the house.

" Carry on, Inspector ! " Sir Clinton advised. "I leave the rest of the round-up to you. But keep exactly to what I told you."

Armadale hurried off, and within a few seconds the chase had been set afoot.

" We must see if we can wipe your eye this time, Mr Clifton," the Chief Constable observed. " It's a run over the old ground, you notice."

Michael Clifton nodded in answer.

" If you'd let me run him down I'd be obliged to you," he suggested. " You've given him a longish start, certainly ; but I think I could pull him in."

Sir Clinton made a gesture of dissent.

" Oh, no. We must give him a run for his money. Besides, it wouldn't suit my book to have him run down too early in the game."

The fugitive had reached the edge of the pine-wood as they were speaking, and now he disappeared from their sight among the arcades of the trees.

" The moon will be down in no time," Cecil pointed out as they ran. " Aren't you taking the risk of losing him up in the woods there ? It'll be pretty dark under the trees."

He quickened his pace slightly in his eagerness ; but the Chief Constable restrained him.

" Leave it to Armadale. It's his affair. We're only spectators, really."

" I want the beggar caught," Cecil grumbled, but he obeyed Sir Clinton's orders and slowed down slightly.

A few seconds brought them to the fringe of the wood ; and far ahead of them they could see the form of the burglar running steadily up the track.

" Just the same as before ? " Sir Clinton demanded from Michael.

" Just the same."

Through the wood they went behind the police squad. At the brow of the hill, where the trees began to thin, Armadale called a halt. They could hear him giving orders for the formation of his cordon. When his men began to move off under his directions the Inspector came over to Sir Clinton.

" He'll not slip through our hands this time, sir. I'll beat every bit of cover in that spinney. He can't get away on either side without being spotted. We'll get our hands on him in a few minutes now. I suppose he's armed ? "

Sir Clinton shook his head.

" I should doubt that."

The Inspector failed to conceal his surprise.

" Not armed ? He's sure to be."

" We'll see in a minute or two," the Chief Constable answered. " You'd better get your beaters to work, hadn't you ? . . . Ah ! "

In the silence they heard the sound of a faint splash from the direction of the quarry.

" History's repeating itself pretty accurately, isn't it ? " said Sir Clinton, turning to Michael. " That's the kind of thing you heard the other night ? "

" Just the same," Michael admitted.

But as the line of constables moved forward he could not help contrasting their methodical work with the rather haphazard doings of the pursuers on the earlier occasion. Armadale had evidently issued stringent orders, for not a tuft of undergrowth was left unexamined as the line slowly closed in upon the hunted man. Every possible piece of cover was scrutinized and beaten before the cordon passed beyond it.

" Very pretty," Sir Clinton commented, as they moved up in the rear of the line. " The Inspector must surely have been training these fellows. They really do the business excellently."

Michael suddenly left the path they were following and stepped across under the trees.

" I'm going to have a look at that Fairy House myself," he declared. " That's where I found Maurice after the last show. I want to be perfectly certain that it's empty."

He opened the door, leaned inside the building, and

then came back to his companions. Something like disappointment was visible in his expression. He was taken aback to see glances of sardonic amusement exchanged between Cecil and the Chief Constable.

" Drawn blank, have you ? " Cecil inquired.

" There's no one there at present," Michael admitted.

" I don't think the constables would have missed a plain thing like that," Sir Clinton remarked mildly, though with a faint undertone of correction in his voice.

Before Michael had time to reply they heard Armadale's voice. The cordon had passed completely through the spinney and was now on the edge of the marble terrace.

" Come along," Sir Clinton urged. " We mustn't miss the final scene."

They hurriedly joined the line just as Armadale ordered a last advance.

" He's somewhere on this terrace," he told his men. " See that he doesn't break away from you at the last moment."

Sir Clinton turned to Michael.

" Just the same as before ? "

Michael made a gesture of assent.

" I'll admit that this is more businesslike."

The Constabulary line crept forward almost foot by foot, subjecting every one of the marble seats to the most rigid scrutiny. Inspector Armadale's anxiety was more and more apparent as the cordon advanced without securing the man for whom they were searching. At last the whole of the possible cover had been

247

beaten, and the constables emerged on the open terrace. The fugitive had vanished, apparently, into thin air.

Michael Clifton turned to the Chief Constable with an ironical smile.

" *Just* the same as last time, it seems. How history repeats itself ! "

The Inspector hurried across the terrace to where they were standing. It was obvious that he was completely staggered by the turn of events.

" He's got away, sir," he reported in a mortified voice. " I can't think how he's managed it."

" I think we'll repeat that last stage again, Inspector, if you don't mind. Withdraw your men till they're just in front of that last line of seats."

While the Inspector was giving his orders Sir Clinton pulled his case from his pocket, opened it, and thoughtfully tapped a cigarette on the lid. Before lighting it he threw a glance up and down the empty spaces of the terrace from which the fugitive had so mysteriously vanished.

" All plain and above board, isn't it ? " he said, turning to his two companions. " I've got nothing in my hands except a cigarette, and you can search my sleeves if you like. It is required, as Euclid would say, to produce a full-sized burglar for the satisfaction of the audience. It's a stiff job."

He glanced again over the wide white pavement of the terrace.

" A conjurer's usually allowed a little patter, isn't he ? The quickness of the tongue distracts the eye, and all that. Just a question, then. Do you happen to remember what Medusa was able to do ? Turned things into stone when she looked at them, didn't she ? That somehow brings the late Pygmalion to my mind —a kind of association of opposites, in a way, I suppose. But I've often wondered what Pygmalion felt like when the statue came to life."

He turned sharply on his heel.

" You can come down off that pedestal, my friend. The game's up ! "

To the amazement of the group around him, the white marble statue above him started suddenly into life. It leapt down from its base on to the pavement of the terrace, staggered as it alighted, and then, as Cecil and Michael grasped at its smooth sides, it shook itself clear and sprang upon the broad marble balustrade.

" Come back, you fool ! " Sir Clinton snapped, as the figure faced outward to the gulf below.

But instead of halting, the white form gathered itself together for an instant and then dived headlong into the abyss. There was the sound of a splash ; and an appalling cry came up through the night.

Sir Clinton dashed to the rail.

" Below, there ! Get out on that raft at once and pick him up. He's badly hurt. He'll drown if you don't hurry."

The Inspector hurried forward.

" Why didn't you warn us, sir. We'd have had Marden as easy as anything. If you'd only told us what to expect."

Sir Clinton looked round.

" Marden ? That's not Marden. I tell you,

Inspector, if that jump of his meant anything, it suggests that there's no Marden at all."

The Inspector's amazement overbore his chagrin.

" I don't understand . . ." he began.

" Never mind. I'll explain later. Get away down to the water-side at once. See if he's badly damaged. Quick, now."

As the Inspector hurried off, the Chief Constable turned to Michael Clifton.

" History doesn't always repeat itself exactly, you see."

He pulled out a match-box and lit his cigarette in a leisurely fashion. Then, throwing away the vesta, he inquired :

" You see now how he got away from you last time ?"

Michael made no reply. He was examining the pedestal from which the living statue had taken its flight ; and he could see the scores and cuts left by the chisel which had smoothed the standing-place of the original marble figure. Quite obviously, on the night of the masked ball, the same trick had been played ; and while the pursuers were searching all around, the fugitive had stood rigid above them, unsuspected by anyone.

Cecil turned to the Chief Constable.

" Aren't you going down to see if something can't be done for the poor devil ? He must have come a fearful smash on the rocks."

" Poor devil ? " Sir Clinton retorted. " That's not a poor devil. That's a wild beast, if you're anxious for information. But if you're a member of the Society for the Prevention of Cruelty to Animals, I suppose we'd better see that things are done decently and in order. We'll go down, if you're perturbed about him."

It took them some little time to descend to the level of the lakelet. They could see, as they went down, the process of rescue ; and when they reached the water-side, they found two constables stooping over a limp white figure, beside which the Inspector knelt solicitously. As the newcomers approached, Armadale rose and stepped over to them.

" He's done for, sir," he reported in a low voice to Sir Clinton. " His pelvis is smashed and I think his spine must have gone as well. He's paralysed below the waist. I doubt if he'll last long. It was a fearful smash."

Cecil crossed over and peered down at the face of the dying man. For a moment he failed to recognize him ; for the white grease-paint disguised the natural appearance of the features : but a closer scrutiny revealed the identity of the living statue.

" Why, it's the chauffeur ! "

" Of course," was all that Sir Clinton thought it worth while to say.

Armadale brought something up from the water-side.

" Here's the waterproof he was wearing, sir. It's Marden's, just as I told you when I saw him in the museum to-night. When he flung it over the edge of the cliff as we were coming up, it landed on a broad bit of rock instead of sinking like the Pierrot costume, the other night."

Sir Clinton was silent for a moment. His glance

wandered to the broken, white-clad figure on the ground, but no pity showed on his face. Then he turned back to Armadale.

" See if you can get a confession out of him, Inspector. He won't live long at the best ; and he might as well tell what he can. We can't hang him now, unfortunately ; and he may as well save us some trouble in piecing things together. For one thing, he's got a bag or a suit-case lying around somewhere in the neighbourhood with a suit of clothes in it. You'd better find out where that is, and save us the bother of hunting for it. If you manage to get anything out of him, take it down and get it witnessed. Bring it down to Ravensthorpe at once."

He paused, then added as if by an after-thought :

" You'd better search these tights that he's wearing. There ought to be five of the medallions concealed about him somewhere. Get them for me."

He turned to Cecil and Michael.

" We'll go back now to Ravensthorpe. Unless I'm far astray in my deductions, there's been another murder there ; and we must keep the girls from hearing about it, if we can."

As they walked through the pine-wood, Sir Clinton maintained a complete taciturnity, and neither of the others cared to break in on his silence. His last words had shown that ahead of them might lie yet another of the Ravensthorpe tragedies, and the shadow of it lay across their minds. It was not until they were approaching the house that the Chief Constable spoke again.

" You've spun that yarn I gave you to the girls ? "

" They know there was some stunt afoot," said
Cecil, " but they were to keep out of the way, in their
rooms, until we were clear of the house."

" One had to tell them something," Sir Clinton
answered. " If one hadn't, they'd have been pretty
uncomfortable when all that racket started. You
managed to scare him out very neatly with the row you
raised when I blew my whistle."

" The girls are sitting up, waiting for us," Cecil
explained. " They said they'd have coffee ready when
we came back."

" The deuce they did ! "

Sir Clinton was obviously put out.

" I'd been counting on their going back to bed
again. Then we could have got Marden's body away
quietly—if he's been murdered, as I think he has.
There's no use upsetting people if you can avoid it.
Ravensthorpe's had its fill of sensations lately and
there's no need to add another to-night."

He reflected as he walked on, and at last he seemed
to hit on an expedient to suit the circumstances.

" The bottom's out of this case now," he said, at
last. " There'll be no trial ; so there's no need for
any more secrecy, so far as I can see. I'll be giving
nothing away that I shouldn't, at this stage of the game."

He threw away the end of his cigarette and looked up
at the bulk of Ravensthorpe before them. Here and
there on the dark front the yellow oblong of a window
shone out in the night.

" Suppose I spin them a yarn," Sir Clinton went on.

" I can keep them up until dawn with it. After that, they'll sleep sound enough ; and while they're asleep, we'll get Marden's body away in peace and comfort. It'll spare them the shock of finding another corpse on the premises ; and that's always something gained."

When they reached Ravensthorpe, Sir Clinton turned to Cecil.

" You'd better go and close the safe in the museum. No use leaving things like that open any longer than's necessary. I must go up to Marden's room now. I'll be back again in a minute or two."

Ascending the servants' staircase, Sir Clinton made his way to the valet's room. The door was locked ; but when Sir Clinton tapped gently, a constable opened it and looked out. At the sight of the Chief Constable, he stood aside.

" He's been murdered, sir," the man explained in a whisper.

" I guessed it might be that," Sir Clinton returned.

" Whoever did it must have chloroformed him first," the constable went on. " There was a pad of cotton-wool over his face ; and his throat's cut."

The Chief Constable nodded in comprehension.

" That would prevent any sounds," he said. " Brackley was a first-class planner, there's no doubt."

The constable continued his explanation.

" We came up here as you told us, sir ; and when we heard your whistle we slipped into the room, expecting to arrest him according to your orders. But he was dead by that time. It was quite clear that he'd been murdered only a short time before. Your orders didn't cover the case, so we thought the best thing to do was to lock the door and wait till you came back. You'd said we were to keep him here till your return, anyhow ; so that seemed to be the best course."

" Quite correct," Sir Clinton commended them. " You couldn't have done better. Now you'll need to wait here till morning. Keep the door locked, and don't let any word of this affair get abroad. I'll see about removing the body in due course. Until then, I don't want any alarm on the subject."

He stepped across the room, examined the body on the bed, and then, with a nod to the constables, he went downstairs once more.

255

CHAPTER XV

"IT's a pleasure to meet Sir Clinton again," Joan observed when they had finished their coffee. "For the last ten days or so, I've been dealing with a man they call the Chief Constable. I don't much care for him. These beetle-browed officials are not my sort. Too stiff and overbearing fo· me, altogether."

Sir Clinton laughed at the hit.

"Sorry," he said. "I've invited one of your aversions to join us. In fact, I think I hear him at the door now."

"Inspector Armadale?" Joan demanded. "Well, I've nothing against him. You never let him get a word in edgeways at our interviews. Grasping, I call it."

The door opened and the Inspector was ushered in. As he entered, a glance passed between him and Sir Clinton. In reply, Armadale made a furtive gesture which escaped the rest of the company.

"Passed in his checks," Sir Clinton interpreted it to himself. "That clears the road."

Joan poured out coffee for the Inspector and then turned to the Chief Constable.

"Cecil promised that you'd tell us all about everything. Don't linger over it. We're all in quite good listening form and we look to you not to be boring. Proceed."

Sir Clinton refused to be disconcerted.

"Inspector Armadale's the last authority on the subject," he remarked. "He's got the confession of the master mind in his pocket. I haven't seen it yet. Suppose I give you my account of things, and the Inspector will check it for us where necessary? That seems a fair division of labour."

"Very fair," Una Rainhill put in. "Now, Joan, be quiet and let's get on with the tale."

"Before the curtain goes up," Sir Clinton suggested, "you'd better read your programmes. First of all you find the name of Thomas Pailton, *alias* Cocoa Tom, *alias* J. B. Foss, *alias* The Wizard of Woz : a retired conjuror, gaolbird, confidence-trick sharp, etc. As I read his psychology, he was rather a weak character and not over straight even in dealing with his equals. In the present play, he was acting under the orders of a gentleman of much tougher fibre.

"The next name on the programme is Thomas Marden. The police have no records of his early doings, but I suspect that Mr Marden had cause to bless his luck in this respect, rather than his honesty. I'm sure he wasn't a prentice hand. As to his character, I believe he was rather a violent person when roused, and he had a deplorable lack of control over a rather bad temper.

"The third name is . . . ?"

"Stephen Racks," the Inspector supplied in answer to Sir Clinton's glance of inquiry.

"*Alias* Joe Brackley," Sir Clinton continued. "I think we'll call him Brackley, since that was the name you knew him by, if you knew him at all. He was nominally Foss's chauffeur. Actually, I think, he was the brain of the gang and did the planning for them."

" That's correct," the Inspector interpolated.

" Mr Brackley, I think, was the most deliberately unscrupulous of them all," Sir Clinton continued. " A really dangerous person who would stick at nothing to get what he wanted or to cover his tracks.

" Then, last of all, there's a Mr Blank, whose name I do not know, but who at present is under arrest in America for forging the name of Mr Kessock the millionaire. He was employed by Mr Kessock in some capacity or other which gave him access to Mr Kessock's correspondence. I've no details on that point as yet."

" This is the kind of stuff I always skip when I'm reading a detective story," complained Joan. " Can't you get along to something interesting soon ? "

" You're like the Bellman in the *Hunting of the Snark*, Joan. ' Oh, skip your dear uncle ! ' Well, I skip, as you desire it. I'll merely mention in passing that an American tourist came here a while ago and asked to see the Leonardo medallions, because he was writing a book on Leonardo. He, I believe, was Mr Blank from America ; and his job was to see the safe in the museum and note its pattern.

" I must skip again ; and now we reach the night of the robbery in the museum. You know what happened then. Mr Foss came to me with his tale about overhearing some of you planning a practical joke. His story was true enough, I've no doubt ; but it set me

258

thinking at once. I may not have shown it, Joan, but I quite agreed with you about his methods. It seemed a funny business to come straight to the police over a thing of that sort. Of course he had his reason ready ; but it didn't ring quite true, somehow. I might have put it down to tactlessness, if it hadn't suggested something else to my mind.

" That pistol-shot which smashed the lamp was too neatly timed for my taste. It was fired by someone who knew precisely when the keeper was going to be gripped, and it was fired just in time to get ahead of Foxton Polegate in the raid on the show-case. That meant, if it meant anything, that the man who fired the shot was a person who knew of the practical joke. But on the face of it, Foss was the only person who knew about the joke, bar the jokers themselves. So naturally I began to suspect Foss of having had a hand in the business. It was the usual mistake of the criminal —trying to be too clever and throw suspicion on to someone else.

" Now Foss wasn't the man in white, obviously ; for he came to see me while the man-hunt was still in full cry. So at that stage in the business I was fairly certain that at least two people were in the game : Foss and someone else, who was the man in white. That looked like either the valet or the chauffeur, since they were the only people I knew about who were directly associated with Foss while he was here. But this incognito business at the masked ball had made it possible for outsiders to come in unrecognized ; so the man in white might be a confederate quite outside our range of knowledge. One couldn't assume that either Marden or Brackley was in the show at all.

" I learned, later on, that Foss had synchronized his watch with yours, Cecil ; and that, of course, made it pretty plain that he was in the game. There was also another bit of evidence which suggested something. If either the valet or the chauffeur was the confederate, then they could easily enough have found out from the servants what costume Maurice meant to wear that night—a few questions to his valet would have got the information—and they could have chosen the Pierrot costume for their own runner in order to confuse things. That suggested that Foss's servants might be in the business ; but it proved nothing really. The white Pierrot costume was chosen mainly for its conspicuousness, I'm sure.

" Now I come to the disappearance of the man in white."

" Thank goodness ! " Joan commented. " It gets more interesting as it goes on, does it ? That's something to be thankful for."

" One does one's best," Sir Clinton retorted, unperturbed. " Now the vanishing of that fellow could be accounted for in various ways, so far as I could see. First of all, he might have slipped down the rope into the little lake. That was what the rope was meant to suggest, obviously. But fortunately one of the hunters had the wit to keep an eye on the lake ; and it was pretty clear the man in white didn't go that way. Then there was the possibility of his being concealed in the cave ; but that was ruled out by the search of the cave.

Thirdly, the gang might have hit on the opening of one of the secret passages of Ravensthorpe. Candidly, I ruled that out also. It seemed next door to impossible. But if you exclude all these ways, then there seem to be only two possibilities left. The first of these depends on the man in white having a confederate in the cordon who let him slip through. But the chance of a slip-through of that sort escaping the notice of the rest of the hunters seemed very small. It seemed to me too risky a business for them to have tried.

" The final possibility was that the fugitive disguised himself as something else. Well, what disguise would be the best ? It's a question of camouflage, and they had only a few seconds to do the camouflaging You can't dress up as a drain-pipe or a garden-seat in a couple of seconds. So we come down to something that's human in shape but isn't really human. In a garden, you might pretend to be a scarecrow ; but up on that terrace a scarecrow was out of the question. And then I remembered the statues.

" Suppose somebody had gone up there in the even-ing and had chiselled one of the statues off its base. The broken marble could be heaved over into the little lake and the bare pedestal would be left for the fugitive.

" I ought to have thought of that," Michael inter-jected. " It's so obvious when you think of it. But I didn't think of anything like that at the time."

" My impression then," Sir Clinton continued, " was that the man in white had white tights on under his Pierrot dress. His face and hands were whitened, also ; so that as soon as he stripped off his jacket and trousers, he was sufficiently statuelike to pass muster in that light. His eyes would have given him away in daylight ; but under the moon he'd only got to shut them and you'd hardly notice his whitened eyelashes. In the few moments that you left him, while the cordon was being formed, he took off his Pierrot things, wrapped them round the weight he'd used in breaking the case's glass, and pitched the lot over the balustrade. That would account for the splash that was heard."

Sir Clinton paused to light a cigarette.

" That theory seemed to fit most of the evidence, as you see. It explained why they'd chosen that parti-cular place for the disappearing trick ; and it accounted for the splash as well. Further, it suggested that there was a third man in the gang : the man who smashed down the real statue. They'd leave that bit of work to the last moment for fear of the damage being seen accidentally beforehand. Now Foss was at the masked ball, so it wasn't he. The man in white might need all his powers in that race, so it was unlikely that he'd been up there on a heavy bit of manual labour just then, for the shifting of that statue, even in pieces, can have been no light affair. That suggested the use of a third confederate. But I'm no wild enthusiast for theories. I simply noted the coincidence that this theory demanded three men and that Foss's party contained three men : himself, the valet, and the chauffeur.

" Now, for reasons which I'll give you immediately, it seemed likely that this affair was only a first step in a more complicated plan. On the spur of the moment,

I decided it was worth while taking a hand. So I got a patrol set round the spinney and issued orders that no one was to go up to the terrace until I'd been over the ground. I took good care that everyone knew about this ; and I took equally good care not to go there myself. I rather advertised the thing, in fact. That was to assure the fellows that no one had seen the empty pedestal. They were pretty certain to rout about for information ; and they'd hear on all sides that no one had been up to the terrace. That left the thing open for them to try again if they wanted to.

" Another thing confirmed my notions. When the Inspector was dragging the lake, he got a largish piece of marble out of it. That fitted in with the view that the broken statue was down in the water in frag-ments, hidden by the weeds. It all fitted fairly well, you see.

" Then came another bit of evidence—two bits, in fact. The village drunkard put abroad some yarn about seeing a White Man in the woods ; and a little girl saw a Black Man. That might have been mere fancy. Or it might have been true enough. When the hunters had gone, the pseudo-statue would come down off his pedestal. Suppose he wandered off into the wood and was seen by old Groby. There's your White Man. But he couldn't possibly get back to the house in white tights. He'd want to get in as quietly as possible. What about a set of black tights under the white ones ? When he took off the white ones, he'd be next door to invisible among shadows ; and he'd be able to sneak in through a window in the servants' wing—in the shadow of the house—fairly inconspicuously. Perhaps that's how it happened."

" That was it," the Inspector confirmed, looking up from a sheet of paper which he was consulting from time to time.

Sir Clinton acknowledged the confirmation but refused to lay much stress on the point.

" I thought it possible," he said, " but it was merely a guess. In itself the evidence wasn't worth anything; but it fitted well enough into the hypothesis I'd made."

He turned to the Inspector.

" Did you get the five medallions as I expected ? "

Armadale put his hand into his pocket and withdrew the five disks of gold, which he handed over to the Chief Constable. Sir Clinton took the sixth medallion from his own pocket and laid the whole set on the table beside him.

" They say," he went on, " that the more *outré* a crime is, the easier it is to find a solution for it. I shouldn't like to assert that in every case. But there's no harm in paying special attention to the bizarre points in an affair. If you cast your minds back to the case as it presented itself to us on the night of the masked ball, you'll recall one point which undoubtedly seemed out of the common."

He glanced round the circle of listeners, but no one ventured to interrupt.

" Here was a gang of thieves bent on stealing something. One of them—Foss—knew that in the show-case there were three medallions and three replicas. The medallions were of enormous value ; the replicas were worth next to nothing. Foss, I was sure—and it turned out afterwards that I was right—Foss knew that the real medallions were in the top row and that the replicas were in the lower row."

He arranged the six disks on the table as he spoke.

" And yet, with that knowledge, it was the replicas which they stole and not the real medallions. Amazing, at first sight, isn't it ? To my mind it was much more bizarre than the vanishing trick. And, naturally, it was on that point in the case that I fixed my attention. These weren't blunderers, remember. The rest of the business showed that they were anything but that. The way they had seized upon that practical joke to serve their ends was quite enough to prove that there was a good brain at the back of the thing. That joke wasn't in their original programme, and yet they'd taken it in their stride and turned it to account in a most ingenious way. They weren't the sort of people who would make a mistake about the positions of the replicas. If they took the electrotypes instead of the real things, it was because the electrotypes were what they wanted.

" Why did they want them ? That question seemed to thrust itself forward in front of all the others which suggested themselves in the case ; and it was that question that had to be answered before one could see light anywhere."

He leaned forward in his chair and glanced at the two rows of medallions on the table before him for a moment.

" If one thinks about a point long enough, it often

happens that all of a sudden a fresh idea turns up and fits into its place. I think it was probably the notion of the pseudo-statue that put me on to this affair. There you had a fraud imposing itself on some people simply because they had no reason to suppose that any fraud was intended. I doubt if any of you people, Mr Clifton, gave a second glance at these statues that night. You simply regarded them as statues, because you knew that statues were on all the pedestals in normal circumstances. You were off your guard on that particular point.

" That idea seemed to give me the key to this mysterious preference for replicas. If they'd taken the real medallions that night, with all the fuss that was made, then you Ravensthorpe people would have known at once that the true Leonardos had gone ; and, naturally, with the theft of them dated to a minute, the risk was considerable. But suppose that the theft of the replicas was only the first stage in the game, what then ? They had the replicas ; you had the real medallions. Foss, as the agent for Kessock, had every excuse for asking to see the medallions again.

" Now at that point there would come in the very same subconscious assurance that played into their hands in the case of the statue. Maurice would know for certain that the three things in his safe were the real Leonardos. He'd fish them out for Foss to examine ; and he'd put them back in the safe without any minute inspection when Foss handed them over. The replicas would be off the board—lost, gone for good. He'd never think of them."

Sir Clinton glanced mischievously at Joan before continuing.

" As it happens, I can do a little parlour conjuring myself. It comes in handy when one has to live up to the part of Prospero or anything like that. I know what one can do in the way of palming things, and so forth. And as soon as I hit on this idea of the case, I saw how things might be managed. Foss would fake up some excuse for handling the real medallions ; and during that handling, he'd substitute the replicas for the Leonardos. Maurice, having apparently had the things under his eye all the time, would never think of examining the medals which he got back from Foss's hands. He'd simply put them back into the safe. Foss would have the real things in his pocket ; the deal would fall through ; Foss & Co. would retire gracefully . . . and it was a hundred to one that no minute examination of the medallions in the safe would be made for long enough. By that time it would be impossible either to find Foss or to bring the thing home to him even if you did find him.

" You see the advantages ? First of all, the only theft would be one of the replicas, which no one cared much about. Second, the date of the real theft would be left doubtful. And third, this plan gave them any amount of time to dispose of the real things before any suspicions were aroused at all, as regards the genuine Leonardos. My impression is that they had a market for them : some scoundrelly collector who'd pay high to have the Leonardos even if he couldn't boast publicly that he had them."

"That's correct, sir," the Inspector interposed. "Brackley had a market, but he wouldn't tell me who the collector was."

Joan rose from her chair, crossed the room to a small table, and solemnly came back with a tray.

"Have some whisky and soda," she suggested to Sir Clinton.

"You find the tale rather dry?" he inquired solicitously. "Life's like that, you know. Inspector Armadale really needs this more than I do. He's been a long time out in the cold up yonder. I'll take some later on, if you don't mind."

Joan presented the tray to the Inspector, who helped himself.

Sir Clinton waited till he was finished with the siphon and then continued, addressing himself to Joan:

"Perhaps the story has lacked feminine interest up to this point. We'll hurry on to the day when you, Maurice, and Foss had your talk on the terrace. Down below was Foss's motor, serving two purposes. It was there if they had to make a bolt, should things go wrong. It also allowed the chauffeur, making a fake repair, to watch what went on in the museum. I gather that he meant to keep an eye on his confederates.

"At that moment, Foss had the three replicas in his pocket; and he was looking for some excuse to carry out the exchange. He led the conversation on to Japanese swords and so forth. I suspect Brackley supplied the basis for that matter, enough to allow Foss to make a show of information. Then Foss brought up the subject of his 'poor man's collection' of rubbings. I've no doubt he forced a card there—induced Maurice to offer to let him take rubbings of the medallions. That would be child's play to an ex-conjurer with a smart tongue. He got his way, anyhow.

" But then came a complication he hadn't expected. You, Joan, got interested in this taking of rubbings. I admit it was hard lines on the poor fellow. It was the last thing he could have anticipated."

" Thanks for the compliment ! " Joan interjected, ironically.

" Well, it wasn't in the plan, anyhow," Sir Clinton went on. " It meant an extra pair of eyes to deceive when the exchange was made ; and as the exchange was the crucial move in the whole scheme, your company—strange to say—was not appreciated. In fact, you made Mr Foss nervous. He wasn't quite as cool as he could have wished ; and my reading of the situation is that he bungled his first attempt at the substitution and had to prolong the agony by pretending to take a second rubbing of the first medallion he got into his hands.

"He had more luck with his second attempt, even with your eagle eyes on him ; and he stowed away Medallion Number One in one of the special concealed pockets which he had in his clothes. But he desired intensely to be relieved of your company ; and he proceeded to draw your attention to someone calling you. Of course that voice existed solely in his own imagination. But it was quite as effective as a real voice in getting you to leave the museum ; and then there was one onlooker the less to bother him in his sleight-of-hand.''

Sir Clinton paused to light a cigarette before continuing. Inspector Armadale, laying down his paper, turned to the Chief Constable as though expecting at this point to hear something which he did not already know.

" The next stage is one of pure conjecture," Sir Clinton went on. " Foss is dead, and I haven't had any opportunity of interrogating the other actor : Marden."

Inspector Armadale smiled grimly at the way in which the Chief Constable evaded any reference to the valet's murder.

" Possibly Inspector Armadale has a note or two on the matter," Sir Clinton pursued, " but even if he has, it can only be something like ' what the soldier said,' for Brackley could have merely second-hand evidence at the best. Take the case as the Inspector and I found it. Foss was dead, stabbed with the Muramasa sword. On its handle we found the finger-prints of Maurice, and no others. Under Foss's body we found an undischarged automatic pistol with his finger-prints on the butt. We noticed curious pockets in Foss's clothes ; but they were empty. And we found no trace of any of the medallions about the place. Maurice was *non est inventus*—we could see no sign of him. Marden had cut his hand in a fall against one of the cases. He'd wrapped it up with his handkerchief in a rough sort of way. The case containing the Muramasa

270

sword was open, and the sheath was lying in it, empty, of course.

" It's only fair to Inspector Armadale to tell you that he suspected Marden immediately. What I'm going to give you is merely the case as it presented itself to me."

Armadale looked slightly flustered by this tribute to his perspicacity. He glanced suspiciously at the Chief Constable, but Sir Clinton's face betrayed no ironical intention.

" He may be pulling my leg again," the Inspector reflected, " but at least it's decent of him to go out of his way to say that. It's true enough, but not exactly in the way that they'll understand it."

" Marden had a very complete story to tell us. He'd come to the door of the museum with a parcel which Foss had sent him to post. He'd found the address was incomplete and came back to get Foss to finish it. He stayed outside the door and he heard a quarrel between Maurice and Foss, ending in a struggle. When he burst into the room, Maurice was disappearing at the other end and Foss was dead on the floor. Then Marden slipped on the parquet, fell against a show-case, cut his hand, and tied it up in his handkerchief. Then he gave the alarm.

" The parcel with the incomplete address was the first thing that interested me. We opened it and we found in it a cheap wrist-watch in perfect condition, apparently. The Inspector tried it for finger-prints. There weren't any of any sort, either on the watch or

271

the box in which it was enclosed. That seemed a bit rum to us both.

"The only thing that seemed to fit the case was this. Suppose Marden wanted to keep an eye on Foss. This parcel would give him the excuse of bursting in on his employer at any moment. Assume that Marden himself had made up the parcel and that Foss had nothing to do with it. It was wrapped up in paper on which the address was written. You know how one writes on a parcel—not the least like one's normal handwriting if the paper is crumpled a bit in the wrapping-up. That would make a bit of rough forgery of Foss's writing fairly easy. Further, if by any chance the parcel fell into the hands of the police—as actually happened—there was nothing inside to show that Foss hadn't wrapped it up himself. Nobody else's fingermarks were on it at all. It had been wrapped up with gloved hands. And the contents were innocent enough : only a watch being sent to a watch-maker to be regulated, perhaps. If it had been a letter, then to carry the thing through properly they'd have had to forge Foss's writing all the way through, in order to make it look genuine if it happened to be opened.

"But if that theory were adopted, a lot followed from it. First and foremost, it meant that Marden was the boss and his nominal employer was an underling in the gang, who would have to back up any story that Marden liked to tell. Secondly, it pointed to the fact that Marden didn't trust Foss much. He wanted an excuse to get at Foss at any moment—which is hardly in the power of a simple valet. When he thought Foss needed watching, all he had to do was to trot up with his little parcel, just to let Foss see that he was under observation. Thirdly, this dodge was worked at a crucial stage in the game—when the replicas were being exchanged for the Leonardo medallions. Doesn't that suggest that Marden didn't trust Foss very much ? It looks as if Marden was none too sure that he'd get a square deal from Foss once the real medallions had changed hands. Am I right in my guesses, Inspector ? "

" They didn't trust Foss to play straight, sir. Brackley was quite open about that."

" And it was Brackley's idea ? The parcel, I mean. It looks as if it came from his mint."

" He said so, sir. Foss knew nothing about it, of course. It was a surprise for him. They knew he'd have to pretend he knew all about it when Marden brought it to him."

" That finishes the parcel," Sir Clinton continued. " But it had suggested one or two things, as you see. The most important thing, from my point of view, was that this gang was not exactly a band of brothers. Two of them suspected the third. Possibly the split was even more extensive.

" The next thing was the valet's story. According to him, Maurice stabbed Foss, after a quarrel which Marden couldn't overhear clearly. Unfortunately for that tale, the blow that killed Foss was a powerful one. What Marden didn't know was that Maurice had sprained his wrist that morning. I doubt if a sprained wrist could have achieved that stab. There was no

273

proof, of course ; but it seemed just a little doubtful. Then Marden said that from the door he couldn't catch the words of the quarrel, although the voices were angry in tone. I tried the experiment myself later ; and it's perfectly easy to overhear what's said in the museum from the position Marden said he was in. So that was a deliberate lie. On that basis, one could eliminate most of Marden's tale as being under suspicion.

" What really happened in the museum ? Maurice is gone, Foss is dead, Marden won't tell. One has just to reconstruct the thing as plausibly as one can. My impression—it's only conjecture—is this. Marden was listening at the door and he could see some parts of the room, since the door was ajar. Foss had succeeded in substituting one replica for a real medallion. To get Maurice's eye off him, he asked to see the Muramasa sword. Maurice went to get it, leaving Foss at his rubbing—visible to Maurice all the time. Foss made the exchange of the second replica at that moment. Maurice came back with the Muramasa sword—and of course in doing that, he put his fingerprints on the handle in drawing the blade from the sheath. Marden, at the door, saw him do this and made a note of it. Just as Maurice came back to Foss, he was suddenly taken ill. He had the third real medallion in one hand ; and as he passed Foss he picked up the two replicas—which he believed to be the other two real medallions. He went to the safe and hurriedly put on a shelf the two replicas ; but the other medallion, in his other hand, he forgot all about. He shut the safe and staggered into the secret passage."

Inspector Armadale looked frankly incredulous.

" Do people take ill all of a sudden like that ? " he demanded. " Why should he want to rush off all at once ? "

Sir Clinton swung round on him.

" Ever suffered from rheumatism, Inspector ? Or neuralgia ? Or toothache ? "

" No," the Inspector replied with all the pride of perfect health. " I've never had rheumatism and I've never had a tooth go wrong in my life."

" No wonder you can't understand, then," Sir Clinton retorted. " Wait till you have neuralgia in the fifth nerve, Inspector. Then, if you don't know yourself that you're unfit for human society, your friends will tell you, soon enough. If you get a bad attack, it's maddening—nothing less. Men have suicided on account of it often enough," he added, with a meaning glance at Armadale.

A light broke in on the Inspector's mind.

" So that was it ? No wonder I couldn't put two and two together ! " he reflected to himself ; but he made no audible comment.

" Now we come to a mere leap in the dark," Sir Clinton continued. " I believe that as soon as Maurice was out of the way, Marden went into the museum and demanded the medallions from Foss."

He put down his cigarette and leaned back in his chair. When he spoke again, a faint tinge of pity seemed to come into his voice.

" Foss was a poor little creature, hardly better than a rabbit in the big jungle of crime. And the other two were something quite different : carnivores, beasts of prey. They'd picked him out simply on account of his one miserable talent : his little trick of legerdemain. He was only a tool, poor beggar, and he knew it. I expect that when he saw what sort of company he'd fallen into, he was terrified. That would account for the pistol he carried.

" His only chance of a fair deal from them lay in the fact that he had the real medallions in his possession ; and he meant to hold on to them. And when Marden demanded them, Foss revolted. It must have been like the revolt of a rabbit against a stoat. He hadn't a chance. He pulled out his pistol, I expect ; and when that appeared, Marden saw red.

" But Marden, even in a fury, was a person with a very keen mind. Perhaps he'd thought the thing over beforehand. He was evidently one of these sub-human creatures with no respect for human life—the things they label Apaches in Paris. When the pistol came out he was ready for it. Foss, I'm sure, brandished the thing in an amateurish fashion—he wasn't a gunman of any sort. Probably he imagined that the mere sight of the thing would bring Marden to heel.

" Marden had his handkerchief out at once. Probably he had it ready in his hand. He picked up the Muramasa sword, leaving no finger-marks of his own on it through the handkerchief. And . . . that was the end of Foss."

Sir Clinton leaned over, selected a fresh cigarette with a certain fastidiousness, and lighted it before going on with his tale.

" That was the end of his feeble little attempt to get the better of his confederates. The money in his pocket-book didn't give him the escape he'd hoped for. All his precautions to leave no clues to his real identity played straight into the hands of Marden and Brackley.

" Marden's immediate problem, once he'd come out of his fury, was difficult enough. I suspect that his first move was to search Foss and get the medallions out of his pockets. Then he was faced with the blood on his hands and on his handkerchief. He had his plan made almost in a moment. He went across, deliberately slipped—he was an artist in detail, evidently—smashed against the glass of one of the cases, cut his hand, and then he felt fairly secure. He wrapped up the wounds in his handkerchief—and there was the case complete to account for any stray blood anywhere on his clothes. He tried the safe, for fear Maurice was lurking inside ; and then he gave the alarm."

Sir Clinton glanced inquiringly at the Inspector, but Armadale shook his head.

" Brackley had nothing to say about all that, sir. Marden gave him no details."

" It's mostly guess-work," Sir Clinton warned his audience. " All that one can say for it is that it fits the facts fairly well."

" And is that brute in the house now ? " Una Rainhill demanded. " I shan't go to sleep if he is."

" Two constables were detached to arrest him," Sir Clinton assured her. " He's not on the premises, you may count on that."

Inspector Armadale's face took on a wooden expression, the result of suppressing a sardonic smile.

" Well, he does manage to tell the truth and convey a wrong impression with it," he commented inwardly.

" Now consider the state of affairs after the Foss murder," Sir Clinton went on. " Marden and Brackley were in a pretty pickle, it seems to me. They had three medallions which Marden had got when he rifled Foss's body. But *they didn't know what they'd got.* They weren't in the secret of the dots on the replicas. For all they knew—knew for certain, I mean—Foss might have bungled the affair and the things they had might be merely replicas. If so, they were no good. I can't tell the difference between a medallion and an electrotype myself ; but I believe an expert can tell you whether a thing's been struck with a die or merely plated from a mould. These two scoundrels, I take it, weren't experts. They couldn't tell which brand of article they had in their hands.

" There was only one thing to be done. They'd have to get the whole six things into their hands, and then they'd be sure of having the three medallions. So they fell back on their original scheme of plain burglary. That, I'm sure, had been their first plan. They'd sent their American confederate to see the safe a long while ago ; and no doubt he'd reported that it was an old pattern. Hence the otophone, by means of which they could pick the combination lock. The otophone was still on the premises : I'd left it for them. But they were up against one thing.

" I'd put a guard night and day on the museum.

That blocked any attempt at burglary unless they were prepared to take the tremendous risk of manhandling the guard. If the door had merely been locked, I don't think it would have given them much trouble. I'm pretty sure there's a very good outfit of burglar's tools mixed up with the tool-kit of the car, where it would attract no attention. But the guard was a difficulty in the way."

Without making it obvious to the others, Sir Clinton made it clear to Armadale that the next part of his story was meant specially for the Inspector.

" I've given you the view I held of the case at that point. I felt fairly certain I was right. But if I'd been asked to put that case before a jury, I certainly would have backed out, It was mostly surmise : accurate enough, perhaps, but with far too little support. A jury—quite rightly—wants facts and not theories. Could one even convince them that the vanishing trick had been carried through as I believed it had ? It would have been a bit of a gamble. And I don't believe in that sort of gamble. I wanted the thing proved up to the hilt. And the best way to do that was to catch them actually at work.

" There seemed to me just one weak point in the armour. I counted on a split between the two remaining confederates, if I could only get a wedge in somehow. I guessed, rightly or wrongly, that the Foss murder would strike the chauffeur as a blunder, and that there might be the makings of friction there. The chauffeur's watching the museum under cover of the fake repair to the hood suggested that he mistrusted the others. I suspected that Marden might have stuck to the stuff he'd taken off Foss's body. If Brackley hadn't got his share of that swag, he'd be in a weak position. I gambled on that : everything to gain and nothing much to lose. I had the chauffeur up for examination again ; and when I gave him an opening, he deliberately gave his friend away by letting me know he'd seen Marden and Foss together just before the murder. And when he did that, I blurted out to Inspector Armadale that the guards on the terrace and the museum door were to be discontinued. Brackley went off with those two bits of exclusive information. He didn't tell them to Marden. He saw his way to make the balance even between himself and his confederate. If he kept his news to himself, he could burgle the museum safe ; get the remainder of the six medallions ; and then he'd be sure of getting his share of the profits. Neither of them could do without the other in that case.

" In actual practice, Brackley went a stage farther than I'd anticipated. He schemed to get Marden's loot as well as the stuff from the safe. I needn't go into that side-issue."

Again Inspector Armadale suppressed his amusement at the way in which Sir Clinton chose to present the truth.

" The rest of the tale's short enough," Sir Clinton went on. " Brackley determined to burgle the safe. If pursued, he decided, he'd repeat the vanishing trick on the terrace ; for I'd convinced him, apparently, that the *modus operandi* of it was still unknown to us.

Probably he went up there and satisfied himself that no one came near, after the patrol was taken off. He got himself up for the part : whitened his face ; put on white tights ; covered himself with Marden's waterproof as a disguise and to conceal his fancy dress ; put on a big black mask to hide the paint on his face, lest he should give the show away if an interruption came. And so he walked straight into the trap I'd laid for him.

"We saw the whole show from start to finish. I even let Cecil and Mr Clifton into the business, so that we'd have some evidence apart from police witnesses. We saw the whole show from start to finish."

Sir Clinton broke off his story and glanced at his watch.

"We've kept Inspector Armadale up to a most unconscionable hour," he said, apologetically. "We really mustn't detain him till sunrise. Before you go, Inspector, you might tell us if my solution fits the confession you got out of Brackley—in the later stages, I mean."

Inspector Armadale saw his dismissal and rose to his feet.

"There's really nothing in the confession that doesn't tally, sir. Differences in detail, of course ; but you were right in the main outlines of the affair."

Sir Clinton showed a faint satisfaction.

"Well, it's satisfactory enough to hear that. By the way, Inspector, you'd better take my car. It's in the avenue still. Send a man up with it, please, when you've done with it. There's no need for you to walk after a night like this."

Armadale thanked him ; declined Cecil's offer of another whisky-and-soda ; and took his departure. When he had gone, Cecil threw a glance of inquiry at the Chief Constable.

"Do you feel inclined to tell us what you made of my doings ? I noticed that you didn't drag them out in front of the Inspector."

Sir Clinton acquiesced in the suggestion.

"I think that's fairly plain sailing ; but correct me if I go wrong. When you heard of Maurice's disappearance, you saw that something was very far amiss. You had a fair idea where he might be, but you didn't want to advertise the Ravensthorpe secrets. So you came back one night and went down there. I don't know whether you were surprised or not when you found him ; but in any case, you decided that there was no good giving the newspapers a titbit about secret passages. So you took him out into the glade by the other entrance to the tunnel ; and then you came up to Ravensthorpe as though you'd come by the first train. The Inspector tripped you over that point, but it didn't matter much. He doesn't love you, though, I suspect. I'd no desire to make matters worse by interfering between you ; for you seemed able to look after yourself. Wasn't that the state of affairs ? "

"There or thereabouts," Cecil admitted. "It seemed the best thing to do, in the circumstances."

Sir Clinton showed obvious distaste for discussing the matter further. He turned to the girls.

"It's high time you children were in bed. Dawn's well up in the sky. You've had all the excitement you need, for the present ; and a good sleep seems indicated."

He gave a faint imitation of a stifled yawn.

" That sets me off," said Una Rainhill, frankly. " I can hardly keep my eyes open. Come along, Joan. It's quite bright outside and I'm not afraid to go to bed now."

Joan rubbed her eyes.

" This sort of thing takes more out of one than twenty dances," she admitted. " The beginning of the night was a bit too exciting for everyday use. How does one say ' Good-night ' in proper form when the sun's over the horizon ? I give it up."

With a gesture of farewell, she made her way to the door, followed by Una. When they had disappeared, Sir Clinton turned to Cecil Chacewater.

" Care to walk down the avenue a little to meet my car ? The fresh air and all that. I rather like the dawn, myself, when it happens to come my way without too much exertion."

Cecil saw that the Chief Constable was giving him an opening if he cared to take it.

" I'll come along with you till you meet the car."

Sir Clinton took leave of Michael Clifton, who obviously intended to go to bed immediately. As soon as he was well clear of the house, Cecil turned to the Chief Constable.

" You skated over thin ice several times in that yarn of yours. Especially the bits about Maurice. Toothache ! Neuralgia ! That infernal Inspector of yours swallowed it all down like cat-lap. From his face, you'd have thought he picked up an absolute cert. that no one else could see. I almost laughed, at that point."

He changed suddenly to a serious tone.

" How did you spot what was really wrong with Maurice ? "

" One thing led to another," Sir Clinton confessed. " I didn't hit on it all at once. The Fairy Houses set me thinking at the start. One doesn't keep toys like that in good repair merely on account of some old legend. They were quite evidently meant for use. And then, Cecil, you seemed to have some private joke of your own—not a particularly nice joke either—about them. That set me thinking. And after that, you dropped some remark about Maurice having specialized in family curses."

" You seem to have a devil of a memory for trifles," Cecil commented, in some surprise.

" Trifles sometimes count for a good deal in my line," Sir Clinton pointed out. " One gets into the habit of docketing them, almost without thinking about it. I must have pigeon-holed your talk about the Fairy Houses quite mechanically. Then later on I remembered that these things were dotted all over your estate and nowhere else. On their own ground, the Chacewaters were always within easy distance of one or other of these affairs. Ancient family curse ; curious little buildings very handy ; one brother grinning—yes, you did grin, and nastily too—at them, when you know he hates another brother like poison. It was quite a pretty little problem. And so . . ."

" And so ? " demanded Cecil, as Sir Clinton stopped short.

" And so I put it out of my mind. It wasn't the sort of thing I cared to think much about in connection with Ravensthorpe," Sir Clinton said, bluntly. " Besides, it was no affair of mine."

" And then ? "

" Then came Michael Clifton's story of finding Maurice in one of these Fairy Houses. And the details about the queer state Maurice was in when he was found. That came up in connection with a crime ; and crimes are my business. Why does a fellow crawl away into a place like that ? Why does he resent being dragged out of it. Why won't he even take the trouble to get up ? These were the kind of questions that absolutely bristled over the whole affair. One couldn't help getting an inkling. But that inkling threw no light on the crime in hand, so it was no affair of mine. I dropped it. But . . ."

" Yes ? "

" Maurice wasn't an attractive character, I'll admit that. I loathed the way he was going on. But I like to look on the best side of people if I can. In my line, one sees plenty of the other side—more than enough. And by and by I began to see that perhaps all Maurice's doings could be explained, if they couldn't be excused. He was off his balance."

" He was, poor devil," Cecil concurred, with some contrition in his tone.

" Then came the time I forced you to open the secret passage. Your methods were the very worst

you could have chosen, Cecil. I knew perfectly well
that you hadn't done anything to Maurice. You're
not the fratricidal type. But you very evidently had
something that you wanted to conceal behind that door.
You were afraid of my spotting something. The
Inspector jumped to the conclusion that it was murder
you were hushing up. By that time I had a pretty
good notion that it was the Ravensthorpe family secret.
Once I saw that passage of yours, dwindling away to
almost nothing, the thing was clear enough. With
the Fairy House clue as well, the thing was almost
certain. And finally, you gave the show away completely by what you said beside Maurice's body."

" Chuchundra, you mean ? "

" Yes. I remembered—another of these docketed
trifles—just what Chuchundra was. He was the
musk-rat that tried to make up his mind to run into
the middle of the room, but he never got there. Then
I asked you if the trouble began with A. Of course
it did. Agoraphobia. I suppose when Maurice was
a kid he had slight attacks of it—hated to move about
in an open room and preferred to sidle along by the
walls if possible. That was the start of the nickname,
wasn't it ? "

Cecil assented with a nod.

" It evidently cropped up in your family now and
again. Hence the Fairy Houses—harbours of refuge
when attacks came on. And that underground cell,
where a man could shut himself up tight and escape
the horror of open spaces."

" I'd really no notion how bad it was with Maurice,"

Cecil hastened to say. " It must have been deadly when it drove him to shoot himself."

" Something beyond description, I should say," Sir Clinton said, gravely.

He glanced over the wide prospects of the park and then raised his eyes to where great luminous clouds were sailing in stately procession across the blue.

" Looks peaceful, Cecil, doesn't it ? Makes one rather glad to be alive, when one gets into a scene like this. And yet, to poor Maurice it was a mere torture-chamber of nausea and torment, a horror that drove him to burrowing into holes and crannies, anywhere to escape from the terrors of the open sky. I don't suppose that we normal people can even come near the thing in our imaginations. It's too rum for our minds —outside everything we know. Poor devil ! No wonder he went off the rails a bit in the end."

》》 If you've enjoyed this book and would like to discover more great vintage crime and thriller titles, as well as the most exciting crime and thriller authors writing today, visit: 》》

The Murder Room
Where Criminal Minds Meet

themurderroom.com

www.ingramcontent.com/pod-product-compliance
Ingram Content Group UK Ltd.
Pitfield, Milton Keynes, MK11 3LW, UK
UKHW040434280225
455666UK00003B/55